# "I COULD GO AS A MAN."

"You have no idea how much trouble you—and I—would be in if you were unmasked."

For the first time, Rob saw a flicker of wariness cross her face. "I wouldn't be."

He smelled trouble. "You don't know what it's like out there. Day after day of travel, heat, insects. That spirit gum'll irritate your face—you'll take off your whiskers for a spell and the next thing you know, everyone in the train will be whispering. Soon enough—"

Ros held up her hands as if in surrender. "Okay. I take your point, Mr. Lewis. I'd rather travel as a woman anyway, for just the reasons you describe." She appraised him impartially. "What if I had a man to look after me, just not a father or a husband, since I have neither."

"Who?"

"You."

He choked. "What kind of damn fool—"

She watched him with a strange, reserved expression on her face. "I'd make it worth your while."

Worth his while? He stood up, sending his chair tumbling away in his haste. "What makes you think I'd—"

She laughed low in her throat. "The way you look at me."

Dear Romance Reader,

In July 2000, we launched the Ballad line with four new series, and each month we present both new and continuing stories set everywhere from medieval England to the American West—the kind of passionate, romantic stories you love best, written by the most gifted authors. At the back of each book, we tell you when you can find subsequent books in the series that have captured your heart.

This month, Kelly McClymer continues her sparkling *Once Upon a Wedding* series with **The Impetuous Bride.** When a spirited young woman flees England to avoid matrimony, she never imagines that she'll be forced to wed in America's Wild West—or that her new husband will be quite so appealing! Then the ever-talented Linda Lea Castle concludes her dramatic saga, *The Vaudrys,* with **Embrace the Sun.** A Scottish lass harboring a dangerous secret risks everything when a wounded Englishman falls into her dooryard . . . and into her heart.

Next up, Sandra Madden introduces the second book in her wonderfully atmospheric *Of Royal Birth* series, **A Prince's Heart.** A British lieutenant fighting the Irish Rebellion loses his heart to the enemy— a lovely Irish lass who leads him on a journey of discovery that he'll never forget. Finally, Kate Donovan concludes her sweetly romantic *Happily Ever After Co.* with the charming tale of a woman looking for a husband to save her ranch—and a man who can't resist playing the hero in **Fool Me Twice.**

These are stories we know you'll love! Why not try them all this month?

Kate Duffy
Editorial Director

ONCE UPON A WEDDING

# THE IMPETUOUS BRIDE

## KELLY McCLYMER

**ZEBRA BOOKS**
KENSINGTON PUBLISHING CORP.
http://www.kensingtonbooks.com

*To Jim—*
*thank you for being such a great pinch hitter!*

# Chapter One

*Saint Joseph, Missouri, 1854*

Just as his opponent jumped the three red checkers deliberately left open on the board, Rob Lewis's shoulder blade began to itch. Trouble. The itch always meant trouble. He surveyed the checkerboard. Everything was set. Homer was grinning, his eyes lit with pleasure at the three pieces Rob was willing to sacrifice for the final win.

The old man was blind to the trap. He didn't even scowl when the stranger dared to interrupt their game without a by-your-leave. "Gentlemen."

Rob looked up from the game and swiftly sized up the impertinent fellow who had demanded his attention. Another eager emigrant. Young—his voice still had a slightly feminine pitch. Steady blue eyes, a confident set to his rather slender shoulders, and a glint of determination in his gaze. All to his credit.

However, he also had an impressive set of sideburns, a positively elegant handlebar mustache that gleamed with oil, and a tailored set of clothes that must have cost him a pretty penny, judging by what Rob knew from years as the son of a famous senator. Not to mention that the fellow didn't have enough sense not to interrupt a man in the middle of a game.

"Give us a minute to finish up here." Rob gave as genial a nod as he could muster, considering the hellish last few weeks he'd just spent ferrying Tom Rich and Joss Hennesee to their just rewards. He couldn't say which exasperated him more—the men with prices on their heads, or the eager tenderfoot fools who wanted to head West. Still, a man had to earn a living—if he didn't want to live at his father's beck and call.

"Shouldn't be long." Homer chuckled as he captured Rob's pieces.

Apparently the stranger was in no mood to wait. He raised a brow and repeated his request as his gaze met Rob's squarely. "Captain Hellfire?"

Impatience was a common enough malady among the emigrants; Rob tried not to hold it against the fellow. "Could be."

The stranger turned piercing eyes on Rob's opponent in checkers for a moment—long enough to take in Homer Cantor's milky eye and the white stubble on the four chins, which didn't lend themselves to easy shaving. Dismissing Homer as a possible candidate for Captain Hellfire, he turned his gaze back on Rob. "Do you have room in your company for another party?"

Homer scowled at the intruder and slapped the table, making the checkers dance. He said to Rob, "Take your turn, dammit. I want that whiskey."

Rob considered his move for a minute, as if he didn't

already know exactly what he planned to do, and then eliminated one of Homer's black pieces.

Instead of turning on his expensively heeled boot and departing, the stranger prompted him in polished tones. "On what does your decision depend?"

He scraped his shoulder against the splintered wooden back of his chair. "On who's asking."

"Then what do you say to someone who's outfitted and ready to go?" There was a definite light of challenge in the blue eyes, and Rob groaned silently.

*No*—but Rob didn't say it aloud. "Give me a minute to finish my game, then I'll talk business." He wasn't exactly sure why this one seemed like trouble—and he didn't want to find out. But he wouldn't be cavalier with his decision—he needed the money.

"Very well." The stranger did not move away, but stood studying the checkerboard with a calculating look.

"You can play the winner, if you dare," Homer said. No doubt the old man anticipated a new, and perhaps more easily beaten, opponent. "Best player pays for the whiskey."

The stranger declined with a brisk shake of his head. "I'm afraid I'm more partial to cards or dice."

"He's cowed by your skill, old man." Knowing that Homer's next move would be his last, Rob didn't hurry him. Homer grunted with laughter and began to make his move.

"If you do that, sir, Captain Hellfire here will capture all your men with his next move."

"What?" Homer examined the chessboard. "How?"

The emigrant lifted a finger, clad in expensive leather gloves, to point out the trap that Rob had set for him.

"Well, I'll be . . ." Homer sat back, rethinking his move. He grinned at Rob. "Seems this stranger knows the game better than either of us."

"Seems so," Rob said grudgingly.

Homer glanced up at the man. "What would you suggest I do, mister?"

"I hardly think it would be sporting of me to tell you how to win the game. Do you?" The stranger flashed a dimple, knowing the damage was done.

Trouble with a capital *T*. Rob couldn't resist a grumble at the upset. "You already did."

"Nonsense." Another shake of the head that made the mustache sway. "I just provided a friendly warning, nothing more."

Homer frowned at the pieces. But Rob knew he'd see soon enough what to do. Homer was skilled at the game, just not usually as good at looking a few moves ahead as Rob. His mouth stretched into a grin when he saw what to do, and he snapped the checker into place with a flourish. "Your turn, my friend."

Rob made the only move he could. He'd known he'd risked putting himself in this position when he went for the win. But Homer wouldn't have seen it if it hadn't been for the emigrant.

Homer suddenly pounced on the board with a crow of triumph as he cleared it of all Rob's red pieces. "I won!" he announced to anyone who would listen.

Phineas Bartley, up on a ladder to retrieve a wheel of cheese for a shop customer, halted what he was doing to call encouragingly, "First time in years, Homer! You're losing your touch, Captain Hellfire."

"Pay me," Homer demanded with an almost childlike glee.

Rob rose in surrender. "Okay, old man, let's get that whiskey I owe you now."

He scraped back his chair to rise, but the stranger stood so close Rob couldn't get up without knocking him over.

He sighed. With the delay he was facing, he needed all the parties he could find. Several of those who'd intended to leave with him had joined other companies and headed out. "How many in your party?" The itch under his shoulder blade returned.

"Five."

"Five wagons?"

"Five people."

How much trouble could such a small group cause? "Any single women?"

There. The stranger raised a disdainful eyebrow before he answered pretty sharply, "None."

He prodded, looking for the fly in the ointment. "Any women or children at all?"

There was a slight hesitation before the answer. "One woman. One child."

"How old?"

"Three weeks."

A newborn, then. Sometimes that worked out better than the adventuresome toddlers. "This her first?"

"Yes."

"How old's the woman?"

"Eighteen."

He suppressed a groan. There was trouble. A woman—no, a girl—with a newborn infant, traveling without another experienced woman to help her. "The trip's hard on anyone—especially a woman just out of childbed—not to mention the baby."

"Others have done it."

"Might be best to wait a few months, let her get her strength back."

"Impossible." At last the emigrant's patience broke. "I have made inquiries, and all are agreed that you are the best wagon master in these parts." The left eyebrow lifted elegantly again, stopping just short of mockery.

"A veritable legend. Please don't tell me that a young woman and her infant so terrify you that you will refuse to let us travel with your company. And, might I add, pay handsomely for the privilege."

*Legend.* Rob scowled and then shrugged, as if the money didn't matter to him one way or another. The itch was back. But there would be other women, married women who had experience with birthing babies, traveling in the train. There always were.

Still, something about the stranger made him hesitate. He might be determined, but he was young, slender, and almost boyish in his fancy duds. "How much flour you got?"

"A thousand pounds."

"Not enough."

"According to my research, that should be more than enough for five of us. I've also packed rice, sugar, dried fruit, and beans." The man's voice rose to an almost feminine pitch for a moment as he pulled out a neatly clipped newspaper article, unfolded it, and read from a listing of supplies: " 'A thousand pounds of flour . . .' "

Research? Was that why he sensed trouble? Emigrants who hadn't made the trip, except by virtue of the newspaper accounts, often thought they knew more than they did. "That'll feed the five of you, but you'll need some to trade with the Indians."

Rob waited for the stranger's response. Would he argue? Pitch a fit?

But the stranger merely swept him with a narrow-eyed assessment. Decisively, the fellow nodded briskly and pulled out a pencil to jot down a note. "How much more?"

"Another hundred pounds, maybe."

The note made, the pencil slipped back into his

pocket, he nodded. "Then I'll be sure to have it when we start."

Rob sighed. Why couldn't he just tell this emigrant no? There were other trains, other captains who could deal with the trouble that was hiding somewhere here. "How many oxen? Horses? Cattle?"

"Four yokes. All eight no more than five years old. A milk cow, and twenty head of cattle."

Rob almost agreed then. An itchy shoulder blade was no reason to turn down good money. Still, there had been that odd look in the blue eyes when he'd answered about unmarried women. "Ain't got any sisters, do you?"

A smile curved the man's mouth, making it almost too pretty under the glossy brown mustache. "Five, as it happens—but all safely across the sea in England. There's just me—and my servants."

Servants; it figured the fancy gent wouldn't want to dirty his own hands. "Fine." But if he thought he'd get away without a little hardship, he'd be sorely disappointed soon enough. "For two hundred I'll see you safe to San Francisco."

"Excellent." The stranger held out his hand as if to shake on a bargain.

Rob ignored the hand. "Be here ready to move out in three weeks." The fellow had moved just enough for Rob to brush by him and make his escape. "Come on, Homer, let's get that whiskey I owe you."

"Three weeks?" Again, the voice took on a higher timbre. "I thought you were scheduled to move out tomorrow." He strode over to the board the shopkeeper had put up to keep track of all the emigrant groups leaving for the western parts. " 'Captain Hellfire. April second.' "

Rob pushed Homer before him, hurrying him toward the door. "Go on over and get your whiskey, Homer."

"I won; you're supposed to pay for me."

"Tell Howard I'll be in to pay in a minute." He felt more lighthearted than he should, knowing that whatever trouble was traveling with the emigrant wasn't going to be his. "Unless this fine gentleman here wants to pay."

With a frown, the stranger tapped the board again. "April second."

As Homer scurried away, Rob shrugged and then strode over to the board to scrawl a three after the two, making the date April twenty-third. He didn't spare a glance toward the young Englishman, just pushed out the door. The bustle inside the store was nothing to what was out in the street. He stopped a moment to chart a clear path through the emigrants preparing to head out and the residents trying to milk as much money from them as possible before they left civilization.

"Captain Hellfire?"

Rob turned; the emigrant had followed him. The fellow's lips were thinned, but his indignation was in check as he asked briskly, "What is the reason for your delay?"

"Just got in from the last trip. Have some business to attend to."

The sunlight struck the stranger, burnishing the mustache and sideburns to an almost unnatural sheen. The itch began again as the persistent fellow smiled. "If you could forgo your business and take off tomorrow, I'd compensate you well."

"Sorry. You could always go elsewhere. Other trains."

"I suppose I must." Disappointment mingled with some other emotion Rob couldn't determine. "Despite your legendary, although no doubt somewhat exaggerated reputation''—the fellow had the brass to give a doubtful twist to his mouth—"I cannot wait three weeks."

"Exaggerated?" Rob drawled. "Hell, mister, the myth of Captain Hellfire is no exaggeration—it's a pack of half-truths masquerading as a legend."

"I can see that." The stranger surprised him with an answering grin rather than a scowl. He reached into his pocket. With an unerring aim, he flipped a coin through the air. "That's for your time—and the old man's whiskey."

Rob pocketed the coin with a nod. He didn't need to bite it. Gold. For a moment, he felt a twinge of regret that the fellow wouldn't be traveling in his company. He crossed to the saloon, where Homer had already finished his first hard-won whiskey and was working on a second. The new checkers champion grinned as he held up his half-full glass. "Malachi stood me another, in honor of beating you."

"Are you losing your touch?" One of the saloon girl's sidled up to him.

"Only with checkers." Rob laughed as he gestured for a glass of his own. The two hundred would have been nice. But he'd rather avoid trouble if he could.

He smiled at Theresa. "Scratch my back for me, would you?" Her fingers found the spot and he sighed as the itch finally disappeared.

Ros scratched discreetly at the itchy whiskers attached to her face as she watched the man they called Captain Hellfire dodge the traffic in the busy street with a lithe grace. Too bad. They'd have to find another wagon company to join. Despite the undoubted truth of his final comment, she thought he'd be a safe man to travel with.

After all, he had been smart enough to set up that series of moves to win the game—despite the risk of losing if his opponent had noticed what he was up to. Which he wouldn't have—if she hadn't pointed it out. He'd been annoyed, but not unduly so. Another point in his favor.

She bent her head and twitched her face, unable to make the itch go away. She wasn't used to wearing the whiskers for so long anymore. The spirit gum was irritating her skin and the unnatural facial hair was hot and bothersome. No matter. Without them anyone would guess she was a woman, and that she could not risk. Four people's futures depended on her maintaining her disguise. Five, if she counted her own.

She allowed her gaze to wander over the other emigrants so visible in this last station of civilization. Where was that young couple with the toddler and the baby heading? Whose train had they entrusted their goods and their lives to? What about that family with the older woman, a youngster on her lap, two half grown behind her and a nearly grown girl watching a handsome young emigrant unloading a wagon nearby? How did they know which wagon master to trust?

She sighed. She'd let Moses decide what to do. It was only right, after all. The fate he was deciding was his own, his family's, not hers. She only intended to go far enough with the company to provide him cover.

It would be a disaster if anyone guessed he was not a freed man this close to civilization. But once he was established as her trusted servant, she could ride away and let everyone think she'd left him in charge of her goods until she could rejoin the company. To do that in good conscience, she'd have to make certain they traveled with an experienced and fair-minded wagon master.

Moses was still stocking the wagon with goods when she found him wedged in a narrow alleyway by the feed store. Though the sight of a black man was common enough in slave-owning Missouri, Moses still incited stares from passersby. His skin was truly black, an ebony that now shone with sweat from the hard work of packing in sacks, barrels, and crates of dry goods for the long journey ahead.

His size drew stares as well. He was over six feet tall and broad as a barn. What was most striking about him, however, was his hairless head. He had taken to shaving it when he had worked the fields on Rose Point Plantation. Ada had demanded he continue the practice once he'd been chosen to work as butler in the Big House.

Moses stopped his work, a canvas sack of flour still slung over his shoulder, when he caught sight of her.

She shook her head. "Captain Hellfire isn't leaving for another three weeks. Do you have another wagon master in mind, or should I make inquiries about who else is leaving in the next day or two?"

"We don't have a choice," he answered grimly. His anger was a part of him, a part she had grown used to in the years of working to help slaves escape. But the frustration that bubbled up from him was new—caused by his unexpected decision to run away after years of helping others slaves get away.

"Of course we have a choice. He may have been the best, but there are other good companies we can join."

Moses shook his head. "Can't do it this week for sure."

"What do you mean?"

"They don't have all our supplies." She had never heard his voice convey such hopelessness before. Not even when they crouched in a swamp, surrounded by baying hounds and one shot each in their shotguns. "A company of six hundred just come through and wiped out all the supplies to be had."

"What are we missing?" Maybe they could make do somehow. There were forts along the way—although they charged outrageous prices for their goods.

Moses looked down at his list. "The tent—shopkeeper says he should have some in next week."

They couldn't do without that. "Maybe—"

He shook his head and pointed to the list. "We also missing half the flour, all the beans, and most of the iron and wrought nails. Can't do without them."

No. He was right. "Captain Hellfire says you'll need another hundred pounds of flour, as well." She didn't want to accept the fact that they were well and truly boxed in. Not here. Not now. "Let me talk to the shopkeeper—"

"Wouldn't bother." He slung the sack down violently.

"You don't know—"

He stopped packing and his voice rumbled with anger. "There's none left. I looked."

Of course he had. Moses had more at stake than she did. "I sent specific instructions, and the date—"

"Someone else offered a little more in cash."

"I would have matched the offer."

Moses smiled at her, a brief flash that reminded her that he seemed older, even though he was younger than her nearly thirty years. "Money in hand always beats money on the tongue, you know that."

She surveyed the busy, dusty streets. "Judging by the chaos, it shouldn't be difficult to find another company, even if we must wait for the merchants to restock."

"I want the best for Fee and the baby. No drunk

who'll get us stuck in the mountains when the snow comes."

Ros nodded. "A reliable leader might be more troublesome to find. Let me make a visit to the saloon and make some inquiries. Surely I can find the names of some other good wagon masters who will head out next week.

"Captain Hellfire's supposed to be the best."

"So his reputation would suggest." Her research had clearly indicated Captain Hellfire was the best wagon train leader across the wilderness. She had been told his trains had never once, in five years, suffered an Indian attack. They also had fewer losses to accident and mischance than any other. "But even he admits that the legend isn't all true."

"Do you think any of it is?"

"He seemed a capable enough man to me—intelligent and certainly not hotheaded." If she'd been so inclined, she might have enjoyed a game with Captain Hellfire. Not checkers, but perhaps poker. She'd liked the way his long deft fingers had handled his game pieces.

"Then why don't we just wait?" They both knew the answer to that. Runaway slaves didn't idle away their precious time in a slave state—not even one on the border of freedom.

"I don't think he's likely that much different from any of the others. Except perhaps that he seems more even-tempered than I'd have expected for a man with his nickname." Ros shook her head. "Captain Hellfire was playing checkers."

"Maybe there's more than one Captain Hellfire? What was his Christian name?"

"I didn't ask and he didn't give it," Ros said sharply, annoyed with herself. "I suppose I have the time to see

if I can find out." Could there be more than one wagon
master with that ridiculous nickname? Come to think
of it, he hadn't even agreed that he went by the nickname, had he?

Moses interrupted her train of thought with a low
warning. "Think we got trouble."

# Chapter Two

Could this day get worse? Ros consciously made herself relax—she didn't want to warn anyone watching that she had grown suspicious of them. "Where?"

"To the left of that braying donkey. They been watching me."

Ros glanced surreptitiously toward where Moses indicated. The men weren't hiding their interest. She felt a chill down her spine. She recognized one of them: Jericho. Damn. She'd known Jackson wouldn't just let Moses run away without pursuit. But they'd left a false trail that led north to Canada. No one should have been so close on their tail.

"I don't know if he's studying you because he's talked to Jackson, or just because he's a greedy, suspicious bastard." She moved up close to the wagon so that she could speak as softly as possible. "How much more to load?"

"Just this."

"And the cattle?"

"In the grass outside of town. Saleratus and Lemuel's watching 'em."

"We'll have to leave them there."

"They'll be fine." Moses undoubtedly was more worried about the cattle than the sixteen-year-old twins who had proven time and again on the harrowing trip from South Carolina to Missouri that they could take care of themselves.

"Where's Ophelia and the baby?" Moses's wife could prove a difficulty in extracting themselves from this situation. She hadn't wanted to run away. If Moses hadn't told her that he was taking the baby with or without her, she wouldn't have come at all.

Moses hefted the sack into the wagon, back in motion at last. "She's in the milliner's to get a length of blue ribbon."

"Ribbon?" Ros couldn't help the bite in her voice. "When is she due back?"

"An hour ago." Moses hitched up a shoulder as if to shake off his concern. "First ribbon she ever bought herself new—always got Miz Ada's castoffs before. Says she's not going into the heathen wilderness without it."

Heathen wilderness. Did the girl think a blue ribbon would protect her? Ros sighed. "Very well. I'll go retrieve her from the shop and we'll go to ground until we can get fully provisioned and find a place on a company."

"Where will we go?"

"Promise Creek."

"Thought you didn't want to bother Miz Lewis this trip?"

Caroline would be worried. Caroline was always worried, despite her desire to help on the Underground Railroad. For that reason, Ros had deliberately chosen not to stay in her home on this trip. "Plans have gone awry before. She's our best chance."

"What to do about them?" Moses indicated the men, who still watched them openly.

"If we leave too hastily, they're likely to follow, and who knows what they'd do with no one around?" Ros had been in such situations before. For that matter, so had Moses.

Damn. Too bad their supplies weren't ready. She'd just head out and take her chances on the trail, if she could. Surely they could meet up with and join a suitable company once they were on their way.

She said, "Maybe we should do a tortoise and hare?" They'd done that before when they were in trouble. He'd sneak off and she'd meet him later. She had a bad feeling about it this time, though.

"If I can be the rabbit—I don't like the evil in them eyes."

She nodded. "You take the wagon, since you've been loading it. Leave it with Lem and Sal to watch and wait for me right outside of town. Hide in the trees by the crossroads. I'll gather up Ophelia and meet you there in an hour, after I make sure we're not followed."

Her uneasiness increased as she helped Moses finish loading and securing the wagon. The moment he went around to the front to climb up into the wagon, the men crossed the street toward them.

"Hey, boy!" Moses stopped, though Ros knew him well enough to recognize the tension in his shoulders, which meant he'd take the wagon and run at the first sign that things would get ugly. She wished she had her shotgun handy.

The man who'd spoken—not Jericho, but one of his companions—smiled, big and friendly. "Where you headed?"

"West, sir," Moses said obsequiously.

"You free?"

Ros relaxed a little at the question, ill-mannered as it was. They didn't know for certain he'd run away, or they wouldn't have asked such a thing. No doubt they were fishing to see if they might pick up a little easy money.

"He belongs to me." She forced herself to relax, to fall into the role she always adopted on the road. With the most highbrow accent she could manage, she said, "Magumbo and I are in a hurry, gentlemen, and I don't appreciate your interrupting him at his work."

"Who're you?" The ruffians glared at her—or rather, glared at what they thought was a man.

"I am Lord Hightower." Ros put all her thespian ability into the role of supercilious patrician to distract them. "And this is my slave, Magumbo. Now step aside. As you can see, he is very busy—we are heading west tomorrow."

The men moved backward infinitesimally. "Lord, huh? We don't have no titles here."

Furious, Ros answered sharply. "Why do you think I'm heading west? I'm hoping for some semblance of civilization on the opposite edge of the continent, as there is surely none to be found here. Go, Magumbo— we have a schedule to keep."

Moses ducked his head, no doubt to hide any smile her performance might have provoked, and chucked the reins, which made the slow-moving team ease into the steady stream of emigrants heading through town.

She didn't relax, not even when the men made no move to stop him. There was an attentiveness in their gaze that didn't bode well for the future. Even if they hadn't seen his description yet, once they had, there was no doubt they'd remember.

"Don't it scare you to own such a big buck?" Jericho's man asked. "You being on the small side—for a man?"

Ros bristled, as she knew any man would at the insult. "Not at all. I would trust Magumbo with my life." Since that was the truth, she let her conviction ring in her words.

"Really? I wouldn't trust him farther than I could throw him." His laugh was high, almost a whine.

The men moved away, but their attention remained fixed on the wagon slowly inching down the road to freedom. Suddenly Jericho straightened, and his idle watchfulness turned into determination. With a sharp command to his men, all three unhitched their waiting horses.

Ros watched in dismay, unable to warn Moses of the danger. With the crowd and confusion, the men would have no difficulty in following the ungainly conveyance.

Looking for any distraction that might halt the men, she spotted an overladen dray cart. Desperate, she quickly stepped out in the path of the team pulling it. "Lout!" she cursed loudly, as if the driver were at fault and not she, to startle the horses.

Unfortunately, the horses were much too sensitive for the crowded conditions. They not only shied away from her, they reared back and plunged sideways into the crowded traffic way.

The overburdened cart balanced on two wheels just long enough for anyone in its path to get out of the way before it fell to the ground, spilling potatoes under the wheels and hooves of anyone in the vicinity.

Not even a man on horseback could make his way

through the chaos now, she thought with satisfaction, until she realized the dray's team was about to bolt.

Rob Lewis stepped out of the saloon just in time to see the English gentleman deliberately spook the team of cart horses. Rob watched the dominolike effect the small action had as he pushed his way through the crowd. If the team bolted ... Even as he had the thought, they did. He cursed, too far away to do any good.

To his surprise, the Englishman he had not credited with much fortitude grabbed the slack reins and bodily hauled the team to a halt. As he hung all his weight, to force the horses' heads down, the dray man's curses could be heard clearly above the din. The man had jumped clear of the cart as it fell and was putting his whip to poor use on the Englishman.

Whether the slender man could have prevented the team from bolting just with the slight weight of his body Rob would never know as a half-dozen men joined their efforts to his. When Rob arrived the original team had been forcefully settled and the dray man had been grabbed up and bodily moved away from the scene so that he could not whip those who were working to calm the uproar.

And an uproar it was. At least a dozen more horses and countless cattle and sheep had decided to take the opportunity to let their dislike of the crowded street be known. Rob knew a little about stampedes, and his stomach clenched as he anticipated the worst. But as quickly as it had begun, the furor ended. Now there was only the need to pick up the goods that had been tossed into the street during the commotion.

A whistle blew and loud shouts ensued. Apparently a

few resourceful boys had taken the opportunity to snatch a ham that had been jostled out of an emigrant's wagon. Everyone was checking to make sure they hadn't lost anything in the commotion. Except the Englishman, whose gaze followed three men very closely.

Rob stopped a moment to observe. The men were in a hurry. At least, they had been. Now they were cursing, trying to convince their frightened mounts to pick a way clear of the chaos. He recognized one of the men: Jericho. He made his living tracking down and returning runaway slaves. The itch under Rob's shoulder blade grew so intense he shrugged his shoulders.

Were the Englishman's servants escaped slaves? He didn't want to know. That was the trouble he'd sensed when the fellow had been near. Rob didn't want escaped slaves on his train. Especially not the slaves Jericho was tracking.

He approached the Englishman from behind, not wanting to spook the man before he could speak to him. As if sensing him, though, the fellow turned when he was a few feet away. There was a self-satisfied look in his eye that confirmed Rob's instincts. He'd intended to cause the dray to overset.

As the fellow watched Jericho and his men search fruitlessly for a quick way out of the mess, he smiled. The dimple Rob had seen before flashed again. His satisfaction was so intense that he did not seem to realize that the cart man's whip had taken him on the cheek, cutting a neat slash that now welled with blood.

Rob fished out a handkerchief and held it out. "You're bleeding." When the other man didn't seem to understand what he meant by it, he pantomimed by holding it up to his own cheek for a moment.

Startled, the man raised a hand to his cheek and

smeared the blood on his fingertips. When he drew
back his hand and saw the blood, he did an odd thing.
He laughed, a high, husky laugh. "I'm fine. These cart
men should look where they're going." Shaking his
head at Rob's offer, he drew out his own handkerchief
and carelessly dabbed at the gash. The cloth came away,
and Rob saw the wound was not as deep or as long as
he had first thought. Lucky for the Englishman.

"I don't think you were in much danger, unless it
might have been from Jericho and his unhappy friends."

"Who?" The squint in the eyes spoke of more danger
than he would have expected from a slender dandy like
this.

"Did you find another train to join?"

"As it happens, some of my supplies were bought
from the shopkeeper I ordered them from before I
could claim them. I'll have to wait at least a week."

"Major Hartnell has a train leaving next week. He's a
good man." And an underground railroad sympathizer.
But that wasn't anything to spread around, not even to
this reckless Englishman. "He'd likely get you and your
. . . servants . . . safely West."

"Thank you for the advice." The Englishman nodded
almost regally, making Rob feel an absurd desire to bow
deeply and sweep off his hat.

"My pleasure." *Just as long as you're not traveling with
me.*

"By the way, I have been meaning to ask—" The
fellow suppressed a small smile. "Is there another Captain Hellfire, by any chance?"

Goddamn that balderdash about him. "Not as far as
I know."

"How disappointing." With that, at last, the Englishman struck off through the destruction he had single-
handedly set in motion. Rob nearly choked when he

saw the fellow lift his hat jauntily to Jericho's group as he passed.

"Fool," swore one of Jericho's men. But in an instant he was occupied with calming his rearing horse as the Englishman disappeared in the crowd.

"What a mess."

Rob turned to see Ben Smith, one of Saint Joe's deputies, staring at the overturned cart, which was being righted by a half-dozen men. He nodded in agreement. "Not the first time, though."

"Nor the last," Ben agreed. "These emigrants are always doing some fool thing or another. I'll be glad to see them go."

Rob shook his head, not believing him for a moment. "Your livelihood will go with them."

Ben's grin widened until the short squat figure resembled a gargoyle with a star pinned to its chest. "Not mine. Not yours either."

True. Rob glanced about to see if anyone was listening. "I suppose there will always be someone willing to break the law."

"Hope so, or I *will* be out of a job."

"You sound like you plan to do this when your whiskers are all white as snow."

Ben looked surprised. "I plan to do this until I cock up my toes and go meet my maker. Don't we all?"

The thought did not appeal to Rob, but he didn't want to say so. Wasn't that his problem? Hadn't his esteemed father always told him that he never stuck to anything long enough to make a success? He didn't need to hear Ben's version of the old scolding.

"Which reminds me—" Ben dug in his pocket and pulled out a telegraph cable. "Pinkerton wants you on this right away."

Rob took the paper without glancing at it and tucked

it into his breast pocket. "He'll have to wait. I have business to tend to."

Ben frowned. "He won't be happy."

"I haven't been home in almost a year, Ben." Rob didn't want to explain, but he knew he'd better if he wanted to keep the job with Pinkerton. The agency liked to think any man that worked for them was on the job anytime, anyplace. Pinkerton was ambitious and zealous, and he expected the same of his men. But even a driven man understood family, didn't he? "I owe my wife some money. And I want to see my daughter."

"I'd take care of it myself, but the sheriff needs me here right now." Ben spat loudly. "Can't you take care of this job quick, before you tend to your own business?"

Rob wondered why he argued with Ben at all. The man was a confirmed bachelor who considered children an unfortunate plague upon the earth. "My daughter's only seven. Takes her at least a week before she'll even come close to me, when I've been away this long."

"Then leave a week later with your train. You can still make it through. You're Captain Hellfire." Ben laughed at the nickname.

"I wish you wouldn't call me that." He wished Ben hadn't bestowed the nickname at all.

"Don't be modest, Captain. Thirty-five wagons and a hundred and twenty people led safely through a prairie fire? You deserve that name."

"Dumb luck and a good stiff easterly breeze is all that was, Ben." It was an old argument, and one he had no chance of winning. Rob watched Jericho and his men disappear into the crowd in the same general direction the Englishman had gone.

"Maybe that careful streak in you is what makes you the best leader on the trail. And the best man Pinkerton's got—besides me, of course. Not that we're allowed to say so.''

Rob grinned, and echoed his friend's often expressed thought—''Of course not; we couldn't do our jobs for the women throwing themselves at us if they knew what dashing fellows we were.''

Ben nodded serenely and got back to the point. ''So I can tell Pinkerton he can count on you?''

Rob took out the paper and unfolded it. There were only a few words—Pinkerton was a frugal bastard when it came down to it. ''I'll do it.''

''Knew I could count on you.'' Ben slapped his back heartily.

Rob shook his head. ''Wait until I come back without any holes shot in me,'' he said cautiously. ''I've got a terrible itch under my shoulder blade right now.''

Ben just stared at him implacably.

''Fine. It'll go down easy as stealing candy from a babe.'' No use thinking black thoughts. He cheered himself up with a hope that when he came back, the English greenhorn and his runaways would be long departed.

He sighed as he looked at the wire one more time and then carefully shredded the paper and let the wind take it to be scattered and pounded under wagon wheels and horses' hooves, into the mess of potatoes being ground into the dirt. ''Where'll I find him?''

''Out by the abandoned Hartford farm.''

He knew the place Ben described. As he turned to leave he stopped and called over his shoulder. ''I'm not promising to make this clean and neat—if I have to drag a dead body back because it's quicker, I will.''

Ben just laughed. He shouted an answer, one just enigmatic enough that anyone else who heard it couldn't be sure who or what they were talking about.

"Boss pays the same for a gutted pig as he does for a live one."

The image brought to mind the Englishman—with Jericho and his men on his trail. He hoped the foolhardy fellow knew how to hide.

"Miz Fenster, these wheels gonna fly off if you don't slow down." Moses's voice was deepened in his panic and his words cut through the noise of the creaking, rattling wagon as it hurtled forward in the moonlight. They were near safety. But not if the men were close enough to see them.

"Can you see them behind us?" she shouted, ignoring his pleas to slow down and urging the sweating team faster.

Moses turned to look back, his body half raised from the seat as he studied the shadows the bright moon cast across the landscape. "No. I think we lost them."

Not for long. Ros's instincts were on high alert. That Jericho and his men had found them at all spoke of their single-minded determination. She didn't dare underestimate them again.

"We're going to racket apart." Moses's plea was not for himself, but for his wife, who clung to the back of the wagon like a frightened leech. And for his son, tied with strips of cloth and leather to his mother.

"If we stop they'll catch us." Ros could hear Ophelia's whimpers from the back of the buckboard but closed her mind to them. Instead she concentrated on Moses. She had seen his determination. "Do you want to be caught? Do you want Ophelia and your boy caught by Jericho?"

Moses cursed once and then leaped into the back of the buckboard. She could not hear his words, but his voice was deep and soothing. Soon, Ophelia's sobs and whimpers stopped—or at least were covered by the noise of the racketing buckboard. The woman had survived much worse; she knew how to hang on. And there wouldn't be safety for any of them if they slowed and were caught by Jericho and his men.

At last she had to slow, or she would have dashed them all into a ditch hidden in shadows, or the side of the barn meant to safeguard them.

Moses climbed forward again and took the reins from her, hauling back hard so that the team recognized the urgency of their stop. "I think we lost them."

She didn't know if he said it because he believed it, or in order to soothe Ophelia. "Not likely. We've just gained ourselves a bit of time to hide . . . I hope."

Moses vaulted from the seat and raced ahead of the slowing team to open the doors. The barn rose before her, a two-story shadow with a slightly lighter shadow where the doors gaped as Moses pushed them open. Good for Caroline; she must have known that someone might need to hide in a hurry and had left the main doors unbarred. Ros would have to thank her. She'd been a surprisingly good Underground Railroad conductor, considering her delicate nature.

The carriage hurtled in, the team barely able to stop before they ran into the other side of the barn, where the doors were properly barred shut for the night.

# Chapter Three

Ros dropped the reins and threw herself from the buckboard, landing nimble and sure on the packed dirt floor strewn with straw. "Hurry, Ophelia," she called as loudly as she dared, knowing their pursuers could be at their heels.

Moses lit a lamp and closed the barn doors again. He couldn't latch them from the inside, but they fit snugly together, and Ros prayed not much light would escape to signal their whereabouts.

"Are we safe?" Ophelia began to wiggle out of the wagon, the squirming handful of infant making her awkward. The sound of rustling in the hay of the wagon mingled with the sounds of the horses' labored breathing.

"Not yet, but soon." Ros strode to the far edge of the barn, into the last stall, where an ancient horse stood sleeping, propped against the wall. There wasn't much room, but her movements were swift and sure as she knelt and cleared the straw from the floor, exposing a wooden trapdoor.

With a grunt, she took the metal ring in both hands and lifted the door. She turned to find Ophelia crowded behind her, looking with fear at the gaping darkness of the hole at her feet. "I can't go in there."

Moses stood behind her, the light from the lantern making a crazy pattern of shadows across his face, so that she could not see his expression as he said confidently, "Sure you can, Fee. You're the bravest woman I know."

Ros kept her face impassive. Ophelia, brave? The woman she had discovered in the milliner's too afraid to choose a red ribbon in case the blue would prove to be more flattering? Love certainly did turn a man's brain to mush.

Barely keeping her impatience in check, she took the lamp and shooed them down. "Go."

Still Ophelia stood, staring down into the hole.

Moses pushed her gently one step at a time closer to safety. "You'll be safe down there, Fee." He brushed a finger gently against his son's cheek. "And so will he."

Abruptly, one step from the hole, Ophelia stiffened. "Not without you."

Moses hugged her swiftly. "I'll be down as soon as I unhitch the team and rub them down."

Ophelia gazed up at him. "Promise?"

Moses whispered, "Promise."

Still Ophelia didn't move. Ros thought the woman would turn hysterical, but instead, she obediently disappeared down into the darkness with only one tiny whimper after Moses said gently, "Fee. Please. For the baby."

Moses moved to unhitch one horse. Ros argued, even as she unhitched the other. "I can do this."

"Time's not our friend right now."

"If they find you—"

"They won't." He continued working, rapidly and thoroughly. "And they won't find anything to say these animals been transporting runaways, either."

Ros took up handfuls of straw and spread them over the areas the team had disturbed with their hasty entrance as Moses led each horse into an empty stall. Without a word, she began to rub down one as he worked on the other. The horses were settling to their water and feed when the sound of pursuit came at last.

Both took the time to throw blankets over the horses' backs before heading for the trapdoor. The sleepy horse did not look pleased to have them in her stall again as Moses climbed down in the hole and pulled the trapdoor closed after himself. Ros heard Ophelia let out a cry of relief, which was quickly muffled, no doubt by a swift hug from Moses. What such a strong man saw in a helplessly clinging vine she couldn't imagine.

"Make sure you don't make any noise. There's blankets and food down there. I'll come get you in the morning." Ros slapped the querulous horse on the withers and watched for a moment as she stomped about her stall in annoyance, destroying any signs that humans had been there—any signs that there was a trapdoor and two runaways with a baby hiding beneath it.

She went to the unlatched barn door, but it was too late. Jericho and his men were there, she could hear them.

As quickly and soundlessly as she could, Ros wiggled her way out a little hole in the wall that Gwyneth had showed her once. It was large enough for a child and an adventurous dog; it must be large enough for a determined woman dressed like a man.

As she squeezed out, holding her breath, she heard Jericho and his men enter the barn. Damn. She'd gone this long without ever coming face-to-face with the bounty hunter; she didn't want to ruin her lucky streak now. Afraid to move and make some sound that would draw their attention, she stopped, her back pressed up against the rough planks as she tried to listen and place Jericho and his men.

Above the sound of a restless horse raking hooves through the straw, she heard them tramp heavy-footed through the barn. They weren't hiding their movements. Why should they? They had the law behind them.

"Damn. I coulda swore . . ."

"Are they ghosts, now? Able to disappear with a team in a few minutes?"

"Barn doors don't unlatch themselves."

"Maybe they . . ."

With a curse, "Let's go. While we waste time here, they're getting away."

"Or they're hiding outside, waiting for us to leave before they come in."

"First we'll try the house." Jericho.

Ros nearly cried out when a cold nose poked her hip and an enthusiastic animal began to push against her and whine. Tora. For a moment she wished the huge Great Dane had one ounce of protective instinct. But she was a puppy at heart, despite her seven years.

"Hush, Tora," she whispered in the dog's ear. "They'll hear you."

"What's that?" Footsteps pounded toward her hiding place. Before she could decide how to get herself—and the eager dog—into the house without drawing the attention of the men, Tora heard their voices and within a moment had wiggled through the hole in the wall of the barn to investigate.

Prepared to leap to the dog's defense, Ros had the latch half lifted even before she heard the sound of hammers being drawn. "Look at that creature."

With one hand, Ros tore at the whiskers attached to her face with spirit gum. If she'd only had a skirt she could fool them. But there wasn't time. She'd just have to be a woman who wore men's clothing.

"Hey, lookit." One of the men laughed and Ros froze. "He's a big one, but I think he's too dumb to be mean."

From the whining and yipping sounds, Tora was making her general cowardice known. Slowly, Ros lowered the latch and backed away from the barn door.

"Here, boy, want a biscuit?"

Tora barked her begging bark, half sharp demand and half whining plea.

"He's a friendly fella, now."

*She. She's a friendly diversion that's going to save my neck.* Ros didn't wait another moment longer. Tora had proved she could take care of herself. A mad dash across the yard and Ros slipped into Caroline's unlocked house without discovery.

Rob watched the abandoned farmhouse as he crouched behind a dilapidated shed. Ben's information appeared to be a little off. For an abandoned farm, it was looking pretty lived in. As the afternoon had rolled along, Rob had had ample time to appreciate the newly planted garden just outside the kitchen.

During the day he'd seen neither hide nor hair of Barker. There'd been a woman washing and hanging her clothes to dry. There'd been three rough-and-tumble boys scattering feed to the squawking chickens that inhabited a small fenced in area—when they weren't escaping from the various holes in the dilapidated wire fence and being chased around the house by the littlest boy.

Rob had watched all afternoon, not just to see the

man he was hunting, but looking for any sign that there was a man living here. He hadn't found one. The oldest boy, no more than ten, had milked the cow that was tied to a shade tree. The woman had gotten her brood washed at the pump and put to bed and then spent a few minutes in the rocker on the rickety porch as the sun set. Alone. Barker had not appeared.

Rob had been tempted to take the evidence and go back to Ben empty-handed. After all, there'd been no men's clothes on the line, and it looked like the woman had done her week's washing. Still, if Ben said Barker was here, then he most likely was. Maybe he'd gone off hunting to feed this brood. If so, he'd be back.

Rob settled back, watching the silent, dark house. His patience was rewarded when, in the full moonlit dark, he could see his quarry moving about at last. At first he thought the figure might be the woman, feeling restless. But a traitorous shaft of moonlight revealed Barker, his face stark in the cold light.

The man sat in the rocker. The creak of the worn porch boards reached Rob and he tensed, thinking Barker was going to crash through, rocker and all. But after a few moments, the boards ceased their protest and Barker began to rock, turning his head from time to time as he stared out into the darkness. Did he sense Rob? Some of these criminals seemed to have an extraordinary ability to smell pursuit.

As if he could read Rob's mind, Barker came off the porch mid-rock and began to walk toward the shed with purpose. Rob tensed, debating whether to step out, or wait for the man to get close enough to rush. But Barker hadn't sensed him. He stepped into the shed and came out with a length of wire and a pair of clippers. As Rob's breathing slowed, Barker walked over to the chicken fence and set about repairing the holes through which the chickens had been escaping during the day.

The woman came out, a gray shadow. Rob had seen that time hadn't been kind to her, although she'd been quick with a smile for her boys during the day. Her voice was low but carried in the still of the night. "Frank. You need a lantern."

"Too dangerous." Barker stopped mending as she approached.

"Still?" There was a sadness and an impatient disbelief in her voice.

"Maybe forever, Anna. I told you that."

"I know. I just wish . . ." Her voice trailed off and she held out a plate of something. Supper, Rob supposed. Whatever stew she'd dished up for her boys earlier. He guessed he might as well let Barker eat in peace. His last meal in freedom, so to speak. At least for a good long while.

The woman smoothed her hand along Barker's arm as she spoke to him, her words so low Rob couldn't hear anything but the wistful tone. Barker took the plate and wrapped his arm around the woman's waist. She laughed, a silvery sound of pleasure that seemed at odds with her worn face.

The hard ground under him suddenly felt harder and the night chill he'd been ignoring seeped into his bones mercilessly. All of a sudden Rob understood why Barker was here instead of on the road, skipping from place to place to avoid being caught. Of course, he thought, wouldn't it be a woman who'd bring the bank robber down?

She'd probably told him she loved him. Probably thought she did. Judging by the three boys, she'd been putting up with his bank robbing ways for some time. Did she know? And if she did, why would she insist he settle down here, where he'd be easy pickings for any lawman? Why not head west, where the law was scarce?

Rob shrugged off a bat that'd swooped low from behind. Didn't matter, he supposed. Right now, while Barker was fixing up the place and eating his supper in the dark, she had made him a target for Ben and Rob and the Pinkerton Agency.

He had told Ben he'd take the man dead or alive, but seeing him there, taking care of his woman and unaware that his free days were at an end, Rob couldn't do it.

He watched, waiting impatiently for the woman to go inside. When she did, he drew his gun and left the shelter of the shed.

Barker didn't look up at Rob's footsteps, just said, "Anna, I'll never get this fence finished if you don't quit pestering me."

" 'Fraid you're not going to get that fence mended tonight—maybe not for five to ten years, Barker."

The bank robber leaped to his feet, brandishing the wire clippers. He stopped when he saw the moonlight glinting off the barrel of Rob's gun. Abruptly, he relaxed, dropping the clippers to the ground and raising his hands in the air. "Didn't aim to be found so soon. Got a porch to fix soon's I mend the fence."

Rob shrugged. "Sorry."

"Ain't we all."

Rob gestured with the gun to the little copse in which he'd sheltered his horse. It was at least half a mile away. "Best get going, before the moonlight wanes."

Barker hesitated, his eyes going from Rob's gun to Rob's eyes, measuring his chances to overpower him. That was the way of bank robbers. They were gamblers of a sort.

Rob hated gamblers. He gestured again. "Get moving. We haven't got all night."

He heard the sound of a rifle being primed and his shoulder blade, which had not bothered him all afternoon, began to itch like the blazes.

"He ain't going nowhere, mister."

"Anna." Barker smiled and lowered his hands. "Good girl. Give me the rifle, sweetheart."

Rob's stomach clenched and he prepared to fire, but the woman's words stilled him.

"Walk away, mister. Walk away and leave us to our lives."

"Anna," Barker protested, but when he moved, Rob tensed as if to shoot and Barker stopped moving.

"I can't walk away, Miz Barker. Your husband here's left some good folks a good bit poorer and the law wants to talk to him."

"If the law wants to talk to him, it ought to have sent two men."

"I promised to take him in dead or alive."

"Well, you ain't taking him alive. And if you shoot him, I'll shoot you."

Barker grinned. "She's a dead aim, too."

Anna said gruffly, "Have to be, don't I, with my man gone all the time?" She shot the ground once, by his feet. "Now git before I change my mind and shoot you anyway."

Rob recognized defeat when he saw it. At least for now. He walked away, but the itch grew until it felt like he had a burning target branded between his shoulder blades.

The house was silent and dark, save for the dim lamp Caroline left in the kitchen for any runaways who might want to use it as a safe place to shelter in the night. Ros followed the faint glow, stripping off her man's garb as she went. Would Jericho actually come into the house?

Anyone in town could tell the men that Caroline and Gwyneth lived alone, that Mr. Lewis hadn't been home in more than a year. That she lived alone with her daughter and taught school in the little one-room schoolhouse in town. A quieter mouse than Caroline Lewis couldn't be found. And Gwyneth was just a child. No threat there.

In her male disguise, Ros would be hard to explain. But that was easy enough to deal with. She'd simply dress as a woman. No one would think anything of Rosaline Fenster visiting Caroline. They were cousins of a sort, and Rosaline had visited before. In fact, she'd visited often enough to know the little house even in the dim light. She wouldn't wake Caroline. If Jericho did choose to come to the door, she wouldn't want to count on the woman's ability to lie without detection.

Ros made her way into Gwyn's room, pushing through the curtain that separated the child's room from the kitchen just as Tora began to bark. The little girl barely made a discernible shape under her covers. Ros stripped off her whiskers and sideburns quickly, pushing down the regret that made her throat burn. She did not want to put anyone in danger—especially not this little girl.

If only the wagon train had left as scheduled . . . She pushed aside the thought. They could be caught as easily on the other side of the Missouri as here.

Gwyneth let out a little snore and regret blossomed again. She should have chosen somewhere else to go to ground. Should never have let Caroline offer her home as a stop for weary travelers. At the time it had seemed a brilliant idea.

Indeed, Caroline had not protested when Ros

explained the good she could do, just by leaving her door unlocked and a lamp burning in the kitchen at night for those down on their luck who might need a safe hiding place for a short while.

Ros rescued her pistol from the waistband of her trousers. She'd do what she needed to protect them if there was trouble. It was the least she could do for bringing Jericho to their doorstep.

Tora barked again, her play-with-me bark. The dog was practically at the kitchen door. Down to the man's shirt that served now as a nightshirt, she kicked the discarded clothing under the bedstead. She dove beneath the covers, moving as carefully as possible so that she would not wake the child.

Gwyneth turned restlessly in her sleep, and Ros smoothed back her hair and hushed her lightly. Maybe the men would go away. Maybe Gwyneth would never have to be frightened by them.

But her hope was in vain, because a scant moment later the men were banging on the door, calling out a warning about dangerous runaway slaves.

The harsh shouts invaded the peace of Caroline's little home and Ros couldn't bear the sound. Swearing, she felt about for Gwyneth's robe. It would be too small, but perhaps the men wouldn't notice. She could pretend to be Caroline.

She had found the robe and stuffed one arm into the sleeve when she heard Caroline stirring in her room next to Gwyneth's. Too late. She heard Caroline stumble sleepily into the kitchen and prayed she would understand what was happening and not reveal everything in her fright.

The glow of the lantern increased as Caroline turned up the wick. Ros swore softly; in her haste, she hadn't pulled the curtain in Gwyneth's bedroom doorway all the way closed. Now she had a view of Caroline, in her nightdress and robe, a shawl pulled around her shoulders. She held a rifle aimed toward the door.

She held it right, too. Ros was pleased. During the last round of lessons they had, Caroline hadn't been able to hit the side of the barn. But the men wouldn't know that, the way she gripped the weapon as if she was confident of her own abilities.

Her hand gripping her own pistol, Ros positioned herself so that she could see, and yet anyone glancing in would not realize that she was awake. She felt Gwyneth come awake next to her and pressed a palm to the child's mouth briefly to indicate the need for silence. When the child snuggled tightly against her, hampering her gun hand, Ros pushed her away gently.

Caroline's voice was raspy with sleep as she asked, "What do you want?"

Jericho's voice was rough with suspicion and anger as the men pushed into the kitchen. Big. Rough. Dangerous. "Slave's runaway."

Caroline looked small and vulnerable in the midst of them. "What's that to do with me?"

"We thought he might have come here."

Caroline's arm swept a gesture around her kitchen. "Does it look like I have a slave here?" Her hand was visibly trembling.

"If he did, you might want to take note he's not just a runaway."

"No?"

"No. He murdered a woman. Might have done worse, too, but I don't want to say out of respect for her husband."

Caroline shivered, an all-over-body shiver that made Ros's throat tighten. Would she believe the men? Would she tell them where they might find Moses?

"Goodness. I hope you get him. But he isn't here, I assure you."

One of Jericho's men had found the bread safe and hacked himself a piece of bread while Caroline spoke with Jericho. He turned now, drawing the bread knife theatrically across his throat with one hand as he stuffed bread into his mouth with the other and mumbled, "Dark, ma'am. You wouldn't want to have your throat cut in your bed."

"That's why I have this." Caroline hefted the rifle, and the men eased back a bit in respect.

"Where's your man?"

"Gone."

"If you don't mind, then, we'll take a look around, make sure you're safe."

# Chapter Four

Ros tensed. Should she play the helpless female? Damn. Or would she make matters worse if they questioned her short-cropped hair?

With Gwyneth trembling beside her and Caroline surrounded by three barely civil men, Ros struggled to decide what to do. The men would stop being even so much as semi-polite to Caroline if they thought she was harboring a slave sympathizer and possibly slaves as well.

But Ros was not just any sympathizer—her connection to the man they hunted would be clear as soon as they caught sight of the slash on her cheek. They might decide that Caroline had been used unwittingly and leave her in peace. But if they knew that Moses was here . . . Perhaps she should hide under the bed? That way Caroline might be able to brazen her way out of the situation without Ros making it any the worse.

She started to ease out of the bed, but Gwyneth clutched tight around her middle. Ros held her breath as she tried to pry the warm little arms away from her, but the child held on with the tenacity of a bulldog.

"Take a look around? My little house?" Caroline didn't seem too concerned at the thought. Didn't she know Ros could be hiding here? Didn't she know—Ros wanted to curse as Caroline said pleasantly, with a sweet dependency, "Mighty nice of you. I don't know what this world is coming to when a woman isn't safe in her own home."

"That's what we're here for, ma'am." They approached the curtain separating off Gwyn's bedroom, and suddenly it was much too late to hide. As a last resort, she slid farther under the covers, pretending to be asleep. With one hand, she pressed on Gwyn's chest to indicate the child should stay still. Gwyn's cold little hand crept into hers. Would the men try to wake them?

As they drew near, though, Caroline said softly, "I'd appreciate it if you don't wake up my daughter. She's recovering from the cholera."

"Of course." They veered from the room as if it held certain death. And no wonder; cholera was a nasty disease. Clever Caroline to think of it. Ros squeezed Gwyn's hand in comfort as the men moved through the rest of the house quickly, giving wide berth to Gwyn's room. Though they made a great deal of noise and bluster, they seemed more than glad to find nothing.

Jericho said with a rusty streak of disappointment, "Guess there's no runaways hiding here, then, ma'am."

Caroline gave one of her silly little girlish laughs. "Thank goodness." Normally that laugh made Ros grit her teeth, but this time it made her smile. Caroline didn't sound bright enough to be hiding slaves. Even Jericho wasn't likely to keep wasting his time.

One of the other men said in a surprisingly genial tone, "I'd lock your doors if I were you, ma'am."

"Of course. I will. Thank you for suggesting it."

"No trouble, ma'am. I'm surprised your husband—"

Ros tensed at the mention of Caroline's absent husband. Thwarted from their hunt, would these men find another way to amuse themselves tonight? She had little respect for Jericho, but his reputation was for catching slaves, not raping women.

Caroline did not seem to worry about their intentions. "My husband would be quite cross with me if he were to learn I hadn't locked the door, I assure you gentlemen."

"When's he due home?" The man was persistent.

"Never mind that." Jericho, however, was restless to get back to his hunt. "See that you listen to him from now on, ma'am. Never know what kind of riffraff will consider an open door an invitation."

Caroline gave her little laugh again. "Oh, I won't be so careless again. I promise."

As soon as they were gone, Caroline bent to turn out the lantern. After three unsuccessful attempts, she leaned against the table, and Ros could see that she was swaying. Before she could leap up to help, Caroline collapsed to the floor in a crumpled heap.

Gwyneth was out of bed in a streak of white cotton nightgown. "Mama, what's the matter? Get up."

Ros followed, pushing the little girl away from her mother. "Give her some room, Gwyn." Caroline held out her hand and Ros helped her struggle to her feet. "Clever of you to say that Gwyneth has cholera."

"First thing that came to my mind," Caroline said, her voice dry and hoarse.

"First . . ." Ros could feel the fever burning in her through the layers of clothing she wore. Damn.

"I've been poorly for a few days."

"But you'll be better soon, Mama. Just like me. I'll be your nurse like you were mine."

"I know you will, baby." Every movement Caroline made seemed to be painful. But she didn't collapse again. "Your travelers safe?"

"For now."

Caroline glanced at Gwyneth with a motherly smile as she murmured, "A murderer, Ros?"

"He's not. I swear it."

"Good, then. I'll rest easier tonight." Caroline sagged against her, bonelessly. "Help me back to bed, would you?"

"Of course." Ros realized that the woman weighed nearly nothing at all. She could have been holding a shadow rather than a flesh-and-blood human being.

He'd been right to worry. He hadn't gone more than a few steps before Barker called out, "Stop right there and put your hands in the air."

Rob did as he was told, though his instincts clamored for him to turn and fire. There was too much chance he'd hit Anna instead of Barker. He was perfectly willing to accept a shootout that would leave one man standing—his natural preference being himself doing the standing, of course. Anna messed up the simple equation.

As if aware of her own part in the drama and regretful of it, she said, "Frank. You're not going to kill him." Her tone was as sharp as if she were reprimanding one of her boys.

"Anna, be sensible." Barker, the bank robber who'd coldly held trembling women at gunpoint while he robbed their bank, said pleadingly, "I can't take care of you or the boys if I'm swinging at the end of a rope."

The woman's breath caught audibly. "Hang?"

Unable to use his gun to free himself, Rob unholstered his next best weapon—his tongue. "You won't hang, Barker."

"He won't?" She latched on to his assertion quickly, as he'd hoped she might. "Are you sure?"

"Been doing this long enough, ma'am. Your husband is wanted for bank robbery, nothing worse." Nothing worse. He supposed if she'd stayed with him for so long that she wouldn't consider her husband's occupation too terrible.

Barker said sharply, "I'm wanted dead or alive. I saw the poster."

"Once the law has a man, it tends to want to keep him alive—long as he hasn't killed anyone. You haven't, have you?" Rob was relatively certain that Barker hadn't even shot off his gun during his robberies. But he held his breath as he waited for an answer.

"Nope. Never killed anyone; only scared them and took their money."

Anna Barker spoke again, quietly, as if she were in a church on Sunday morning. "What *would* happen to him?"

What would she consider acceptable? Rob was prepared to lie for a moment, but then he decided he'd better not underestimate Anna Barker again. "Prison."

"For how long?"

"Anna . . ."

"For how long?"

Rob shrugged. "Five years?"

"Is that right?" she asked her husband.

"If I'm lucky."

Anna Barker turned to him, her eyes fierce. "Can you see that he's lucky?"

Seemed like a lot for a woman to ask of a man who was looking at the end of his days on earth. "Yes."

"Anna, you can't believe him."

"Frank, if you go to prison for five years, then you can come home. For good. No more running."

Rob could hear the hope in her voice. Evidently Barker could, too. "Anna—"

"Please, Frank. For me. For our boys."

Without another word, Barker put down his gun and slumped to the ground. Another man might have overpowered him, clobbered him good for the threat, to keep him cowed on the trail home. But Rob couldn't. The man had been brought to his knees by his wife. That was enough cowing for any man.

"Thank you, ma'am," Rob said, tipping his hat to Anna Barker.

"Don't thank me," she said wearily. "I want him home with me for good. If I thought killing you would do it, I'd shoot you myself and be glad of it."

"She means it, too." Barker seemed to admire that in a wife.

"Let's go." Rob gestured to the man, and they began walking away again. He could feel Anna Barker's eyes on him, but his shoulder blade didn't itch at all. Nevertheless, he was careful to keep close enough to Barker that she'd not dare risk a shot in the harshly deceptive moonlight.

Once they were out of range, he breathed a sharp sigh of relief and stopped. "Just a minute, Barker."

The bank robber turned to him, a weary question written on his features. "What is it? Are you lost? I ain't going to help you, if you are."

"I know where I am." Rob brought out his manacles. "I just want to make sure I know you'll stay where I put you."

An urge to resist thrummed through the bank robber, and Rob prepared to shoot first, ask questions later. But just as suddenly as the urge came, it apparently left. Barker obediently put his hands together and allowed himself to be cuffed. "Glad you didn't do it in front of her."

Rob let out a gust of laughter. "She'd have shot me then and there."

Barker grinned but didn't deny the accusation. "She's a good woman. Don't know what she sees in me."

"Ever thought she might be better off without you?"

"She won't hear of it."

"I'll see she and the boys get someplace safe."

"They *are* someplace safe."

"An abandoned farmhouse—"

"I bought it. It ain't abandoned no more."

"You bought it?"

"Woman deserves something for her loyalty, after all these years."

"Guess so."

"The boys'll help her take care of the place. I do wish I'd gotten to fix the porch, though. She likes to rock a spell in the evening."

"She seems like a woman who can manage. After all, she's been doing it for a long time."

Barker turned his head, as if to hide some emotion he didn't want Rob to see. "I'll be back in five years and she won't have to do it alone anymore."

"Not if you quit robbing banks."

"You think she'll let me rob another one, after she gets me home safe and sound with no bounty on my head?" Barker shook his head sharply. "I wish I'd met her a little sooner. Might never have thought bank robbing was good work."

\* \* \*

In the morning, Ros woke to sunshine and the solemn perusal of a seven-year-old. Gwyneth. "I put out bread and butter for the travelers."

She obviously expected praise for this accomplishment, so Ros obliged. "Thank you. I expect they're quite hungry after the long night."

"They didn't come up, even though I told them it was safe."

"You shouldn't do that, Gwyn. Your mother wouldn't like you to put yourself in danger like that."

"I know. Mama says I'm to pretend there's no one there, no matter what. She always puts out the bread and butter. But I had to do it today because she's sick and I'm her nurse. Nurses don't let sick people do things that will make them weaker."

"They don't?" Ros smiled at the authoritative tone in the child's tone. "What do they do?"

"They make broth and put wet cloths on the forehead and talk real quiet so the sick person can sleep."

"How long has your mother been sick?"

Gwyn counted patiently on her fingers. "Four days."

"Then I'm sure she'll be better soon." Ros didn't want Gwyneth to see her concern. Four days? Caroline had been sick alone with Gwyneth for four days. How much longer would the illness last? Normally, with Jericho on her heels, she would have left that morning. But with Caroline ill . . .

"She's awful sick."

"I know." Ros took the child by the hand and swung her off the bed. Following, she added, "Why don't we take care of her together today, so that she can get well twice as fast?"

"Gwyneth." Caroline's voice was weak but certain. "Now that Auntie Ros is here, you must go to school today."

A pout pushed out the child's lower lip. "But I don't want to."

"It is your duty."

"Mrs. Watson's not a real teacher. She can't even spell good."

"She can't spell well," Ros corrected helpfully, and then bit her tongue as she realized that she had just helped underline Gwyn's disrespect.

"You could teach school, Auntie Ros."

"No, I could not."

"But you have before, and Mrs. Watson only does it when Mama can't. And she truly can't spell."

"I have taught school, Gwyn, that's true." For a month. A disastrous month of rules and regulations and tight-waisted skirts. Never again. Although there was no need to say so to Gwyneth now. "But with your mother unwell, I think I'm needed here."

"Yes, Gwyn. Now wash your face and hands while Auntie Ros fixes you a lunch pail so that you will not be tardy."

Gwyneth protested. "I could help take care of you. And I know more than Mrs. Watson already."

"Gwyneth Amanda Lewis!" There was a ghostly remnant of a mother's sharpness in her tone, but it served well enough to prompt Gwyneth to obey.

Ros leaned in the doorway, "A mother's way, even from the sickbed." Caroline did not look well. What color she had was more limp dishrag than her usual cream-colored complexion.

Caroline smiled, but there was a touch of sadness there. "Her lunch pail is by the stove. She likes the crusts cut off her bread and the butter spread liberally. There are apples in the barrel. Make sure you get one without a worm in it."

Ros went off to accomplish the unfamiliar task. Tora,

as if to make amends for turning traitor last evening, watched the buttering of the bread without a single beggar's whine.

Gwyneth returned and took the bucket as if it contained something nasty. As Caroline's daughter, though, she remembered to say politely, "Thank you, Auntie Ros."

"I'll take good care of her while you're gone."

Gwyneth nodded and then abruptly hurled herself at Ros, hugging around her waist with enough strength to steal the breath from her.

Ros patted her head, much as she might have patted Tora's. "Hurry on, now. You don't want to be tardy."

"Thank you for being patient with her, Ros." Caroline had made her way out to the kitchen to prepare a cup of tea for herself. "I know you don't much like children."

"She's a sweet girl, Caroline. You've done a wonderful job." Ros took the kettle from her shaking grip and poured the hot water into the teapot, over the fragrant tea leaves, releasing a pleasant odor that helped mask the smell of sickness for a moment.

She didn't know much about nursing, but she had enough common sense to know a woman who looked as if her legs couldn't support her shouldn't be standing, so she shooed her into bed, following with the tea.

The tea didn't stay down long, and Caroline's quiet, desperate retching was followed by tears. "I don't know if I'm going to survive this."

"Of course you will."

"If I don't, I want you to take Gwyneth to San Francisco."

Ros tried not to look surprised. She knew that Caroline's father and stepmother were there, visiting her sister—but to transport Gwyneth so far. . . . "Are you certain?"

"You were going with Moses anyway."

"Only partway," Ros protested. "And then I was going to pretend to have to leave for business reasons and entrust my servants to finish the trip in my stead." It was a good plan, though she knew it rankled Moses to have to pretend that his hard-earned future, all stashed in the wagon, was Ros's and not his.

"I don't know why we have to talk about this; you're going to be fine." Ros gathered the soiled linens for a good hot washing. Her brother-in-law R.J.'s sister was studying to be a doctor and had been emphatic on her last visit that cleanliness and washing in good hot water could halt the spread of much disease. "Besides, they'll be home soon."

"No. They're going to wait until Jeanne has her baby. That won't be until the fall."

Babies. It seemed like an epidemic in the family. Even her own twin had contributed two in the last five years. "I take it they've forgiven her for marrying an Indian, then."

"Theo is more civilized than my youngest sister. They were delighted when she married him. They have finally forgiven her for becoming famous for her stories of the West."

"Why? Her stories are so gripping—I think they are responsible for Moses and Ophelia setting their sights west rather than north toward Canada."

"I find them too bold for Gwyneth."

Ros would have argued the sentiment, but just then Caroline was overcome by another bout of nausea.

Ros thought she'd rather be facing Jericho at gunpoint than here with a sick woman and no way to help.

"Just rest, Caroline. I'll see to Gwyneth while you recover."

Caroline drifted to sleep and Ros took the teacup away and went out into the barn to talk with Moses. He was currying the horse who'd guarded his hiding place.

"Caroline's got cholera."

Moses's hand hitched in its smooth rhythm. "Gonna stay awhile, then?"

"I am. You and Ophelia might be better off taking the baby somewhere safer."

"Ain't nowhere safer 'til we cross the river."

"They're saying you killed her."

"Me?" His lip curled in surprise and a certain touch of admiration. "Not surprising he'd do that. Master . . ." Moses straightened, resting his hand on the horse's back. "Mr. Hawkins probably got himself believing it, too."

"Probably. But it means they'll be looking hard for you, even if you cross the river and make it all the way to the Pacific coast."

"Can't be helped."

"I suppose it can't." Ros sighed. To her it was a simple concept—men and women owned themselves; no one else had the right to own a human being. And it was that way in most of the civilized world. But the laws of the South had not yet been corrected, which put Moses—and anyone who helped him—in grave danger.

"You want me out of here? Protect that little missy who brought the food this morning?"

"No." Ros shook her head. "You're safer here—if you stay out of sight."

"I suppose I can do that for a few weeks—considering I won't never have to hide once I cross that river."

"I hope so." Jericho, on the track of a murdering slave, might not give up so easily.

# Chapter Five

Ros thought of Caroline lying ill inside. Possibly dying, though she didn't want to admit it. "How are Ophelia and the baby?"

"Well enough."

"Do you think Ophelia will understand she must stay hidden?"

"I'll make sure she does." Moses glanced toward the trapdoor with a grim expression. "I won't let nothing send us back there. I'd rather we all die first."

"Let's see that it doesn't come to that." The sentiment wasn't unusual for one who'd risked his own life to see others safe only to have them become frightened and jeopardize everyone around them. "I'll head back on my own and make the arrangements for the wagon train and check on the boys. Once we know when we start, I'll sneak you and Ophelia into town and over the river, and then you'll be on your way to your new home."

Moses nodded. "Soon."

"I have to wait a few days before I go, just to make sure Caroline is well again." Ros thought of how much willpower it must have taken the sick woman to face down those men. She owed her that, and probably more.

Caroline was out of bed when Ros returned. She sat propped at the kitchen table, a shawl around her shoulders, a pen in her hand and papers scattered about. Her eyes were red-rimmed from tears her eyes were too dry to shed.

"What are you doing?"

"I need to write some letters." Her eyes closed, as if she were embarrassed at the way she felt. "Just in case—"

"Caroline, you need to rest. You'll never get well if you don't."

"Then you write them for me."

Ros helped her back to bed, biting her tongue to keep from scolding Caroline for her foolish fears. She was a young, healthy woman. If she took care of herself, she would recover. Gwyneth had. She wouldn't think of the countless others the illness had taken, just of the ones who survived. As Caroline must.

Caroline fell into bed. "The first letter is for Gwyn."

Ros almost protested but decided not to bother. Caroline could be obstinate as any mule when she wished something done. Surely it would be better to humor her in this.

"I want you to give it to her on her wedding day." Caroline made a choked sound. "She'll be beautiful, I know she will."

"You'll be there," Ros answered with determined cheer.

" 'My dearest . . .' " Caroline paused. "No . . . 'my darling daughter. I wish I could be there to hold you on this special day. Know that I am watching from heaven and sending you all my love. I know that you have chosen a good man, because I told Auntie Ros to make sure—' "

"What?" Ros stopped writing, startled.

"It's important, Ros. I want Gwyneth to be like you— I want her to wait until she finds the right man, not just jump at the first handsome man to make her heart beat faster."

"I'm certain she won't."

"Well, you didn't, and that's why I'm asking you to see that she doesn't make the same mistake I did."

Caroline's voice, weak and hoarse with emotion, conveyed a a lifetime of a mother's hopes and dreams between fitful lapses into a restless sleep. Ros dutifully transcribed them, wishing the dull ache behind her eyes away.

When Caroline finished with a three-sentence salutation of eternal love and hopes for the future, Ros sighed with relief and waved the ink dry. With a flourish, before Caroline could decide to rewrite the whole thing, she folded it, sealed it, and addressed it to Gwyneth. "There." She put it on Caroline's bedside table and said briskly, "Now you can give it to her yourself, when you dance at the wedding."

"One more. To Rob."

"Your husband?"

Caroline laughed weakly and then turned away, her body wracked by a spasm of retching. She lay back against her pillow, her face the same color as her carefully bleached sheets. Her eyes closed, and Ros put the pen down.

Two hours later, she found that Caroline had not forgotten. " 'Dear Rob . . .' " She stopped, as if she couldn't continue.

Ros helped her swallow a spoonful of water, but she didn't keep it down. With a gasp, she managed to force out the words. Ros bent near to hear them the first time, not wishing to make her repeat even one. " 'Love your daughter as you could not love your wife. P.S. Please try to see her two weeks out of every year, at least until she marries.' "

The stark words looked overwhelmed by the blank expanse of cream-colored paper on which they were written. "Is that all?" She hoped so.

Caroline smiled. "Dear Ros, don't fret. Rob and I . . . We . . ."

"I'm sorry." Uncomfortable with the conversation, Ros said stiffly, "I assumed you and he had an arrangement that suited both of you." Caroline's request for Ros to keep Gwyneth from marrying the first man who asked her made sense now.

"Rob needed a wife like you." Caroline's breath gasped out on a spasm of pain. "Instead he got me."

Her words caught Ros by surprise. "I'd make a terrible wife."

"No. You're strong."

"You've seen to your own needs, Caroline. And to Gwyneth's as well."

"I need a man to take care of me. To hold me." She drifted off, her words nearly inaudible. "Not like you."

*Not like you.* Caroline had meant the words as a compliment, but they struck Ros to the heart. She'd like a man to hold her—as long as he was willing to let her go when she wanted to go.

She said softly, looking down at Caroline struggling for breath, even in her sleep, "The woman who faced down Jericho and his men when she was shaking with fever is the bravest woman I've ever known."

When she returned from feeding the chickens, Caroline was sitting up, her cheeks rosy. "Ros."

As she approached, Ros noted that the brightness in

her eye was the brightness of fever, not health. The woman clutched a small leather-bound book in her hand.

"I want you to give this to someone for me." Caroline seemed hesitant, even more so than her illness might cause, as she held out the book with a trembling hand.

"I promise." Ros took the book, meaning to put it aside for later, until she realized what it was. "This is your diary. Do you want me to give it to your husband?"

Caroline shook her head, and her eyes glowed with an unearthly fire. "My neighbor. He will understand. You'll find his name on the last page . . . and many others as well."

Caroline gave a rattling sigh and leaned back against her pillows. "Thank you."

"Do you think you can sleep now?"

"Yes."

"You will most likely regret this a year from now, you know? Telling me all these secrets."

Caroline shook her head. "No. You'll never tell anyone my secrets." Suddenly she shot forward to sit bolt upright in bed. The lack of strength was shocking when she grasped Ros's hand. "Promise me you'll take care of Gwyneth."

Ros said helplessly, "I'll keep her safe until you're well again."

"I can sleep now." Caroline sank back against the pillows one last time. Ros sat in dawning horror as she noted Caroline's pallor, and the stillness of her chest where her breathing labored no longer. The room was silent. Caroline had been right about death.

As she reached forward and touched the still-warm skin and confirmed that there was no movement of air, no life left in her, Gwyneth came through the door, her small booted feet pounding like a drum on the floor.

"No." Ros stood, blinded by her tears.

"Is Mama awake?" the child whispered.

"No."

"When she wakes up, I brought her some flowers to make her feel better." One grubby hand held a fist of spring flowers.

"Gwyn. I'm afraid your Mama isn't going to wake up." She heard her voice as if it was coming from somewhere else. Someone else. Was that the right way to tell a child her mother was dead? Ros didn't know.

How had she been told? No doubt Miranda, her eldest sister, had taken them all up in a huge tight group and hugged each one of them as she used some fairy tale or other to explain that their parents were never coming home. But she couldn't remember. And she didn't believe in fairy tales.


"Hey, mister! How far's Saint Joe?" The emigrant driving the wagon seemed energized by some sense of destiny. His smile was brighter than one would expect from someone who'd obviously spent a goodly amount of time on the driver's seat. His family crowded around behind him, little ones, five or six of them.

"Not too far. Get there today, for sure."

"Today?" The emigrant's wife sounded doubtful, as if she thought Rob would deliberately lie to her.

He tipped his hat to her. "Yes, ma'am. I just rode out of there this morning."

"On horseback."

"Nice horse." The emigrant looked enviously at his mount. Rob wouldn't have been surprised by an offer to buy the animal. Emigrants were like locusts on the road as they passed by.

"I haven't traveled that fast," he confessed. "You

folks should be able to make town before dark, if you don't throw a wheel."

"Mighty obliged," the emigrant said with another smile, and he rumbled off with all his hopes and dreams packed behind him. His wife just frowned and made a small harrumphing sound that conveyed that she'd believe his words when she saw Saint Joe for herself. A pragmatic woman. The emigrant was lucky in some ways.

Sometimes he thought his marriage could have been a tolerable one if Caroline hadn't been so dead set on having a fairy-tale prince for a husband. He could have told her . . . he *had* told her such things didn't happen to girls who said yes to the first man who asked. She'd sniffed back a sob and informed him that he hadn't been the first to ask her to marry him. He'd somehow bitten his tongue on the most damning reply, that he hadn't been talking about the marriage offer he'd made her after they'd become lovers.

He'd been such a young fool. The senator's son, full of promise and pride. Maybe if he had not been so awed by her unconventional family—a dowager duchess for a stepmother, a duke for a stepbrother. And all so different from the mannered Washington society in which he'd grown up. He hadn't guessed that Caroline was the conventional one in the brood.

The betrayal he'd felt when she refused to go farther west with him had been bitter. Worse still was the relief of not having to see the disappointment he brought to her expression daily, no matter how she tried to hide it from him.

She had expected things of him that he could not give her. Of course, to be fair, how was she to know he would quit his promising job with the government and get bitten by the wanderer's bug?

Rob shifted in the saddle. What kind of a sign was it

when a man could argue with his wife when she was still ten miles distant? He thought Barker was such a man—and look where it had gotten the bank robber. A musty jail cell, a most certainly hasty trial, and a spell in the federal penitentiary. All so he could go back a man without a price on his head to what? A fiercely loyal woman like Anna Barker and those sons of his.

For some reason, he couldn't forget Barker's woman. She'd known what her man was, but she'd also known what he could be, and she'd been willing to demand he be that man. Would his life have been different if Caroline had made the same demands on him? Or he on her? He shrugged off the gloomy ruminations. *What ifs* did no one any good.

Still, Anna Barker's firm, clear gaze haunted him. She'd saved his life, and maybe her husband's soul, without a flinch of doubt. Maybe he ought to stop worrying about what might have been and sit down with Caroline and figure out what would be. He took a swig of water to ease his dry throat and nodded to himself.

No more avoiding the question. He'd ask if she meant it when she wrote that she wanted a divorce. If she did, he wouldn't fight her. And whatever happened, at least they wouldn't be pretending it was normal to see each other a few weeks a year. A few celibate weeks of acting like strangers who had to pretend they knew each other to fool a little girl with big eyes and a bigger heart.

The determination sent a shiver of dread down his spine, but he shook it off. They were going to have a serious talk as soon as he'd washed the dirt of the road off himself and had a bite to eat. Even if she ended the discussion by driving him off at the business end of a shotgun.

Anything had to be better than going on as they had been for the last five years.

* * *

"Miz Fenster . . ." Sallie Black raised her hand.

Ros sighed. "If you must, but be quick about it, and I'll not let you go again until spelling."

"Yes, ma'am." Sallie, the prissy daughter of the local preacher, flounced from the room.

"Anyone'd think she was going to some cotillion rather than a privy." Anson Walters was a troublemaker.

Ros looked up and gave him a hard stare. "I have an extra word for you, Anson. *Termagant.* Spell it and use it in a sentence three times, please."

"Miz Fenster—"

"Before Miss Black returns and the others start their test, Mr. Walters."

"Yes, ma'am." Anson did not challenge her authority, which surprised her. She had been waiting these last three days for him to defy her completely. Perhaps it was just the death of his previous schoolteacher that had rattled his somewhat inflated confidence.

Ros looked at her watch as Sallie walked back in. Noon. The funeral was at one. They'd all attend; school would close early. She stood up. "Put away your books."

The class scrabbled to do as she asked, knowing the spelling test was their last chore before school was dismissed for the day.

Ros found herself as eager as they. This would be her last day to teach. She hated the feeling of fifteen pairs of eyes trained on her. The sense that she must be perfect, make no mistake, allow no foolishness, stifled her natural desire to speak her mind when a child fumbled a lesson or pulled a pigtail.

She had done it for Gwyn, unable to refuse the brokenhearted girl any favor large or small. Gwyn, pale and grieving, but certain her mother would want her to go to school. Certain her mother would want her to have a teacher who knew how to spell.

Ros had done it, knowing that the last bit of normality for Gwyneth would be but fleeting. With the funeral came great change. Caroline would be buried, and they would leave her behind for grandparents and a life far from the one she had known here.

And now, atop her worries about safeguarding the slaves, she had a little girl to transport to the safety of her grandparents' care in addition to the necessity of arranging for them all to head West. She must find a way to sneak Moses and Ophelia over the river without risk of catching Jericho's attention. Outfit a wagon for herself and Gwyneth. She could just imagine what Captain Hellfire would say to an emigrant like sweet, fragile Gwyneth Lewis. He'd cock up both his eyebrows and shake his head.

Ros sighed.

"Line up, please."

The children formed a ragged line, Anson, two inches taller than Ros herself, to Emmaline Murphy, a tiny five-year-old who could read better than Anson and didn't hesitate to point that fact out to him.

Ros raised her brow and tapped her foot until they managed something a bit straighter. She looked at freckled Minnie, who was watching her with a confident smile on her face, pigtails askew and pink tongue peeking through the gap in her front teeth. "Miss Murphy: Spell *sorrow*, please."

Overexcited, the child began to spell with a stutter, which erased the confidence in a flash. She missed an *r* and caught herself up at the end, turning to face the wall before Ros could ask her.

Ros turned her gaze on the next in line. "Sam: Spell *sorrow*, please."

Gwyneth, standing pale and still, would be next. Ros would have spared her the unimportant task, but she could not disappoint the child. Gwyneth was concentrating on her test with such intensity that her top teeth had pressed the blood from her lower lip. She was trying so hard to be a good little girl, as she always did.

Ros couldn't remember what she had done when her parents had been killed. Her sisters had cried, all of them—even baby Kate, who hadn't understood what had happened. Ros couldn't remember doing so. Perhaps she had been like Gwyn, dry-eyed and insistent that life must go on. Even now, with her mother dead, the child did not cry.

Ros knew it wasn't natural. But, shamefully, she was glad of Gwyn's bravery. Ros didn't know if she could handle a tearful little girl who asked why. Why had her mother died? Why hadn't Ros made her well? Why had Gwyneth been left to cope with life alone?

No, Ros knew she was more comfortable with the Gwyneth who insisted on going to school—although she had pleaded with Ros to teach. Caroline would have wanted it that way, Gwyneth had explained patiently when Ros had expressed surprise. Since it was true enough, Ros had had enough sense not to argue with her.

She wondered if Gwyneth would stay calm and self-possessed on the long journey west. If not, if she let loose the torrent of emotion she had somehow capped, what would happen then?

Gwyneth spelled her word correctly and gave a little smile. Quickly it disappeared, swallowed by a look of horror that she had dared to smile on this day.

Ros sighed. She knew very little about children. And a child like Gwyneth was as foreign to her as a Dresden china doll.

To her relief, Mrs. Watson appeared in the doorway. Despite Gwyn's ruthless assessment, the woman seemed better equipped to handle a classroom of fractious children than Ros would ever be. With a sharp clap, Mrs. Watson called, "To the pump to wash your hands and faces. Mrs. Lewis deserves clean hands to pray for her."

The children, reminded again of why they were free of school, grew solemn. Ros understood that for them it most certainly didn't feel real. She remembered seeing her parents laid out for burial. She had knocked on the side of her mother's coffin and asked to come in, to the horror and sorrow of every adult in the room. Would seeing the pine box lowered into the ground make them understand?

"Gwyneth, my dear—" Mrs. Watson shot Ros a hostile look. "Would you like me to help you?"

Ros wasn't sure what kind of help Mrs. Watson offered. Gwyneth, at seven, was much too large to be carried to the cemetery just outside of town.

Gwyneth, however, no matter her sorrow, did not look like she intended to thaw toward her nemesis. She tucked her hand in Ros's quite unexpectedly. "Auntie Ros will take care of me, Mrs. Watson. Thank you for your kind offer."

"See that she doesn't get herself dirty," Mrs. Watson ordered. "A dirty child is no sight for a mother to see as she leaves the earth behind."

Ros started to retort that Caroline could not see. Fortunately, she realized how the words would sound to Gwyneth before she said them and settled for, "Gwyneth is as clean as that handkerchief you've tucked in your bosom, Mrs. Watson, I assure you."

She felt a guilty pleasure. Gwyneth had confided that

Mrs. Watson had another handkerchief in her sleeve, which she used for the purpose for which it was intended. The one in her bosom was for decorative purposes only, a fact the children had discovered when it had been snatched by a small child and put to use on a horrible fit of sneezing.

The woman gave a huff of indignation and left.

Ros turned to Gwyneth and saw that the child was trying not to smile. Evidently she remembered the story as well. "Are you ready?"

Gwyneth hesitated, her blue eyes wide and distant. At last she asked with solemn concern, "Is my face dirty?"

Ros wanted to throttle Mrs. Watson. To put that kind of fear into a child . . . "No. Your face hasn't one speck of dirt anywhere upon it."

Gwyneth didn't seem relieved. She stood on tiptoe and said softly. "Check real good, Auntie Ros. I want Mama to be proud of me."

"She is." Ros thought of the letter Caroline had written for Gwyneth, to be given to her on her wedding day. She had been very proud of her daughter, but how would the little girl ever know that?

The child looked down at the ground and scuffed her foot nervously as she whispered, "Maybe that's why she didn't get better. Maybe I wasn't good enough."

"Nonsense." Ros considered reading Caroline's letter to Gwyneth now. The child didn't need to wait ten or more years to hear that her mother loved her.

"Papa went away because I don't always do what I'm told." She confided the absurdity as if it were fact.

"Who on earth told you that? Not your mother?" Ros couldn't imagine Caroline saying something so hurtful to her own daughter. Had her father—

"Mrs. Watson says little girls like me who don't behave make their fathers so unhappy that they run away."

Mrs. Watson was fortunate that she had shepherded the other children down the street some distance. Otherwise Ros *would* have throttled her.

# Chapter Six

Rob rode into town wearily, hoping to catch Caroline before she left the schoolhouse for home. He wanted to make certain he would be welcome. He didn't particularly care for the thought of his daughter watching her father run out of the house by her mother. Not that he'd blame Caroline.

He adjusted the brim of his hat to block the harshness of the noon sun. Today he'd see her. He would force himself to be honest with her. He didn't know whether to give her the gift he'd brought her first. Would the book—a prized edition of Mary Shelley's *Frankenstein*—soften the uncomfortable silence that might stretch between them as they tried to find the words to express what they both already knew?

He'd try to convince her to come west with him. To settle there, near Jeanne. It was his duty. But if she refused, if she could not leave Missouri, he had to face that it might be time to sever things with her for good.

Maybe, he realized with a shock, she'd be the first to say it.

She'd asked for a divorce. The word itself was like a hot brand of failure. His, not hers. He'd thought at first she'd only said it to hurt him. But maybe she meant it.

The silence had seemed so natural on his ride into town that he did not notice at first when it turned unnatural. There should have been noise. Commotion. The sounds of dogs and men, women and children. Wheels clacking and horses' hooves hitting hard-packed dirt. But there was none of that.

He stopped, a sense of foreboding hitting him with a thud as heavy as the oppressive silence. The town was empty, businesses closed and shuttered in midday.

The silence built on him as if it were a force in itself as he cantered through the empty streets to the neat little building where Caroline taught the dozen or so school-age children in town. There was no one in the schoolhouse. The windows were closed, the area quiet— no laughing children.

The little church building stood silent, though he noticed dried rose petals crushed into the ground by the passing of boots and wheels and horses' hooves. He studied the pink- and red- and cream-colored blotches of color against the unremitting dun of the ground. Not long ago, he thought. He could still smell the lingering scent of roses the traffic had released from the dead petals.

With a sense of growing dread, Rob passed by the few silent buildings that made up the little town of Promise Creek and headed toward home. Past a grove of trees he saw the sight that made his heart freeze. Everyone was gathered at the cemetery—a gaggle of black-clad geese around a simple pine box.

The departed didn't have to be one of his. He told

himself that sternly. But the bitter fear would not recede. Not until he could see for himself. He'd left her alone so long. Was he too late? Could his daughter be gone before she'd had a chance to grow into a woman?

As he pulled up his mount and reined in, joining the crowd on the fringes, they parted for him. Blank expressions from those who didn't know him. Sad little sighs and tears from those who did. He'd come too late, then. Too late.

He reached the casket in a few strides, his vision blurred for some unaccountable reason.

"Papa!"

For a moment he thought the call came from inside the pine box—a lone chiding cry from a daughter he had neglected. And then he found himself nearly knocked off his feet. He struggled for breath as small arms wrapped around his neck, choking the air from him. "Papa, you came."

The girl. His daughter, though there was little enough of him showing in her delicate profile, crushed her cheek to his. She was growing up beautiful and fragile, like her mother. Caroline.

He looked at the box. Looked over the box at the woman standing on the opposite side. Her hair was cut unnaturally short for a woman. She watched him warily, with a trace of shock, as if she had not expected to see him here. As if he were the ghost here, not Caroline.

A motherly woman bustled over to him. "You Rob Lewis?"

He nodded, all he could manage with Gwyneth's arms still tight around his neck.

"I'm Adelenia Watson." Apparently the name was supposed to mean something to him, but he did not know what. She clucked her tongue and patted his arm.

"I'm afraid that your dear wife has joined the Lord's choir to sing the great rewards of Heaven, Mr. Lewis."

Choir? For one moment he thought she wasn't . . . But then he understood. He wanted to ask how but could not bring himself to form the words.

The other woman—the one who had seemed to think him a ghost—stepped around the coffin. He blinked, thinking that her skirts had been torn off in an accident, but he realized that she was wearing the outlandish costume Amelia Bloomer had made famous. At a funeral. At least her costume was black.

Gwyneth tightened her arms around his neck. "Auntie Ros, Papa has come back for me."

She smiled at his daughter. *Auntie Ros.* She addressed him, her voice low with sympathy. "What Mrs. Watson is trying to tell you is—" She hesitated a scant second to glance down at the pine box, as if she wished she could make it go away. "Caroline's gone. Cholera. I'm sorry."

*Auntie Ros.* He couldn't help a sweeping glance down at her outrageous attire. "Who are you?"

She took a step back, as if to allow him to see everything, as if to say she had nothing to hide. "I'm Rosaline Fenster."

He stared into her blue eyes for a moment with a jarring sense of having done so recently. But he had never met the infamous Rosaline Fenster. Had he?

Recognition struggled just below the surface. He saw the whip mark on her cheek. A mark like the Englishman . . . Rosaline, the duchess's hell-bent sister, who liked to play at being a man when it suited her. And who had played that game with him not very long ago.

All the anger he felt suddenly had a channel through which to flow. Her. "Wasn't ruining my checkers match enough for you?" He knew it wasn't fair. A dull voice in the back of his head whispered *cholera*, but he wanted to blame her for it somehow. So he wouldn't have to think of what might have been if he'd arrived earlier.

"The poor man's gone mad with grief," Mrs. Watson whispered loudly to two men who stood awkwardly by.

Miss Fenster, however, merely raised one brow, as if she understood quite well that he was searching for a way to blame her for Caroline's death. "I did all that I could, but she was too weak."

Gwyn, buried her head against his neck and whispered, "Mama went to sleep and we can't wake her up. Maybe you can make her get up, Papa?"

He looked at the neat pine box that held his wife. His wife's cold body. He could smell the pine from the recently sawn boards. He could count each nail that had been hammered into the lid. But he couldn't scrabble up a remembrance of Caroline's face. Couldn't hear even the ghost of her voice, or any of the arguments they'd had. The anger scalding through him subsided as quickly as it had erupted. He felt as if he'd turned to stone.

Gwyneth raised her head, her eyes hot with her plea. "Papa . . ."

Rosaline Fenster suddenly stood beside him, her hand on Gwyneth's shoulder. "Your father can't wake your mother, Gwyn. You know that, don't you?"

"Yes, Auntie Ros." Rob hugged her tighter to him, just so that he wouldn't have to see that disappointed look in her eyes—the look he'd been so good at bringing to Caroline's face.

He'd thought anything would be better than to see her disappointment again. But not this. Not this.

* * *

Ros stared at the man holding Gwyneth. There could be no doubt: The legendary Captain Hellfire was Rob Lewis, Caroline's indifferent husband. She found herself grateful for the walk back to Caroline's little farmhouse, which allowed her time to comprehend that stunning fact.

She hung back, letting him go ahead with Gwyneth and Mrs. Watson. She wanted to observe him. Needed to reconcile the two men into one.

"I thought she was a widow," one young mother of a schoolchild whispered in astonishment.

"I thought she'd just pretended to have a husband— for respectability's sake," confided another.

Few of the townspeople seemed to know him, which shouldn't have surprised her. Promise Creek had been doubling in size steadily every year. The majority of people at Caroline's funeral would not have met him. Now they had, though, they would not forget him.

The ones who knew him by name seemed to know his reputation, too. The tidbits of knowledge—fact and fiction—began to spread through the curious crowd.

"Did you hear he's the son of a senator?"

"He held off an Indian attack with a slingshot."

Even now, she could see the unmarried ladies of the town eyeing him speculatively as a prospective husband, his wife not yet cold in the ground. They were giving Mrs. Watson scathing glances as well, since the woman had installed herself by the widower's side, thus proclaiming her interests to all. Ros had attended enough funerals to know that was common, especially out here, where men still outnumbered women. They'd give him a day or two of sighing sympathy and coy assistance, out of respect for Caroline. Then they'd close in for the kill.

She couldn't blame them. He was a man to make a feminine heart beat fast—powerful, graceful, with a low, deep voice that vibrated through his listeners. Gray eyes that turned molten silver when he was angry. A man to build a legend upon. And the women of Promise Creek had already begun building. Knowing what she knew of him, though, he'd be long gone before they could get a claw into him.

Captain Hellfire. Rob Lewis. And he'd recognized her with an astonishing speed, despite the fact that he'd ridden into town to find his wife being buried and his daughter distraught. His initial anger toward her had flared and died quickly. He'd noticed her unconventional dress, but he hadn't made a comment upon her shortened skirts or the loose-fitting trousers beneath them. His lips had tightened, though, enough to indicate disapproval. What would he say when she told him that Caroline had asked her to take his daughter west?

She hoped he would not make an issue of her sex, but she feared, from the assessing glances he cast her now and then, through the thicket of women that surrounded him, that he very likely would.

Her instinct was to take the runaways and head toward Saint Joe without a backward glance. But she had promised Caroline she would see Gwyneth to San Francisco safely. She couldn't drag the child from her father's arms right now.

She caught a glimpse of Mr. Whitestone—Gwyneth had pointed him out for her earlier at the funeral—and remembered that she had yet to deliver Caroline's diary to him. She pressed her way through the crowd and greeted him with the mixture of kinship and grief that was so common after a burial. "Mr. Whitestone, I'm so sorry."

"I believe I should be saying that to you," he corrected her gently. He was a tall, thin man. Quiet. She knew he had a law practice and shared Caroline's love of books. In fact, she knew more about this man than was entirely comfortable.

"Mrs. Lewis thought you might be best suited to take care of Tora, if you wouldn't object?" The dog was getting on in years and wasn't likely to be able to make the journey.

He bobbed his head quickly. "Not at all. I'd be happy to take Tora in for you."

"Thank you. You don't know how much it eased Caroline's mind to know that you might agree." She pressed the diary into his hand discreetly. He looked down at it, puzzled, resistant.

"She thought this was best left with you," Ros said firmly.

The poor man, understanding, flushed deeply red. He stammered, "Thank you." The misery in his eyes belied his words, though, and he backed away from her as if she had reached into his chest and crushed his heart.

Ros let him go. She had done what she must and she could offer no comfort. Caroline's words would soothe him, or not. She glanced around to see if anyone had noticed the exchange and saw that someone had—Rob Lewis. His gaze was hard upon her, and she could almost see the questions forming in his mind.

Questions she had no intention of ever answering. Before he could make his way through the crush of mourners, Ros turned to the men nearest her. "Mr. Farmer, Mr. Hollings, I've got to get the chickens fed and the cow milked; could you possibly help out?"

"Happy to, Miss Fenster." Mr. Farmer nodded once. "I'll get my Billy to see to the cow while I fork some hay for her." He moved quickly, obviously relieved to have something to do besides stand around and talk about how awful death was, and how shocking that a woman so young should be struck down in her prime.

Clem Hollings bent down from his nearly seven-foot height to say in a barely audible tone, "I'll feed the chickens and change out their water for you, Miss Fenster, but I think you have a tear in your wire. There were chickens in the yard when we all came. Would you like me to fix it?"

"No thanks," Ros said, grasping the opportunity. "I'll do it myself."

"Fixing the fence is a man's job," one of the women nearest her said disapprovingly.

But Clem shook his head, an unexpected ally. "Sometimes it helps a body to do, rather than sit, after something sad like this."

"She could always serve food to the guests."

Ros looked at the women vying for the chance to be the next woman in Rob Lewis's life. "I believe that job is already being adequately handled."

She escaped without further argument, right behind Clem. He stopped a minute after helping her carry the chicken wire to the fence and showing her where the hole was. "I'm right sorry. Mrs. Lewis was always a nice lady."

"Yes," Ros agreed, although it gave her a twinge, knowing that Caroline would have hated being damned by faint praise.

She had barely begun the repair when Mr. Lewis came up behind her. "What do you think you are doing, Miss Fenster?"

"Repairing the fence, Captain Hellfire."

He winced and glanced over to where Gwyneth played with several other children. "I'd rather you didn't use that ridiculous name—especially not in front of my daughter."

"As you wish." She concentrated on her repair rather than looking up at him. "I'm sorry about Caroline. She was a good woman. I wish I could have done more to help."

"I thank you for what you managed to do—it was more than I managed." The faint bitterness in his tone made her curious to see his expression. She was grateful that she had fought the urge to look up at him when he added, "Mrs. Watson has made sure I was apprised of all that you've done."

Ros could imagine what had been said. The woman wasted no time. First she had appropriated Caroline's job and now she was setting her cap for her husband. Ros said, "Adelenia Watson can be quite helpful, I have found, in the short time I've been here. No doubt she was most impressed by my forward-thinking bloomer dresses and short-cropped hair."

He crouched down beside her. "*Puzzled* might be a better word. I don't think she knows whether to treat you like a man or a woman." He reached for the crimping tool. "Let me do this, Miss Fenster."

His hand rested against hers as they both held the crimping tool. His face was inches from hers. She looked at him, prepared to demand he leave her to finish the job. But when their eyes met, the powerful spark of attraction that arced between them was so shocking that she dropped her hold on the tool instantly.

He had just buried his wife today. What was the matter with her? She rose and stepped away from him. Had he noticed? Or had she been the only one to feel it? He wasn't looking at her, but at the repair. She couldn't see his expression.

She said hastily, "I'm sorry you had to find out about Caroline so harshly. I didn't know how to contact you."

"Couldn't be helped, Miss Fenster. Sometimes that's the way these things happen." His tone was pragmatic.

*The way these things happen.* Yes, it was. Death—and attraction toward an inconvenient man, too. She forced her heartbeat to slow back to normal. Inconvenient. More than inconvenient. Impossible. Deliberately, she said, "Caroline left a letter for you."

He didn't ask for it. Didn't acknowledge that he'd heard. "Where's the family? I'd have thought they'd come."

If only they had been able to, things would have been so much easier. "They're in San Francisco visiting Jeanne and her husband."

He stopped mending the fence for a moment to look up at her. "Is that why Gwyneth thinks you're taking her west with you?" There was an undertone of challenge in his voice—and a definite bite of disapproval in his flinty gaze.

"I promised Caroline I would see her safely to San Francisco."

"There is no need, now that I'm here."

She knew she shouldn't feel such relief to have the responsibility for Gwyn taken from her shoulders, but she did. She smiled. "Gwyneth will be delighted to have you home with her at last, I'm certain."

Without replying, he looked down at the fence, gave a final crimp to his repair and stood. "I'll just put this back in the barn."

The barn. Moses. Ros grabbed hold of the wire and tugged. "No, let me."

"I need to take a look at it anyway," he demurred,

walking away, forcing her to let go or be dragged along with him.

"A look at what?" She elected to let go and hurry along beside him.

"The state of the barn, of course." He kept his strides long, as if he wished she would fall away behind him and leave him alone.

"Why?" She asked the question aloud, even though she was more than certain she knew the answer. She wanted to see if he'd be honest with her.

"I need to know the condition of the property in order to sell it."

"Sell it?" Ros managed to get to the barn door before he did and make a great deal of noise raising the latch. To her relief, the barn appeared empty. "Will you take her west with you, then?"

"A company of emigrants is no place for a child." He stowed the wire without looking at her. "Gwyneth will wait here, safely, for her grandparents."

# Chapter Seven

She was furious with his decision to leave Gwyneth in civilization and not subject her to the rigors of trail life. Rob was certain he was right. He took a swallow of his coffee and looked toward the curtained bedroom, which held his daughter.

*Maybe you can wake her up, Papa.* The echo of her hopeful question would haunt him forever. She hadn't seen him in a year, and yet she had looked at him as if he could walk on water and raise the dead if he chose. If he only could. It should by rights be him in the coffin and Caroline left to cope quite capably with raising Gwyneth, no doubt with plenty of support from her family.

Gwyneth had nodded sagely enough when he told her that she wouldn't be going west with Rosaline Fenster. And then she had smiled, her eyes filled with hope. "Will I go with you instead, Papa?"

Rosaline Fenster had tried to warn him with a quick

shake of her head, but he hadn't paid attention. He'd told her that he thought she should stay here and wait until her grandparents came for her. Not risk the rigors of the trail.

"I'll be good, Papa," she had argued, her lower lip trembling.

"No, Gwyneth. You'll have to trust that I know best."

"Yes, Papa." She hadn't trusted that he knew best though; she had curled into a small bundle in his arms and sobbed herself to sleep. Rob had rocked her, held her—all the while aware of the disapproval radiating from Rosaline Fenster as she sat at the kitchen table, cleaning her shotgun with the care and attention another woman might show an infant.

"She'll get over it," he said, more to comfort himself than to placate her.

"She'll have to. Just like she'll have to get over losing her mother."

"Her grandparents will get her soon enough."

She snorted a very unladylike laugh. "That will make her forget losing her mother—and being abandoned by her father."

He glanced down at his daughter, and said harshly, "What good can I do her? I'm a wagon master, not a father. Two weeks a year, a few presents, that's all I've ever done for her. Why should she expect more, now?"

She put away her shotgun and the cleaning supplies. "She's always expected more. And she always will." She bent down to lift the sleeping child from his lap. "It's the way children think of their parents, Mr. Lewis."

Her neck was inches from his nose. She smelled of gunpowder and oil, and without warning he felt a vexatious desire to turn his head into the curve between her shoulder and her jaw and inhale the warmth of her. What was wrong with him?

He'd thought grief had turned him peculiar this afternoon out in the yard—when he'd wanted to strip the leather gloves off her hands and kiss her fingers . . . and her firm mouth . . . Had he been without a woman so long that even Rosaline Fenster could do this to him?

He held his breath until she straightened, Gwyn heavy in her arms.

She turned away from him. To distract himself—to remind himself of the absurdity of his unwelcome desire—he studied her odd costume as she carried the child into the bedroom. He'd never seen a woman wearing such a thing so close up before. She wore a sort of sack of black cloth, belted around her waist and falling a little below the knee.

He closed his eyes as she disappeared behind the curtain to Gwyn's room. The abrupt, unexpected end to the skirt made a man think of the shape of a woman's legs despite the fact that Miss Fenster's legs were safely obscured beneath the baggy trousers she wore underneath the abbreviated skirt.

He had noticed that her trousers were of the same soft black material and gathered into a band around the ankle. As foolish as the costume was, the sight of her feet beneath the trousers, clad in thick-soled, well-fitting gaiter boots made him imagine the shapely ankle and foot beneath the leather.

He heard her return to the room and begin to store away the loaves of fresh bread the mourners had left behind to help the newly grieving. She made several trips to the cellar to put away the jars of soup and beans and corn and beets. More food than he would need for the few days he would be here.

Several of the women had offered to come over to help out with the cooking, with Mrs. Watson being the most insistent of them. But he had convinced them all not to bother.

Why hadn't he felt this attraction to one of them? Why didn't he want to bed one of them? Not that he would have done so. But he'd have understood the urge better. It was only natural a man might want to remember he was still alive by burying himself in a soft, sweet-smelling woman.

But the woman with him tonight was anything but. He opened his eyes, determined to make himself see the absurdity of his desire and conquer it. Rosaline Fenster put the water on to boil and fixed herself a cup of tea before settling in the chair across the table from him.

She stared absently at the curtain of Gwyneth's room, her jaw set. Her silence was damning—all the more for the wildly inappropriate thoughts he was battling. Grief. It must be the choking mixture of grief, anger, remorse, and relief that made him want to . . .

She glanced at him, and their gazes caught for a moment. Her eyes widened, and he forced himself to look away, down at his hands clenched on the arms of the rocking chair. He said defensively, "What would you have me do? Drag her across the country? I wouldn't have time for her then—not if I want my company to make the journey safely."

Miss Fenster looked at him over the neatly ironed red-and-green-striped tablecloth. "Then I guess you'll do what you've always done."

He ignored the plainspoken rebuke in her words. "I'll do what I have to. What else is there?" The table-cloth was a new one that he hadn't seen before. Caroline must have made it sometime in the last year. Red and green had been her favorite colors.

"She could come with me."

"You?" He was surprised she would consider the idea, to be truthful. He had heard the stories of her wild youth from Caroline, who had told them with an edge of wonder and envy. "Did you really waste your youth gambling in London dressed like a man?"

"Of course." She raised a brow, again. An annoying habit on a man or a woman. "No self-respecting dandy would let a woman gamble with him. Could you imagine if he lost?"

"Did he?" There was a sharp light in her eye that made him glad she'd given up her gambling ways.

"Of course." She smiled, a devilish smile that made his shoulder blade itch. "And I assure you I never wasted a moment in a gambling establishment. I always used my time to learn as much as possible about games of chance and men in general."

*Men in general.* Did she mean what he thought she did? The possibilities jolted through him until he had to hold on to the chair to prevent himself from moving toward her. He glanced involuntarily at the curtain to Gwyn's bedroom.

She glanced at his hands, clenched tight on the arms of the chair, and he felt the heat burn through him at the thought that she would proposition him here. In Caroline's house. But all she said was, "Gwyneth is asleep; she can't hear me. Why won't you let me take her to San Francisco? It is what her mother wanted."

He tried to concentrate on his argument. To clear his head of this fog of desire. "The trip is dangerous."

She was obviously unimpressed by such an argument from a man who'd made the trip—and back—five times already. "You've done it. You're still hale and hardy." Her gaze was frankly appreciative as it swept him.

The heat coiling inside him threatened to explode

when she leaned forward and looked him boldly in the eye. "Why don't you take me?"

He drew in a harsh breath. *Take her.* "No." He wanted to. Not to take her west, no, not that. But to take her in his arms. Yes, with every misbegotten fiber of his being.

Ros sat back, shocked by the intensity of the desire he battled back as she watched. She had known he was struggling with an unwelcome attraction to her, just as she had been with him. Still, she hadn't realized how close to acting upon it he was until then.

She hadn't meant to torment him, merely to make the obstinate man uncomfortable enough that he might reconsider his decision to leave Gwyneth behind.

"Caroline wanted you to," she said, hoping the name would dash cold water on the heat building between them in the tiny kitchen. When she saw his hands clench until his knuckles turned white, she realized he had misunderstood her.

"She would never—" he began with a strangled denial.

"Of course not." Ros felt an odd shift inside her. But Caroline would. She had. Absurd. She felt herself retreat from an unsteady cliff edge.

Suddenly, as he realized that she meant only that Caroline had wanted her to bring Gwyneth west, heat disappeared into icy calm and his voice lost its harsh strained quality.

"I can't. You know I can't." He glanced sideways, at the shadowy outline of Caroline's favorite quilt through the doorway of her room.

"Why not?" She heard the doubt in his voice and fueled it. "Why can't you see Gwyneth and me both to San Francisco? Your reputation for safety is legendary, Captain Hellfire."

*"Legend* is the right word for it." He glanced around the small, neat room that was all that was left of Caroline's hopes and dreams. Except for Gwyneth.

"You don't know the things that can happen on the trail, Miss Fenster." He closed his eyes. "I've seen children fall out of wagons, drown in shallow water, carried away by the current, run over during a stampede, desiccated by illness." He opened his eyes, and she could see his will was firm. "You don't know the trail like I do."

"I know what it feels like to lose both your parents at once. Gwyneth doesn't need to. She has a father. Why don't you take her to San Francisco with you? Give her a chance to adjust to the idea of being without her mother before you leave her with her grandparents."

"If I could, I'd stay with her until her grandparents returned east. But I keep my word, and there are people in Saint Joe who are counting on me to lead them."

She nodded, leaning forward to press home her point. "Gwyneth is counting on you, too, now."

His mouth curled downward with a touch of bitterness. "What good am I to a child?"

"You're her father."

"Caroline—" He stopped. "You said she left a letter. Where is it?" There was a look of blind hope on his face, as if he expected the letter would answer his dilemma.

Would Caroline's terse words make her case for her? She didn't know. Ros went over to the little drawer where Caroline kept all her important papers and pulled out a single sheet of paper, folded and sealed.

She brought it to him. As he stared down at the paper, she quickly damped the fire in the stove for the night. "I'm going to bed."

He looked up at her starkly, an ember of his previous desire still burning deep in his silver eyes.

"In Gwyn's bed." A touch of relief flickered over his features. "There are fresh sheets on Caroline's bed, for you."

"Thank you," he said, though she could see the idea of sleeping in Caroline's bed, fresh sheets or not, did not appeal to him.

She paused in the doorway to Gwyn's bedroom for a moment, her eyes catching his. "I'm sorry about Caroline. I truly am. But I would ask you to remember what she wanted for Gwyneth and see that it is done."

He didn't answer her. Knowing it was unlikely, she said shortly, "Pleasant dreams then, Mr. Lewis."

She lay tense and still next to Gwyn, listening. There was silence for a long while, and then the sound of the stove door opening and closing.

She heard nothing else for a long time, and finally, she drifted to sleep herself, only to wake when the light was still a grayish promise of dawn. When she entered the kitchen she stopped. He was still there, folded over the table, his head in his arms, fast asleep.

Even in repose, he looked like a man one could count on. A man who took his responsibilities seriously. Ros knew men well enough to know that for whatever reason, Rob Lewis had wanted her last night.

Another man might not have resisted the temptation, might have decided that grief excused any impulse toward self-control. But he had reined in his impulses with the restraint of the legendary Captain Hellfire. So what had gone so wrong that he had chosen to all but desert his family? Whatever it was, it didn't seem to trouble his sleep. He didn't move a muscle as she moved quietly around the kitchen.

She rekindled the fire in the stove and put the kettle on to boil. He woke when the stove door clanged shut.

From Ros's perspective he seemed to pass from sleep into alertness without any of the usual disorientation.

He sat up, his voice clear as he said, "That wasn't her handwriting." All trace of desire was gone from his gaze this morning. If she hadn't known better, she'd have been certain she imagined it.

"Good morning to you, too." Ros broke six eggs into the skillet. They needed to talk, but she had hoped not to have to discuss the letter with him.

He had other intentions. "Who wrote it?"

"I did." If he wasn't embarrassed to press the matter, then she wouldn't let herself be, either.

"She was too weak to write, so she dictated it to me. They were her words exactly," she said, in case he might think she had embellished anything. Not that there had been much there to begin with.

"Trust Caroline to write down her last thoughts as she lay dying."

"I almost didn't agree," Ros confessed. "I thought she was being overly concerned and would be well within the week."

"She must have been terribly weak. I've never known her to write so . . . succinctly."

"She wrote a longer letter to Gwyneth, for her wedding day. But she said you were a man who appreciated brevity."

He blew out a breath—half laugh, half sigh. "I'm glad you could be with her, at the end. I'm sure it was a great comfort to her."

A comfort? Ros couldn't imagine herself in that role. "It was just blind luck that brought me here. I almost didn't visit at all. If my trip to Saint Joe had been more successful, I'd be well across the Missouri by now."

"I remember." He moved to give room to the plate

of eggs and slice of bread she placed in front of him with a thump.

She sat down, a plate of her own before her. She'd lain restless next to Gwyneth all night. The child had latched on to her father like a drowning man might latch on to a log floating by. He couldn't just leave her with strangers until family came for her. Why couldn't he see that?

She had to convince him to take her, and she could tell it would be difficult. "It wasn't just your postponement—our supplies were bought by someone else and we had to wait for more."

He didn't seem to be softening any more perceptibly toward the idea. "Jericho chasing after you probably didn't help."

She didn't bother to hide her surprise. He knew about Jericho? She knew better than to lie, but caution had told her never to admit more than she had to. "No. But he didn't find me."

He raised one eyebrow as if to encourage her to continue, and then, when she didn't, he said, "I hope your servants took the chance to head north. It would be mighty foolish of them to stay in one place so long."

More foolish than he could know. "North might have been a good choice."

He frowned at her evasiveness, almost as if it caused him some physical pain. "I suppose you still intend to go west."

"As soon as I can."

"Not on my train." He was blunt, which Ros admired. Another man, one not so sure of himself, might have found a way to dodge the question. "A woman alone is trouble, Miss Fenster. And I suspect you—and your servants—will be downright disastrous to any wagon master foolish enough to take you and your company on."

"Even you? The legendary Captain Hellfire? Surely you aren't afraid of a woman alone. Or even a few servants."

"There's a reason for my reputation, Miss Fenster. I don't take chances with those whom I lead." He sighed. "I don't take unmarried women unless they have a father or brother along to keep them in line."

"Well, I can assure you I will get into no trouble on the road. I am no fool." She waited a moment, hoping he would relent.

Couldn't he understand what his abandonment would do to his daughter? His gray eyes remained as distant as rain clouds. Apparently not. "Let me take Gwyneth with me. I will keep her safe."

"You won't even be able to keep yourself safe." He shook his head. "You shouldn't go west. You're asking for trouble. You and your servants would be better off traveling separately—them north and you back home to cause more trouble."

"We're going west. Me and my *servants.*" She did not look away. "And Gwyneth, if you'd just be reasonable. It *is* what Caroline wanted."

He shook his head, and snapped out the truth at last. "Do you think I'd let you take my daughter on the trail with a wagonload of runaways?"

"They're free," she snapped back, annoyed that he was so close to the truth. He wouldn't let it go, she could see it in his eyes. So she tried a different method of persuasion. "And your daughter will be devastated when you desert her so soon after her mother's death. With strangers, no less."

To her surprise, he didn't argue that Gwyneth would not be devastated. He accepted the idea with a wince of pain and then leaned forward over his plate. His gray eyes pinned her with heart-stopping force. "Why don't you send your servants north and stay here with Gwyneth until her grandparents can come to retrieve her? I'll pay you."

"How much?" She had no intention of staying, but she did wonder what value he set on his daughter's welfare.

"Twenty dollars in gold."

"You might find someone reliable for that." She nodded. At least he put some value on his daughter's welfare. "But it won't be me. I'm heading west." She'd promised Moses. She owed Moses. She intended to see him safely west.

"Then I'll ask Mrs. Watson to keep her safe until Caroline's parents can collect her."

"No! I don't want to stay here." Gwyneth's pale face appeared at the curtain. "I want to go to San Francisco with Auntie Ros." Her face was drawn and pale, her eyes still red-rimmed even though they were now dry.

There was an angry, desolate light in her eyes.

# Chapter Eight

"Don't go, Auntie Ros." Gwyneth held on tight to Miss Fenster's legs—which were encased in man's trousers. She looked no different than she had in Saint Joe when he'd thought her a man.

Unfortunately, he could no longer think of her as a man, now that he knew. His foolishness from last night threatened to return when he looked at her legs, appearing almost indecent in men's trousers. He forced his unwanted feelings down. She was leaving. None too soon.

She—or *he*—glanced up at Rob. "I have to—you know why I have to, Gwyn. Some folks have to go far away to be safe, and I have to take them."

Surprisingly, Gwyneth seemed to understand the urgency of that action. "And the baby?" Rob wondered, for the first time, if Caroline had offered a safe house to runaways before. If his daughter's life had been in jeopardy and he hadn't even known about it.

The ridiculous mustache bobbed as she assured Gwyneth, "The baby, too."

"Then you'll come back?"

"As soon as I can." She looked to the dark clouds forming on the horizon. A storm was blowing in; no doubt she was impatient to be away and out of it.

But Gwyneth was persistent. "What about me?"

"Your father is here."

Two pairs of eyes focused on him for a moment and then dismissed him. "But he doesn't like me."

Rob didn't react to the blatant lie. He knew instinctively that it had been uttered to twist a protestation of paternal love out of him. He refused to be manipulated.

Miss Fenster sighed and bent down to whisper in the child's ear. Gwyneth giggled once, nodded solemnly twice, and then stopped clinging to back away and stand with her shoulders squared. "I can, Auntie Ros, I promise."

"I know you can," she said briskly, climbing up onto the wagon seat and starting the team.

"What can you do?" He looked down upon his daughter, who suddenly seemed less innocent than she had before. Had Miss Fenster encouraged her to continue the help to runaways? Or were his suspicions ridiculous, and Gwyneth had merely promised not to cry—a promise he had wrung out of her himself the last time he left.

She looked at him reproachfully, as if he'd asked her to broach state secrets, and then she left his side to run beside the wagon, waving at Ros. The *gentleman* waved back with a solemn-faced, dignified farewell. Gwyneth's bright blue skirt flapped around her as she ran, exposing a rapid, almost desperate, flash of thin white-stockinged legs.

Rob watched Rosaline Fenster ride away in her ridiculous masculine costume. One part of him couldn't help but admire the tailoring of the suit—which made her shape more manly, even if in a dandified way. He'd thought the whiskers were absurd even when they first met and he had believed her to be a man. Now that he knew that she attached the hairpieces with spirit gum, they struck him as even more absurd.

She had taken long enough to ready her wagon. He supposed if he had been so inclined he might have found her runaways hiding in the wagon. Once, as she packed and harnessed the horses, he had heard what sounded like an infant crying, but the sound had been quickly hushed.

He'd let it go. He didn't have any directives from Pinkerton about any runaways, and he didn't see the need to meddle in what wasn't his business, after all. They were leaving his farm. That was enough.

Gwyneth ran after the wagon, waving and calling good-byes until she was just a small blue dot on the horizon to him, nearly blotted out of sight by the dust raised by the wagon's wheels. For a moment he was afraid she wouldn't ever return. He wondered if this was how she felt when he went away.

To his relief, she returned without needing to be fetched back. Her pace was much slower than her race to keep up with the wagon had been. As she dragged into the yard she looked at him with big, hurt eyes, and she clutched her precious doll—the doll he'd brought her from San Francisco two years ago—to her chest with a ferocity that would have suffocated a real child.

He wished he didn't feel quite so helpless. He had handled dozens of men, women, and children. Surely he could manage one little girl's disappointment in him. Even if she did consider him nothing short of all-powerful. He would explain. She would understand, eventually.

Except that Gwyneth wasn't speaking to him. After that one moment of protest—a moment that nearly broke him because it so vividly recalled the look in Caroline's eyes when he left her alone to head west for the first time—she'd ceased her protests—and any attempts at conversation with him.

He hadn't truly noticed the lack until Rosaline Fenster had gone and the childish chatter had abruptly ceased, except for whispered comments in her doll Sophie's delicate china ear.

He supposed she would get over it, eventually. As he inspected the farmhouse and outbuildings, the garden that Caroline had tilled and planted outside the kitchen, the fruit trees scattered about the property, a dread sense that she might be more like her mother squeezed at his chest.

Caroline had known when he rode away that their marriage was over, that he would never be back to stay. And she had been right. What might Gwyneth imagine his decision to leave her here with Mrs. Watson meant?

She appeared to hold him at fault for her Auntie Ros's hasty departure. But that was for the best. And his desire to keep her safe here, rather than take the risk of bringing her on the trail? He supposed he couldn't expect her to understand why it would be better for her to remain here. All she knew was that she had lost her mother and no one seemed to want to take care of her.

He should have asked Miss Fenster if there was someone more suitable than the disliked Mrs. Watson. She might have only offered her own opinion that the child belonged with her father again. She seemed rather hardheaded when it came to her own opinions. On second thought, it was best that he hadn't asked her.

In the late afternoon, as he was occupied milking the cow, Gwyneth appeared. She smiled beneficently, as if she had decided to forgive him for his boorishness, rather than apologize for her own sulk. She bent to hold the pail for him and deigned to speak to him for the first time since Ros had ridden away. "Papa, why can't I go to San Francisco with you? I'll be good. I promise."

"I know you'll be good." Good. What did that mean when the wagons jolted across the plains, over the mountains, every day? When the sun shone hot? When there were so many dangers they couldn't be counted on the fingers of both hands?

"You're too little for such a rough journey."

Finished with the milking, he lifted the pail and carried it to the kitchen.

Gwen tagged along, nearly running to keep up with him. "Sarah Jane Parker went west last year, and she was only five. I got a letter from her. She's in Oregon now. Her family has two hundred and fifty acres, and her daddy built her her own room in their new house. She has a door and everything." Gwyneth gave a sad glance at the curtain that hung in her own doorway.

Caroline had chosen that cloth the day they moved into this house. Eight months along, she had wanted something cheery—the reds had faded with time until they were just slightly more red than brown. The yellows had faded to near white.

"I could build you a door here." Maybe Mrs. Watson would be willing to move here. Willing to take care of Gwyneth here, where she knew every creak of the floorboard and every blade of grass.

He grew enamored of the idea for a moment. A neighbor who valued payment and wouldn't mind—and then he caught sight of Gwyneth, watching him with sad eyes, as if to ask when he was going to abandon her for good this time.

Damn! Why has Rosaline Fenster been so stubborn? She could have sent the runaways north instead of escorting them on the grueling road west. If she hadn't wanted to stay here, he'd have paid for her to take a steamer to San Francisco to bring Gwyneth to Caroline's family. If she had only done that, everyone would have been happy. And safe.

Why couldn't the stubborn woman just see that was the right thing to do? But then, what could he expect from a woman who thought she could pass as a man at whim?

He thought once about scooping Gwyneth onto the front of his saddle and riding to Saint Joe to tell the blasted woman she could join his company if she'd put a real smile back on his daughter's face. But he fought the urge. She was trouble; he could smell it on her a mile away.

Sooner or later her little game was going to end— and end badly for her and whoever was unlucky enough to be caught with her.

Ros pulled her buckboard over to the side of the road, so the trapper's nearly empty wagon could continue its bouncing and clattering journey by them safely.

The trapper pulled up as he came abreast of her, his smile small but warm. "Got any water on you? I had my last ten miles ago." He had the look of a man not long out of the woods from the winter's business. The shave and haircut were fresh; she could still smell the barber's cologne on him.

Ros handed over the flask she kept under the seat with a smile, even though the fingers of her other hand were wrapped around the shotgun under the blanket next to her. "There's a good spring about a mile ahead of you. By Big Thumb Rock."

The trapper handed back her flask. "I'll watch for it. Thank you kindly." He took his reins from his knee and then stopped, as if struck by a thought. "Traveling through to Saint Joe?"

Ros couldn't see the harm in telling him the truth. "I am."

He frowned, making the newly shaved skin of his face crinkle pinkly. "Might want to keep watch. There's a bunch of bounty hunters at the crossroads slowing things down."

"Bounty hunters?" Ros allowed irritation to show. The trapper would expect it. "At the crossroads, you say?"

"Looking for a couple of escaped slaves, they said. One of them murdered his mistress."

"I'll be on the lookout, then. Thank you, sir."

"Mighty obliged for the water, mister. I'll keep a look out for that spring ahead." The trapper set his wagon swaying down the road again.

Ros could see that he wasn't traveling completely empty. The wagon bed he'd emptied of fur in Saint Joe was piled with sacks of flour, rice, and beans. She wondered if they were supplies for his family or gifts for the lady friend he'd gotten shaved and sheared for.

"Moses," she called out loudly.

"I heard him." His reply was muffled, since the big man was wedged, with Ophelia and Freedom, into the secret compartment of the buckboard.

"Before we get to the crossroads, when there's no one around, I'm going to let you and Ophelia out."

"Safer that way," he agreed.

Ros began to wonder if there would be an inconspicuous place to drop the runaways. The road was crowded with families heading west, local riders heading to and from towns, and trappers with newly empty wagons.

At last, she reached a dip in the road near a copse of trees and stopped. "Hurry!" she called as she swung off the seat and around the back to push the secret latch and open the panel.

Ophelia rolled out first, stiff and awkward. Ros took the baby, Moses scooted toward the opening, to allow Ophelia to regain control of her numbed arms and legs.

Moses, too big to roll in the narrow space, inched himself out as quickly as possible and stretched and flexed his powerful body as his eyes scanned the road in front and behind them.

He took the sack of food Ros handed him. "You'll find plenty of water around here," she told them.

"Tonight after dark, make your way to one of the safe houses. You remember where they are?" She'd shown Moses on a map but hadn't dared commit it to paper for fear it might fall into the wrong hands.

He closed his eyes as if to see the map, and then nodded. "I know."

"I'll get a message to you, or come for you myself, if I can, once I've got everything set for the journey."

Ophelia argued, "But what if they find us?"

"They won't if you do what Moses tells you."

The girl let out a little moan of alarm when Ros snapped the door to the secret compartment closed. "I'd rather be hiding in there than out here."

Moses said gruffly, "We'll be in those trees in less than a minute."

Stubbornly, the girl crossed her arms and argued

more loudly. "All that walking is going to make us easier to catch. I'd rather ride—"

Ros interrupted her complaint. "Jericho won't care what you want. He's at the crossroads and he knows as much as I do about false wagon bottoms."

Ophelia might have argued further, but Moses, spying a rider over the hill in front of them, lifted her in one arm and scooped the baby out of Ros's hold with the other. With a few long strides, they were all hidden in the trees. For a moment the sound of a squalling baby could be heard, but it was soon silenced.

She pretended to be answering a call of nature by the side of the road, her back to the approaching rider. And then she turned and walked back to the wagon as if her heart wasn't beating in her ears. "Afternoon."

"Afternoon," the rider answered with a nod, and then he was past her and she could breathe again. She started up the wagon, wondering if Jericho would be fooled into thinking the runaways were long gone or not.

She didn't have long to wait to find out. Within ten minutes, she came to a tree felled across the crossroads, blocking the path to Saint Joe. There was no sign of the men, but she'd been through this before. No doubt they were waiting to see her reaction. Runaways had been caught before when the driver rousted them from their secret hiding place to help move the tree.

She stopped. Frowned. Muttered to herself. And then she began to back up the team, as if she'd go around the impediment. As if they'd been called, Jericho's two men were at her team's heads, stopping them from moving.

"I say! What is the meaning of this?" she demanded, making the most of her native accent. For some reason, Americans thought that Englishmen were stupid. Ros didn't mind playing on the stereotype if it would get her past Jericho safely.

"Looking for a dangerous runaway."

"Good. Then I suggest you get on with it and leave me to my business."

"Lord Hightower." Jericho showed himself then. "Where's your servant?"

"Magumbo? I had to dismiss him. He turned out to be a disappointment."

The man's mouth twitched in a mocking semblance of a smile. "He turned out to be a murderer."

"I say. You must be mistaken."

He held up a WANTED poster with Moses's face sketched large, and vital statistics emblazoned on it. Ros felt sick. "Damme, that's certainly my man. Who is it he murdered? His master?" Ros feigned a fluttery nervousness. "I say. Do you think he might have been hoping to kill me before I turned him off?"

Jericho's men were grinning, fooled by Ros's performance.

Jericho, however, was not. "Killed his mistress, not his master, though he gave him a good beating. Broke her pretty little neck—after he raped her."

Ada? Dead? Was it possible? Of course it was.

She might have passed the roadblock even then, if Jericho hadn't found the spring latch to the secret compartment and pulled it. The panel fell open. Ros could only thank the stars that Moses and Ophelia were safe.

"I think you'd better step down here."

"I most certainly will not," Ros brazened it out. "And I don't think the man I rented this wagon from is going to appreciate your breaking it. What have you done there?"

But even Jericho's men were not fooled. The big one

reached up to tug her down and everything went—as they said in America—to hell in a handbasket.

He pulled. She resisted, trying to untangle the shotgun from the blanket. Without warning, her attacker backed away. One of her sideburns and half her mustache dangled from his beefy fingers.

Her face felt naked. Exposed. The three men stared at the hairpieces in confusion and Ros took her chance. She leapt from the buckboard on the side away from the men and ran into the nearby grove of trees.

She could hear them behind her, and not very far behind her at that. Fortunately, she had guessed correctly that they'd left their own horses tied there. She untied all three and leapt onto the back of the one she judged the fastest even as she let out a bloodcurdling yell that spooked the horses and sent them running past Jericho and his men.

Unfortunately, the two riderless mounts were not fast enough to avoid recapture. Ros knew the bounty hunters would find her again if she tried to outrun them on the stolen horse. After all, they could rightly claim she was a horse thief and have the whole territory looking for her.

She slowed the horse only enough to prevent a bone-breaking fall as she rounded a bend in the road. With a silent prayer, she slid from the horse's back and rolled down a hill to hide among some boulders by a stream.

Jericho and one of his men were close behind; she heard the thunder of their horses's hooves before the ringing in her ears—from the fall—had ceased. Instinct made her hide longer. In not too long, the third man came riding after his comrades, riding one of her team of horses. Her heart dropped when she saw that he was trailing the other horse as well. She was now on foot, trying to elude three mounted men.

Giving herself a moment to think, she bent by the stream to drink and fill the flask she'd grabbed as she ran. She'd meant to grab the shotgun, but if she had to walk miles, water would be good to have with her.

The clear pool reflected her face, and she groaned. She had one sideburn left, but without the rest of her whiskers, she would rouse suspicion. She was too old to be a hairless boy.

Damn. She'd been found out. Unmasked, as it were. Something so simple: spirit gum loosened by the warm spring sun that shone down to warm her whiskers. She'd forgotten to shift the brim of her hat to shade all of her face as the sun moved in the sky.

She stared at herself for a moment, torn between the desire to curse and the need to break into laughter. She did neither, however, not wanting to make any sounds that might bring attention to her whereabouts.

What was she to do now? With a shrug, she pulled at the lopsided facial hair. The other sideburn peeled off easily. She held it a moment, and then, abruptly, flung it far away, where the stream crossed fast over some rocks heading toward the Missouri. She'd thought it might sink to the bottom, but instead it bobbed and floated like a little rat, heading quickly out of her sight.

She could hear riders thundering back from the direction Jericho and his men had taken. Spotting an overhang alongside the stream bank, Ros pressed herself there, between a boulder and the bank. She didn't have her shotgun, but she wrapped one hand around the hilt of the knife safely sheathed and hidden under the padding of her jacket.

In a moment a few clods of earth fell in front of her and she realized that whoever the riders were, they were stopped on the overhang directly above her.

"Think he fell off and broke his neck?" One of Jericho's men. She recognized the nasal whine.

"Nope." Jericho. "And I don't think he's a he, either."

"What?"

"How many men do you know who wear fake whiskers?"

"You think a girl . . ." The man was too startled to even finish his thought.

"Not just any girl. That English lady, who has a duchess and a countess for sisters, that one Mr. Rossiter told us about. The one that liked to argue against owning darkies. Didn't he say he thought she was helping them escape?"

There was a brief silence before the other man replied. "Well, shoot. A girl. She should be easy enough to catch."

Jericho said agreeably, "Now that we know who we're hunting."

The third man added, "And she'll lead us to the runaways, too. Where do you suppose they got to, if they wasn't in the wagon?"

"Maybe she was riding to meet them."

Jericho took a moment to think on that, and then said briskly: "And we want them all, not just her. Let's head back to Saint Joe. She'll show up there sooner or later, and if the darkies aren't with her, then we'll let her lead us to them."

The men rode away, but Ros could not move for some time. They knew who she was. But not where. She couldn't go to Saint Joe now, without a horse or a shotgun. But she had to get there soon.

# Chapter Nine

Would Moses and Ophelia worry when she didn't show up tonight? Would worry make them do something foolish—like strike out on their own? Still, they knew she needed to get the rest of the supplies for their wagon and outfit one for herself, so they would give her plenty of time before they began to worry.

She sighed. It was going to be a long walk. She couldn't even beg a ride in a wagon bed, with her whiskers gone. An Englishwoman in bloomer skirts caused enough raised eyebrows. No doubt tales of an Englishwoman in men's attire hitching a ride would reach Jericho's ears before she reached Caroline's. . . . No. Not Caroline's anymore. Mr. Lewis's.

She'd have to throw herself on Rob Lewis's mercy. The thought would have been amusing if she wasn't in such desperate straits.

She managed to time her arrival for early morning because the darkness slowed her normal brisk pace and made each mile take longer to cover. Exhausted, she found the sight of the small white farmhouse comforting.

Inside, however, she found that Caroline's neat little house was a shambles. Gwyneth presided at the table, an apron double-wrapped about her tiny form, her cheeks and forehead dusted with flour.

"Auntie Ros. Do you want some breakfast?" The floury little hands indicated a mess of eggs fried to deep brown lace, and a stack of biscuits that looked more like charcoal.

Her father sat with a plateful of the same fare. His eyes assessed her disheveled state from head to toe, his face blank as a just wiped slate, as if he wasn't certain whether to grin or glare.

Ros shook her head. "I'm not hungry, Gwyn. Just tired. I've been walking all night."

Mr. Lewis decided that a mockingly raised eyebrow was suitable for the occasion. "I thought you could take care of yourself."

Ros had no intention of being placed in the position of a child being chastised by a parent. "What makes you think I didn't?"

He put aside his plate and crossed his arms. "What happened?"

She poured herself a cup of coffee, thankful that he had made it, not Gwyn. "Jericho and his men had a blockade up at the crossroads."

He sat forward, just catching himself before he began to swear in front of his daughter. "Did you get caught?"

"Almost."

Gwyneth let out a soft little cry. "And the baby?"

"The baby and his mother and father are safe. They weren't in the wagon when it was stopped."

He looked as though he would say more, but he stopped himself with a glance at Gwyneth.

"It's not your trouble, Mr. Lewis, and I don't expect you to let me do more than stay here another night."

He nodded, his lips pressed together grimly for a moment before he said, "Why don't you clean up and go rest? You can use Caroline's room. I have to walk Gwyn to school."

"Can't I stay home, now that Auntie Ros is here?"

"No. I need to talk to Mrs. Watson, and you know your mama would want you to go to school."

So he hadn't changed his mind about taking Gwyneth along, then?

Ros turned toward Caroline's room, looking forward to a wash and a long nap. She would need them both to face Rob Lewis. She'd never met a more hard-hearted man when it came to his daughter.


Rob didn't have the heart to pierce Gwyn's happiness as she skipped toward school, thinking that with her Auntie Ros back, she might be able to conspire to over-turn his decision. He knew her smile would be fleeting enough once she reached the schoolroom and realized that her mother was not the teacher any longer.

He gave her hand a squeeze when they neared the building and her skip slowly turned to a crawl. Her smile pressed into a tight-lipped expression of dread.

The sight of her teacher, standing at the schoolhouse door with bell in hand, made her reluctant steps slow to the speed of molasses in winter.

Rob tugged her ahead by the hand. "Good morning, Mrs. Watson."

"Why, good morning, Mr. Lewis. How wondrous to see you on this beauteous dawn."

It was a ways after dawn, but Rob didn't point that out to the woman, since he intended to ask her a big favor. "I'm in a bind, Mrs. Watson. I could use your help."

"Of course. Anything."

"I'd like you to stay out on the farm with Gwyn."

She turned pink, even the tips of her ears. "Why, Mr. Lewis, I don't see how that's at all proper."

"I won't be there, so there's no impropriety at all, I assure you. I would never suggest such a thing to a woman as respectable as you, otherwise."

"Where will you be?"

"I'm heading west, and Gwyneth's grandparents won't be able to fetch her for some weeks."

Her face fell. "Oh, I'm so sorry, I couldn't do that. I have three children of my own, you see. And I live in town—the farm, it's so far out." She babbled on for a moment, then brightened. "But little Gwendolyn is welcome to stay with us. And I know she would benefit from my teaching, Mr. Lewis. I could teach her how to make up beds, do laundry, cook, sew . . ." Mrs. Watson was practically singing as she recited her litany.

"Gwyneth is only seven," Rob protested.

"Seven is not too young, Mr. Lewis. My own girls"— she pointed to two thin, pale girls talking quietly— "began learning to be good wives and manage their own homes when they began to walk. They can do everything now, and they're only nine."

"I'm looking for someone to stay with Gwyneth, Mrs. Watson," Rob said firmly. "Can you recommend anyone?"

"No. But I will think on it for you. That cousin— Rosaline Fenster—couldn't she help out?"

"She's not planning to stay much longer."

"Then she's still there?" Mrs. Watson's cheeks turned

pink once again and her voice rose an octave. "She's been staying with you . . . and dear Gwendolyn, of course."

Rob repressed the desire to say, "Of course. She's sleeping in my bed right now, why do you ask?" The woman did not appear to have a sense of humor, and he would not want Gwyneth to suffer from any gossip he would not be here to protect her from.

Unfortunately, Gwyneth didn't share his discretion. "Auntie Ros left yesterday, but she had to come back this morning because her wagon and her horses got stealed by some bad men."

Mrs. Watson's eyes widened. "Oh, my. How frightful."

Gwyneth opened her mouth, probably to explain about the runaways, but Rob interrupted firmly. "Miss Fenster is none the worse for wear, I assure you, Mrs. Watson. And she'll be on her way again as soon as she replaces the stolen equipment and animals."

"That doesn't surprise me." Her twisted smile belied her hearty words. "Miss Fenster seems more than able to take care of herself."

Isn't that the truth? Rob agreed silently. He patted Gwyn's head, suddenly desperate to end this conversation. "Be a good girl for Mrs. Watson, Gwyn."

"Bye." Gwyneth hugged him as if she thought she would never see him again and then hurried into the school building.

Rob tried at the general store, hoping the proprietor might know of a widow lady, or even a sensible spinster, interested in caring for a child out on his farm.

"You've got that woman in the bloomer pants, what you need another one for?"

"Because I need one," Rob answered curtly, not even

caring the kind of gossip his words would bring down upon his head.

The shopkeeper squinted at him over a twisted pair of spectacles so dusty they must have been utterly useless. "You one of them Mormons?"

"No." Rob had nothing against any Mormon. The ones he'd met on the trail seemed overall to be a decent bunch. But the idea of one wife was bad enough—how could a man survive with three or four?

He went home, defeated. Perhaps he could visit the next town over and see if there was an eligible woman available to stay with Gwyneth there.

He arrived home to find the kitchen still suffering from Gwyn's breakfast attack. He began to sweep the flour into a small pile, quietly, so as not to wake the woman sleeping in Caroline's bed. His bed.

A thump from the next room brought his sweeping to an abrupt halt. He stood silent and listened but heard nothing more. Still, he could not shake an uneasy feeling and went to investigate, broom still in hand.

Rosaline Fenster lay flung across the bed as if sleep had taken her midstride. It looked as though she had washed her face and hands, shucked out of her padded jacket, and then been too tired to even crawl under the quilt.

Her bare stockinged feet shifted as he watched, and he saw the reason for the sound that had drawn his attention. One boot lay discarded on Caroline's wedding quilt. The other lay on the floor, where it had evidently just dropped. The curve of her bottom, unmistakable in the trousers she wore, caught his eye for a moment, until he made himself look away.

He picked up the boot that still lay on the bed and placed it neatly beside the other on the floor. She stirred a little, and he watched, almost hoping she would wake so that he could find out what had happened to her. Almost hoping that she wouldn't so that he could watch her sleep a little longer.

He sighed. Why had she been the one to be here when Caroline died? Why couldn't it have been Jeanne, who would have happily taken Gwyneth under her wing and eased his mind without a problem. Or even Sylvia, the youngest half-sister. She had doted on baby Gwyneth the last time he'd seen her.

Miss Fenster was a woman. But not one like he'd ever seen before. She didn't even sleep like any he'd ever seen. And he'd seen his share as he'd patrolled the tents and wagons on watch as he traveled the trails. Most women seemed to tuck in on themselves, protecting themselves like a porcupine protecting its vulnerable belly.

Miss Fenster slept like a man—almost. One arm was curled up close under her head. He could see that her face-washing had been as lackadaisical as her undressing—there was a line of spirit gum on her cheek, faint but clear. But the rest of her—Rob stopped that train of thought as soon as he realized where it was headed.

He must be hard up if he could think that way about a woman like Rosaline Fenster. She was more trouble than a handful of regular women. Did she know how lucky she was that no one had seen her walking home? To have escaped Jericho—even if she did lose her buckboard and two horses?

Hell, if she'd been caught transporting those runaways, she could have been arrested. He wanted to wake her up and shake some sense into her. Make her admit she was taking unnecessary risks. Make her promise to stay here with Gwyneth, where he could be sure they were both safe.

She turned over in her sleep, and her shirt gaped

open, revealing more than he wanted to see, but he couldn't seem to stop staring, to move away. The urge to wake her pounded at his temples. He wanted to tell her how foolish she had been. Wanted to force her out of his house before Gwyneth came home . . .

No; he sucked in a breath on a tiny inward laugh. He wanted to lie down beside her and press himself against her. Into her. Women who wore those bloomer skirts of hers believed in free love. What about women who wore men's trousers? Would she smile if she saw him now, paralyzed with a desire to touch her? Would she welcome him?

From nowhere, a tiny bird tweeted eleven times. Caroline's prized mechanical clock. She'd packed it as carefully as a baby, and it had been the first thing she'd hung on the walls.

He was losing his mind. Free love. There was no such thing. Everything had a price. Rob gave his head a shake to clear it, and then took a spare blanket from the trunk at the end of the bed. The fragrance of roses drifted around him as he shook it out and threw it over Rosaline Fenster, covering her sprawled body, her half-open shirt, and whatever lay beneath.

In the kitchen, he brewed coffee for himself—tea just wasn't strong enough. After gulping half a cup and burning his mouth in the process, he decided to make the repairs he had itemized in his inspection yesterday.

Tomorrow he'd post a notice that the place was for sale.

Ros woke to find herself alone, snugly covered with one of Caroline's extra blankets. The scent of roses made her think of the dried petals that she had seen at Caroline's funeral. The colorful, fragrant petals had been left over from the wedding that had occupied the church the day before.

She'd taken perverse pleasure in noting how the mourners' boots ground them into the ground. But the fragrance had been released as they passed, and she didn't like the reminders it brought her now.

Had he covered her to hide her from his sight? She pushed off the blanket and sat up, stretching and feeling the bumps and bruises she had gotten in her fall into the streambed while she was trying to run from Jericho and his men.

Not too bad. She'd been lucky—if she didn't count the fact that they knew she was a woman. That Jericho had an inkling who she was, even though he hadn't yet discovered her name. Was her image going to be plastered to a WANTED poster in Saint Joe?

She needed to get out of Missouri fast, whether she soon had a price on her head or not. She'd have to convince Rob Lewis that he must take her party into his company. Not that she could think of a single thing that might convince him. She rose and splashed her face carelessly with the water still in the basin. She scrubbed at the stubborn remains of spirit gum on her cheek.

As she moved, she bumped the broom propped against the wall and grabbed at it to keep it from falling to the floor. What was the . . . ? She went out into he kitchen. Rob Lewis was nowhere to be seen. There was the beginning of a pile of swept-up flour on the floor near the stove, but nothing more had been done. Apparently he had started to sweep up the flour and then given up. Then why had he left the broom . . . ? She smiled. Maybe she did have some bargaining power with him, after all.

She shrugged and put water on to boil. While she

waited, she managed to sweep the place clean. After a good strong cup of tea and a slice of bread, she set about making fresh biscuits. After that, she'd find a new horse.

She wouldn't bother to replace the buckboard. She had no use for one without a secret compartment. She'd send a wire home and commission a new one from the wagon maker who had designed this one. A sympathizer to the cause, he could be counted on to be discreet.

The rhythmic sound of wood-splitting began from somewhere outside. The man couldn't be faulted for laziness, she reflected, even if he hadn't been the best husband or father. Ros took a mug of coffee and went investigating. She had a feeling she'd be in a better position if she put a proposition to him than if she waited to hear from him.

She found more than she bargained for when she rounded the corner of the house. He'd been splitting rails for fence repair, and he'd taken his shirt and his undershirt off. His skin glistened with a sheen of sweat from his exertions and, as she watched, every muscle in his back rippled when he brought the ax down hard.

She watched for a while, her throat dry, suddenly unsure of herself. Without a shirt, the man seemed more the stuff of legends. Captain Hellfire. She wasn't just attracted to him; she found him compelling in a way she'd never found another man in her life. But dangerous, too, she discovered. This man splitting rails seemed capable of reacting to her proposition with anger, maybe even violence, instead of curt dismissiveness. She wished she had not left her knife in Caroline's room.

He turned, as if he felt her eyes upon him. For a time their gazes locked. He scowled at her for a moment, as if he could read her mind. As if he knew her confusion. And then he grinned, unexpected and more appealing than she liked to admit. As if he dared her to come near enough that he might touch her.

She ignored the tension low in her belly and held out the mug without moving toward him. "Want some coffee?"

Smoothly, he turned away from her and crossed to the water pump. A few strokes of his muscled arm and water began to flow. He plunged his head into the stream and splashed his arms and upper body as if he didn't know he had an audience. His back still to her, he plucked his undershirt from a propped up rail and slid it on.

When he reached for his shirt, she turned and went back into the house. Whatever she had to say to him, she wouldn't do it until he was dressed. She didn't trust herself. She didn't trust him.

So the man had hidden depths. Most men did; Ros knew that well enough. She had gotten lazy, thinking of Rob Lewis one way. Well, she'd take the warning—laziness was dangerous around Mr. Lewis.

She reconsidered her approach and decided to let him come to her. When he walked into the kitchen with his shirt properly tucked and buttoned, she was ready for him. She had lined up Gwyn's blackened, soggy biscuits and the plate of flour she'd swept from the floor and table, alongside a mug of strong coffee.

"What's that? My dinner?" He looked at her as if he suspected she might actually expect him to eat the mess.

She handed him the coffee and dumped the pile of flour into the scraps she'd saved for the chickens. "Did you find anyone to keep Gwyneth until her grandparents can come for her?"

"No."

Good. But she didn't let herself smile, knowing that

might make him uncooperative. "If you take me to San Francisco, I'll keep Gwyneth out of trouble for the trip."

"I'd be a fool to take you." He said it baldly, unblinking.

"Why?" She didn't pretend to misunderstand him.

"You're trouble three ways to Sunday."

She sighed and dumped out the bowl of biscuit dough she'd been mixing onto the table. "I won't cause any problems. I'll take care of myself and Gwyn. She'll be happy. She'll have her father. It's a perfect solution. What else can you do?"

"Find a *married* woman already in the company to watch her."

"I forgot your rule about unmarried women." She took up the rolling pin and dusted it with flour. "Is that the only problem then, that I haven't got a husband to keep me in line?" She didn't look at him, just started rolling the dough.

He didn't like her tone. The only problem. As if it weren't a big enough problem in itself. "An unmarried woman is just a stick of dynamite waiting to be lit. Men don't like her. Women don't like her. That means I don't like her."

He expected her to argue, but she seemed to consider what he said. "True enough." She put down the rolling pin and took the biscuit cutter in hand. "Most unmarried women are trouble. But that's because they're looking for a man. I'm not."

Her reasonable tone took him off guard, but he quickly rallied. He'd seen the way she'd looked at him in the yard. "There'll be plenty of men ogling you in those bloomer skirts of yours. Or are you planning to wear trousers now?"

"All my clothes are still in the wagon." She cut out biscuits fiercely, and he had a feeling that her inclination would have been to have his hide under her cutter. "So I won't be wearing any bloomer skirts for awhile."

She stopped suddenly. "Do you think Gwyneth would mind if I borrowed a few of Caroline's dresses—just until I can buy new clothes of my own in Saint Joe?"

He didn't know which would be worse—Rosaline Fenster in trousers or in skirts. "I suppose she'd understand. Even a seven-year-old knows trousers are no dress for a lady."

"Well, I'm no lady. I can take care of myself—and that includes dealing with men who find my bloomer skirts a signal that I'd welcome their advances."

He had a paralyzing flash of images—Miss Fenster with a man backed up against a scrub pine, shooting. And Miss Fenster with a man backed up against a scrub pine, riding him. Either one seemed completely possible. And either one was asking for trouble. "No."

# Chapter Ten

She began laying out the cut circles of dough on the pan. "What if I found a husband? Just for the trip. Just to keep from causing any trouble?"

Fortunately, he was prepared to scotch that hare-brained scheme. "Had a woman pretend to be married just to travel out with me. Sent her back with some Indians soon as I found out."

She set the covered pan of dough circles on top of the stove to rise. "Where did you find out?"

"Nebraska territory."

Her expression told him she'd done enough reading to know what that meant. "How did you find out?"

"Her 'husband' took up with another woman and tossed her out of the wagon."

She wadded up the remaining dough and lifted the rolling pin. She eyed him a bit like she was considering whacking him with it. But as she began to roll out the dough again, she said mildly, "Seems like he's the one caused all the trouble."

He couldn't help smiling. "That's what she said." Not that anyone in the company had had any sympathy for her. She'd lied to them, and they weren't prepared to forgive her for it. "She wanted me to make him return the money she'd paid him."

"Did you?"

"I convinced him it was the right thing to do."

"So he was some poorer for his betrayal. Good. He should have kept to their bargain. Why didn't you toss him out of your company?"

The thought had been tempting at the time. "It was his wagon and his livestock."

She cut new dough circles vigorously. "What about the woman he took up with—wasn't she unmarried, too?"

"She had a daddy supposed to be watching out for her. And he was, too. Got out a shotgun and made sure those two tied the knot right there on the trail. We didn't even have to wait to reach an outpost; we had a preacher along with us."

She pressed out two more biscuits with the remaining scraps of dough and added them to the ones already rising. With a sigh, she wiped the table and her hands clean. "Captain Hellfire traveling with a preacher. Interesting."

He didn't think for a minute that she had given up. She was just trying to decide how to approach him next. "I like it. Gives folks some comfort on the Sabbath and when there's burying to be done."

She looked down at the outfit she wore. "I could go as a man."

"You have no idea how much trouble you—and I— would be in if you got unmasked."

For the first time, he saw a flicker of wariness cross her face. "I wouldn't be."

He smelled trouble. "You don't know what it's like out there. Day after day of travel, heat, insects. That spirit gum'll irritate your face—you'll take off your whiskers for a spell and the next thing you know, everyone in the train will be whispering. Soon enough—"

She held up her hands as if in surrender. "Okay. I take your point, Mr. Lewis. I'd rather travel as a woman anyway, for just the reasons you describe." She appraised him impartially. "What if I had a man to look after me, just not a father or a husband, since I have neither?"

"Who?"

"You."

He choked. "What kind of damn fool—"

She watched him with a strange, reserved expression on her face. "I'd make it worth your while."

Worth his while? He stood up, sending his chair tumbling away in his haste. "What makes you think I'd—"

She laughed low in her throat. "The way you look at me."

"I assure you—"

"Never mind. It was a wild thought."

"I just lost my wife."

She raised an eyebrow. "What did Caroline look like?"

The blow was low but accurate. "I know I wasn't around much. Caroline was fine with our life."

She shrugged. "Which is why I thought you might be interested in my proposition. A no-strings-attached deal that would last until we reached San Francisco."

No strings? There wasn't a woman alive who understood that phrase—not even Rosaline Fenster. "Forget it."

"I promise I'd do everything you said."

The images that chased across his mind . . . But no. "I don't believe you are capable of doing as you are told, Miss Fenster."

He might have been even more emphatic in his rejection of her idea, but just at that moment Gwyneth came home from school. She smiled when she saw the circles of biscuit dough. "I didn't think you could cook, Auntie Ros."

"Of course I can. I wouldn't want to starve, would I? I'm not very good at it yet, though. Give me a hand with the stew, would you? I think it needs a pinch more salt."

"Did you make Papa change his mind?"

He expected her to . . . he wasn't exactly sure what. Pout? Complain? But she said matter-of-factly, "I've done all I can, Gwyneth. I think your papa has made up his mind and we had best accept it."

Gwyneth, taking her cue from her Auntie Ros, nodded. He sat with his coffee growing cold as the two prepared supper. Gwyneth chattered about school— apparently Mrs. Watson was not the best at spelling. He thought this was what he had missed the last five years. But then he dismissed the thought. He wasn't cut out for domesticity for much longer than a few days.

He was almost disappointed when the cozy atmosphere was ended and his supper placed in front of him. He grabbed for a biscuit from the steaming basket and realized he had two females staring at him.

"You need to say the blessing, Papa."

He bowed his head and mumbled a few quick words, which apparently amused Miss Fenster and satisfied his daughter.

"I like your biscuits better than mine, Auntie Ros."

"You just need to practice, Gwyn."

"I don't know." She looked doubtful.

"Do you know how many batches I burnt before I learned how?"

"How many?"

"At least a hundred. And I had to eat them all."

Gwyneth giggled, and then grew solemn. "Mama said she would teach me when I was nine."

Rob offered, "I can teach you." Both females looked at him as if he'd offered to give birth to kittens.

"I make camp oven biscuits on the road all the time. That's a good sight trickier than making them in a big old oven like this one here."

"Can you teach me to make camp oven biscuits?"

"When you're nine."

She smiled, as if he'd offered her a big bag of lemon drops. But then her smile disappeared. "No. I'll have to live with someone like Mrs. Watson and you'll forget all about me."

If she'd said it with tears in her eyes, or with a whine in her voice, Rob would not have felt an arrow of pain in his chest. But she'd said it softly, under her breath, like a child reminding herself not to hope for things because fathers leave and mothers die.

She pushed the food around her plate for a moment and then said politely, "May I be excused?"

"Gwyn . . ." Rob didn't know what to say.

"I have to feed the chickens."

"Clear your plate and go." Miss Fenster took the decision away from him, with a glance that suggested he'd better not cross her. And then she left the house, too, without a word to him.

Not that she owed him an explanation. When Gwyneth didn't come back to the house, he decided she was trying to weaken his resolve and didn't head after her. But after an hour, when she still hadn't returned, he went to see what she was doing, determined that she wouldn't wrap him around her finger, no matter what.

He found her on the fence he'd just mended, looking at the distant hills. Miss Fenster leaned against a nearby fence post. They weren't talking, but the silence was companionable, and he didn't have the sense that either of them had grown silent because they were talking about him. Or that they even realized he had joined them.

He put his hands on the fence rail and braced himself against it, remembering when he first taught her to sit a rail—at three. She'd been wobbly and laughing with the falls, certain she'd land in his arms. He'd made sure she always did. "Time to go to bed."

"Okay, Papa." She didn't move right away.

He came up behind her and lifted her off the fence. "Now."

She sighed. "I just wanted to make a picture in my head, for when I don't live here anymore. So I don't forget."

Miss Fenster's voice drifted in the night air. "You'll remember the best things, Gwyneth. We always do, no matter how far we move on."

He carried her into the house, although she was much too big a girl for such things. Once inside, though, she didn't ask for help getting ready for bed. He waited for her to call for him to tuck her into bed and read her a story, as he always had the few weeks a year he was home. But she didn't call him. When he went to check, he found her asleep—or doing her best to make him think she was.

He came back to sit at the table, discovering that Miss Fenster had returned to the house and now sat peacefully rocking in the rocker, her eyes closed.

After a moment, he sighed. "I'm going to regret this, I can tell I am."

"Regret what?" she murmured.

"I'll take you." He added hastily, "I mean I'll let you travel in my company to San Francisco. I'll let Gwyneth travel with you." Hopefully attached like a burr to her aunt's side, just so they were never alone.

He'd thought she might smile, show a little measure of triumph. But she opened her eyes and met his like she was making a solemn promise. "You won't regret it."

He felt the itch begin under his shoulder blade. "If you cause any trouble—any trouble at all—I'll put you off my train. Understood?"

"Completely," she agreed.

The itch only got worse.


It took them all day to cross the Missouri with their wagons, and cattle, sheep, and horses. Ros watched the children play at a makeshift game of pretend while the Saint Joe ferry, a stripped-down riverboat, took them all over—five wagons, a hundred head of cattle, and three dozen people at a time.

"When will we get to San Francisco?" Gwyneth asked at least a dozen times.

"You'll know when you see the ocean."

"But when?"

"When the sea breeze fans you." Ros held hope that the enigmatic answers would serve to soothe the child. They certainly didn't soothe her. If she hadn't been with Moses and Ophelia, she'd have traveled on horseback and left the caravan of wagons in her dust.

She'd hired a teamster to purchase the rest of the supplies and the extra wagon she needed. She hadn't wanted to show her face, knowing that Jericho would be watching for her. To her relief, though she'd surreptitiously scanned all the WANTED posters she'd seen, her likeness had not been upon any of them. Moses, however, had a bounty of two hundred dollars on his head. The likeness of him was near to perfect, too.

She'd gotten word to him that he should cross the Missouri on his own. She'd see to Ophelia and the baby. So far, however, Ophelia hadn't shown up to be seen to.

Would she make the journey without them? She supposed she must; Gwyneth was counting on her.

The two wagons that were hers were loaded on the ferry late in the afternoon. As the wagons lumbered onto the steamboat, Ophelia came running across to greet her. "Miss Rosaline!"

Even though it was warm, the woman had a cloak buttoned around her. Ros supposed it was to keep the fact that she was carrying a baby hidden. She wouldn't have expected the girl to show so much sense. But then Ophelia turned and waved to an older woman. The woman smiled and lifted her hand in a half wave before she frowned in exasperation and disappeared into the crowd.

Ophelia whispered loudly, "Moses says to be sure they load everything carefully. We can't afford to replace much."

Ros wondered if he was somewhere across the river, watching them. His dreams were all packed up in those wagons, so she could hardly blame him for being cautious. She'd seen one wagon tumble in already today—not from their train, thank goodness, or they'd have been delayed another day.

"Mr. Lewis is a careful man." That was an understatement, but there was no need to tell such a thing to

Ophelia. She'd be shocked to hear what Ros had been prepared to offer the man. "He's personally overseen all the loading and unloading, so I don't think Moses need worry about anything but getting himself across the river."

"He left last night. The man took him wasn't back when I left. I don't know if he made it."

"I'm sure he did. He wouldn't let his son go west without him."

Ophelia's doubt cleared and she nodded her head. "He does dote on that boy, Miz Rosaline. I don't think I ever seen a daddy who took such interest in his son while he was a bitty baby. Most times they wait until they grow up enough to talk and run before they notice them."

"His son is a fortunate baby."

Ophelia shivered. "I don't want to think about it anymore. He'll be there. He has to be there. I won't do this without him."

Ros sighed. "Would you go back?"

"It's not so bad where I am. Master don't hate me, like he do Moses."

Ros knew she was going to scare the girl, but it couldn't be helped. "That was before you and Moses left with the baby."

"You think he'd blame me?" She actually began to tremble. "Of course he would. I took my baby. He didn't want me to take my baby."

"You're never going to see him again, Ophelia. And when you cross that river, you'll be out of the slave states forever." Ros tugged her along, worrying about the curious eyes turned on the apparent mistress cajoling her maid to get on the steamboat.

"They're watching us, Ophelia. Do you want them to think you're a runaway?"

"No, Miz Ros." Ophelia straightened and walked along briskly behind Ros, looking perfectly the part of a young servant who knew her place. Ros shouldn't have been surprised. After all, she had been playing that part since she was four years old.

When they crossed the river and stepped onto the banks of the new territory, they set to work getting their supplies in order. Ophelia put the baby, flushed from being cooped up under the cloak, on a folded blanket in the wagon bed as they took a hasty inventory to make certain nothing had been lost.

As they worked, Moses appeared.

"These sacks have shifted; they need to be lashed more tightly," she told him, as if he belonged there, had been there all along. She didn't want to risk word of a happy reunion reaching Jericho's ears. She'd rather he kept on the other side of the Missouri looking for people who were long gone.

"Yes, ma'am." He got right to work, relashing the sacks and making other repairs that needed to be done, both to his wagon and hers. It wasn't until they had moved off a little way to make camp for the night—until he had the tent set up and a fire going—that he stopped and lifted Ophelia in a big hug.

"What you doing, you crazy man?" But she wasn't angry.

"We done it, Fee." The big man bent to kiss the ground. Ophelia giggled and tried to pull him up, but he pulled her down to her knees, pulling the baby from her arms to his to cradle him gently. "Kiss it, Fee."

"What? The dirt? You a fool if you think I will."

"Not dirt, honey," he said gently. "Freedom. No slaves here. Never again."

Ophelia stopped giggling and pressed a kiss to her

palm and then to the ground. "Freedom. I don't believe it yet."

Moses let his son grasp his big finger and said reverently, "You will. 'Cause we're going to hear that word a lot from now on."

"What word?"

"My son's name."

Ros couldn't help asking, "You've finally decided to name him?" Moses had steadfastly refused to give the baby a name, saying that a child's name came when the time was right.

He rose to his feet and held up his son until the baby was staring into his eyes. "I have."

Ophelia smiled up at the baby. "Is it Perseus? I hope it's Perseus. I'm partial to Perseus."

"I may be crazy, but not as crazy as all that."

Ophelia didn't look too pleased. "What, then?"

"Freedom."

Ophelia frowned. "I been thinking—"

Moses's voice was not loud, but it was firm. "Freedom, woman. Do you want him to forget? I don't. Not for one single day of his life."

"You are a crazy man." Ophelia cuddled the baby with a smile on her face. "Do you hear that, Freedom? Your father is a crazy man." She laughed up at Ros, excitement at the journey finally reaching her. "I don't think I'll ever get used to it, Miz Fenster."

"You will," Ros said, as a team of oxen came barreling toward them. They hurried, laughing, out of the way of the bellowing beasts.

Ros saw Rob glance over their way, a preoccupied look on his face as he tabulated the goods, livestock, and supplies in his company. He frowned, and started their way.

Fortunately, he was waylaid by an emigrant with a

question. She said in a low voice, "Moses, you have to stay out of sight for a while."

"The posters." He nodded and, in the way that slaves seem to have acquired, made himself scarce so quickly that if Ros had been superstitious she might have thought he'd used magic.

Rob approached. "Where's Gwyn?"

"She's two wagons over. She's made a friend. It seems they have the same doll. They've decided that Sofie and Betsy Anne are twins separated by a tragic flood that killed their parents."

"Morbid idea."

"They seemed quite cheery—the reunion aspect is joyous, you have to admit, even though there was a tragedy in the past." To distract him from any questions he might have about Moses, she said quickly, "Do you think we'll be able to move on tomorrow? Everything seems at sixes and sevens right now."

"We'll move on. Many companies like to stay a few days to get everyone used to the change, but I've found that it takes just as long moving as it does standing still."

"Not an easy job you have." She felt a bit stiff with him. They hadn't talked much since their last conversation. The strong attraction between them made them both uncomfortable. Neither of them doubted it would be unwise to act upon it. But distance was the wisest way to ensure that. And they'd just agreed to travel together for the next few months.

"Not an easy trip," he answered with a searching glance into her eyes.

Ros thought of the tense wait to board the ferry and the long, slow process of crossing the river. "Judging by today, I can see what you mean."

"Today was easy. Today we have water to drink and wood to burn."

"We'll manage." Ros knew she sounded doubtful. But she hadn't planned on five months of her life going and who knew how long coming back. At least, once she knew Moses and Ophelia were safe, and had deposited Gwyneth safely with her family, she could sail, or take a steamer back home.

"Sure you want to come?" There was a hopeful note to his question she didn't like to hear.

"I promised Caroline." She shook her head. "I'll see the journey through, don't worry about that."

"It's not an easy journey, you know. Not even for the folks who are expecting some reward at the end."

"I expect I'll have my sorrows and my blessings, just like them." Ros gestured to encompass the group. She didn't yet know their names, but bits and pieces of their life stories had already floated to her in half-heard conversations.

She'd heard a mother explaining how long the journey would take them to a child as they waited to load their goods onto the steamship. A son had made a last plea for his father to return to civilization and not risk the arduous journey as they traveled across the river aboard the steamship. But the father had been adamant. If he died on the trail, he'd die with family by his side.

She'd heard women yell at their husbands and children, harried men claim a need to go off to tend to oxen to escape the confusion as they all struggled with setting up camp on the banks of the wilderness. She was certain she would know them all intimately before their journey was out.

The young couple who looked barely old enough to be married, though they were leaving their homes and families far behind to travel west, just the two of them. The family of eight, three wagons of goods, and a Bible clutched in the woman's hands as she counted to make sure she had all her brood accounted for. How many times would she take a count before they were safely in California?

Then there was the grizzled old man and his son, striking out for their fortunes, leaving their bad luck behind—or so they hoped. So they all hoped.

# Chapter Eleven

Sorrows and blessings. A fitting sentiment for the trail. He doubted she knew how fitting. She seemed friendly enough, although he thought she'd looked worried when their glances had caught across camp a while ago. The man he thought he'd seen her talking to worried him. He wished he had gotten a better look. He would have, if only he hadn't had to tell some fool that he'd be scattering his supplies along the prairie for the wolves and Indians if he didn't do a better job of strapping them in.

Rob didn't see the huge black man he thought he'd seen earlier anywhere around. The only potential runaways seemed to be Ros's servant girl, Ophelia, a cocoa-colored, skinny thing who shook when he looked at her, and two nearly grown boys—twins, by the looks of them. He assumed Ophelia was married to one of them, but from their behavior, he couldn't tell which.

They were to drive the smaller of Ros's wagons. Aside

from the timidity of the girl, which could cause trouble in a stampede, a storm, or an Indian attack, he sensed no impending trouble from these three. Unless they were runaways with bounties on their heads.

As if she knew what he was thinking, she said with nearly brazen conviction, "They're hired servants; you've nothing to concern yourself with."

"Servants?" He hadn't seen a poster on any of them. If Miss Fenster wanted to claim she'd hired them to help with the journey, he'd let the tale stand as long as it could. Before he'd left Saint Joe, Ben had given him a stack of WANTED posters and asked him to be on the lookout for the criminals described or roughly sketched on them.

One of the men should be easy enough to pick out— a pitch-black colored man roughly the size of a buffalo from the looks of his sketch. The runaway was wanted for a brutal murder. He was supposed to be on his way west. If so, Rob didn't think he'd hide long. While it wasn't unusual for Negroes to travel west, this one wouldn't be hard to spot. Getting him to the nearest fort might be tricky, but that was Rob's job, and he was good at it.

She hadn't caused a lick of trouble, if he didn't count her *servants* being here. They were all keeping themselves busy. And she'd done her part to make the day crossing the river go smoothly. Still, his shoulder blade itched like the devil when he looked at her standing there, her bloomer skirts already causing talk among the ladies and a different sort of talk altogether among the men.

"Need any help setting up camp?"

She didn't seem offended by his offer, which surprised him. He'd thought she might interpret the offer as a sign that he didn't trust her to take care of herself.

She said pensively, "We've set up the tents, got the coals almost right for cooking, and supper in a pot, waiting to be heated up. The boys have brought the cattle down to the river to drink and set them to graze. After supper they'll keep watch." She smiled. "They're convinced the Indians want nothing better than to steal their cattle."

Rob shrugged. "Some parties don't set out guards this close to Saint Joe. The Indians here are friendly for the most part, and used to our ways. But I set a guard from the beginning to the end."

"Better safe than sorry."

"That's my philosophy." He didn't like the trace of mockery in her tone, but he wasn't going to argue tonight. There was too much that still needed doing.

"Will you have supper with us?"

"Do you have enough for me?"

"You're family. I planned for you to eat with us— Gwyneth has already scratched your name on a cup." She bent down and rummaged in the sack of supplies to pull out a tin cup. She handed it to him with a rueful smile.

Scratched awkwardly in one side was the word *Papa* in lopsided letters. "How can I refuse this invitation?" He handed her the cup. "What time?"

She looked at the fire. "Give us an hour, I think. But don't hold me to it. I'm still learning the secrets of a camp stove."

"I'll have to teach you some tricks."

"There's be plenty of time for that."

Mr. Dudley appeared at his side. "Mr. Lewis, one of my oxen has taken sick."

"See you in an hour." Rob followed Mr. Dudley to the ox. Though the beast's breathing was labored, his eyes and nose were clear, and there was no visible obstruction in his throat. Following instinct, Rob patted the massive ox and spoke to it in low, soothing tones. Nonsense, but it worked like a charm.

"You're a miracle worker." Mr. Dudley was impressed.

"Not at all, Mr. Dudley. Sometimes the trip across the river spooks an animal. I'd keep an eye on this one, though. We don't want a stampede."

Mr. Dudley's eyes widened. "No, sir." Apparently, he'd heard about the dangers of stampedes. Good. "I'll keep Otis for emergencies, use the other two." He pointed to two oxen who were contentedly grazing nearby.

"That would be wise." Rob took special notice of Otis's big white patch near the neck. He'd keep an eye on this animal, too. He didn't like to take chances.

"Would you care to have supper with us? I'm much obliged for your help."

"Thank you, but I'll be eating with my family." He would be invited for supper by almost every family, Rob knew. But this time, he realized, he had a family of his own to join. It felt odd. Almost good. But there was a little nudge of worry to break the feeling. A family sometimes meant divided loyalties.

As he surveyed the grazing animals he looked for signs of sickness or skittishness, trying to ignore the anticipation he felt at the idea of sharing supper with his daughter.

He'd have to work hard not to get himself into a situation where he missed trouble brewing on the train because he was distracted by the thought of sharing the wonders they would see—the hardships they would bear—with Gwyn. And with Rosaline Fenster.

He sighed and walked over to where she squatted before a fire, preparing supper with Gwyneth.

"Changed your mind yet?"

He could have bitten his tongue when he saw the look on Gwyn's face at his suggestion. "You won't make us go back, will you, Papa? We just got started."

The infernal woman just laughed, as if he'd made a joke. "If you can do it year after year, Captain Hellfire, I'm quite certain that Gwyneth and I will manage just fine."

He didn't want to pass off his concern as a joke, so he said rather stiffly, "Best to ask such things directly, I've found."

He sat on a flat stone that Gwyneth had apparently dragged into place for him. He smiled at her. "I'm not used to such a fancy seat on the trail."

She smiled back eagerly. "I put your name on that cup."

He examined it as if he hadn't seen it before, heaping on the praise until he was certain she'd see through it. But her smile got wider and she scooted her rock closer to his with every compliment until she was right next to him.

A baby cried nearby. He thought it belonged to another family, until Ophelia went into the tent and came back with an infant in her arms. He'd forgotten she'd said she had a baby in the party.

He was tiny but ferocious, the way he waved his hands around. He wasn't nearly as dark as his mother, more a milky coffee color that turned nearly red when he worked himself up to a crying fit—which he had done. The servant unself-consciously began to nurse the infant, and the whimpers gave way to greedy gulps.

They all trooped to the river and picked their way down the steep banks to the water to clean their own dishes and the supper pot. He promised Gwyneth he'd show her how to wash her dishes without water when they reached the desert, and she asked if they'd be there tomorrow.

"No, honey, I'm afraid not. We've got weeks and weeks before we're there."

"I can do it, Papa," she said when they were back by the fire again. Her hand crept into his tentatively, as if she was afraid he might push it away. "You'll see. I'm stronger than I look."

"Of course you are." She looked at him so expectantly, he added quickly, "Would you like me to tell you a story about the desert?"

She nodded vigorously. "I like your stories, Papa." After that, he knew he had to stay even though supper was cleared, though his normal habit was to wander the camp, checking to see how the travelers were making the adjustment to long travel. He closed his eyes and told her the story of the sandstorm of '51.

When he opened his eyes, the campfire was dying and Gwyneth lay curled asleep on the ground. He thought he'd almost caught Miss Fenster staring at him, but he couldn't be sure. Now she was looking out over the camp, where other families were in the process of retiring for the night.

He couldn't help thinking about what she had proposed. If he could have thought of a way to do so discreetly . . . But no, he wasn't that big a fool.

Ros wondered if he regretted not taking her up on her offer. She had to admit she had only mild regrets about his refusal. He'd proven he wasn't much of a man to grow attached to a woman, so she'd been sure she'd be safe enough that way. But she liked him. She truly admired him. And she was more than a little attracted to him. What if her heart had gotten pinched in their no-strings deal?

No, they were better off going on as they were. They were doing quite well. The first day had gone smoothly enough and was at a peaceful end. They'd all gone about their business, cooking, eating, tending to the animals, and the wagon lay silent, the twins stretched out on pallets on the ground beneath.

Ophelia had gone down to the river for water to boil for the morning. Ros could see her, walking back in the deepening twilight. When the girl smiled tentatively at a woman from another wagon, heading down to get water, she added in a friendly tone, "Be careful, there's some snakes down there."

The woman did not react. There was no doubt she must have heard. Ros had heard the warning from feet away. Ophelia's face fell a bit, as if she thought she might be chastised for daring to speak above her station.

Ros tossed a stick into the fire. "They don't even look at her," she couldn't help murmuring to the wagon master. Was there anything he could do? "As if they weren't people at all."

"What do you expect? That these folks—who are risking their lives to reach the promised land—will jeopardize all of that to break the law? Or celebrate when someone else does?"

The truth of his comment didn't make it sting any less. "What makes you—and them—think she's not a free woman, Mr. Lewis? For a man who treasures his freedom as much as you do—"

He sat up restlessly. "I don't want to hear what you have to say on the subject, Miss Fenster. For the record, I don't believe one man should own another. I hate the laws and hope one day they're off the books."

"But you'll look the other way until then?" Ros stood up.

"Ophelia isn't complaining." In fact, she hadn't seemed to react to the other woman's insult at all.

"How can she? She is as good as mute in this company."

"Don't pay no nevermind, Miz Ros." Ophelia's voice floated out of the dark to them. "Mr. Lewis is right. These people don't know whether to catch me like a rabbit or treat me like I matter. So they'd rather be safe and do nothing at all."

"I hope she steps in those damn snakes," Ros said, as she rose and scooped up Gwyneth.

Ophelia laughed softly. "She's not stupid, Miz Ros. She might have pretended she didn't hear me, but she ain't going to pretend there's no snakes."

"Amen." The wagon master rose, prepared to prowl the camp looking for potential troubles, his nightly habit.

"Hypocrite."

He scowled at her. "Are you thinking of causing trouble, Miss Fenster?"

"No, I am not, Mr. Lewis. As much as it pains me to say so." With that, she turned, ducked her head, and disappeared into the tent.

His voice drifted to her easily through the canvas of the tent. "Pleasant dreams, Miss Fenster."

"Where do you suppose he's got to, then?" Ophelia had asked the same question repeatedly for the last three days as they walked beside the wagons up and down the hills of the rugged, untamed prairie beneath them.

"He's a wanted man. He doesn't want to bring trouble

to you or Freedom." Ros gave the same answer she had given to the question before. That had been the pattern of the last three days. There was a rhythmic sameness to them, but yet each hour brought a new gift: a field of spring flowers miraculously not yet trampled by the cattle, the laughter and shouts of children as they found some new game to make of a rock or stick or broken and discarded wagon wheel by the side of the road, or the clear spring that helped ease the dust from a dry throat.

Ophelia changed the rhythm with a question she had not asked before. "Do you think the Indians got him?" From the hesitation in her words, Ros could guess that the girl had been worrying about this so much, she was almost afraid to voice her concern aloud.

"They seem friendly enough." Indeed, the Indians they had seen so far had been more interested in trading goods and sharing meals than collecting scalps, despite the more colorful stories she had read. "Moses could always make a friend out of an enemy back home." His ability had been behind much of her success helping escaping slaves; Ros knew it well.

"Almost everyone." The girl's voice was sharp with fear. "If he just could have—"

"Some enemies you can't charm," Ros answered, with a quick look to make sure there was no one else close by to hear their discussion. With some enemies, only complete annihilation would serve to bring peace. "That's why we're leaving them behind."

"You don't have any enemies, Miz Ros," Ophelia protested. "You don't have anything to run from."

"Jericho knows I'm a woman." Ros hadn't meant to tell anyone, but she had to impress the necessity of silence on Ophelia.

"How?"

"One of his men tore off my false whiskers when they stopped my wagon."

"Lordy." Ophelia thought about it a second and then shrugged. "He don't know your name, like he knows Moses's . . . and mine."

"He knows I come from England, and he's heard tell of an Englishwoman helping slaves to run away back home. He could indeed have my name by now."

Ophelia stopped dead and pulled the baby up against herself tightly. "He might know your name?" Her eyes were wide and she shook from head to toe with fear.

Ros cursed her own tongue and asked briskly, "Do you think Caroline's father, Mr. Watson—or my brother-in-law, the Duke of Kerstone—would let him hang me?"

At the mention of the duke's name, Ophelia stopped trembling. For a classless society, the Americans still found a man with a title intimidating—when they weren't trying to prove they didn't give a damn. "I don't suppose they would. But I hope Jericho never learns your name."

"On that point, I agree with you wholeheartedly." Ros looked ahead, where wagons could be seen stretched out as far as the eye could see. "I hope you, Freedom, Moses, the twins, and I are all safely in California before Mr. Jericho realizes we've left Saint Joe."

"Moses said he'd rather die in an Indian attack than go back to being a slave." Once again on the subject of Moses, Ophelia gazed off in the distance, as if she thought she might catch a glimpse of him.

"The papers and magazines make a big story out of Indian attacks," Ros tried to comfort her. "But for the most part, they are uncommon." She might have argued that the attacks were often provoked when the Indians' freedom, land, or family was threatened, but she didn't think that Ophelia, who had never owned as much as a pretty ribbon before, would understand.

"I don't trust them savages," Ophelia muttered. "They act all nice when they come near, but two cows and a horse been gone missing since we stepped foot into the wilderness."

"Moses is not a cow or a horse. He's a man who can take care of himself."

"That's why I married him," Ophelia said. "I see the man working for his freedom and I know he not be like some who just sit around and drink and moan they can't get no work and wish they was slaves again."

"No. If he had been able to buy his own freedom, as he'd planned, he would have worked hard to make a success of his life. He isn't afraid of freedom. Which is why I think he's just fine and waiting until the time is right for you to be together again."

"I hope so. He is one sensible man, even if he is hardheaded. But he ain't never been around savages before." Ophelia stopped dead again. "Maybe his shiny scalp look attractive to them redskins."

Ros wanted to laugh, but she didn't, knowing that Ophelia's concern was genuine. "I hardly think they'd be interested in Moses's scalp. The articles I've read suggest they prefer blond or red hair, the longer the better."

"I suppose so." The thought seemed to quiet Ophelia's worries—at least about Moses being murdered and scalped by savages. There was silence between them for a time. Then, like a hand circling the face of a clock, her question came again. "Where do you suppose he's got to, then?"

Just then, the baby began to fuss. Thankfully, Ophelia was duly distracted from her concerns for Moses by the need to feed him. "I'm going to sit a spell," the girl said as she looked around for a convenient spot. "Seems like the wagons has slowed considerable."

"Have they?" Ros looked forward but could only see two or three wagons before the rest were hidden by the crest of a small hill. The wagons were crawling along, however. Was the road bad? "I'm going ahead to see why."

Ros strode away as Ophelia settled down on a flat rock to feed her son. As Ros reached the next rise, she saw that the wagons had halted and begun to cluster around a small branch of the river.

Three Indians sat on the bank, blocking the way to a narrow bridge they had built. She thought they must be Nemahas, but she wasn't certain. They were dressed brightly—wrapped in red, green, blue, and white blankets. The crowns of their heads bristled with a narrow strip of hair, while the sides were completely shaved—or perhaps plucked.

# Chapter Twelve

She had read that some Indian men plucked the hair from their faces instead of shaving like civilized men. But she knew better, from Jeanne's letters, than to believe all that was reported in the newspapers and periodicals. A great deal of emotional rhetoric sold newspapers. Jeanne said the editors' competitive nature and natural disdain for the intelligence of their readership often led them to shape their stories to the view they wanted the reader to hold, even if a few facts got twisted into lies in the process.

She moved forward, along with many other curious members of the company. Would she be able to tell up close whether they were shaved or plucked? Perhaps Mr. Lewis would know. She would ask him tonight at supper, if she couldn't tell just by looking.

A young woman—married, though she was only sixteen—stopped beside Ros. "What do they want?"

"I suppose they want us to pay to cross the bridge."

This was not the first Indian bridge they had come upon, although it was the most well built. Mr. Lewis had said there would be many more on the journey—some built by trappers, some by settlers, and some by Indians.

"How much do you think they want?" The young woman—Astrid was her name, Ros remembered now—looked worried. No doubt she and her husband—all of eighteen—hadn't gone west expecting to pay to get their wagon over every shallow stream and river branch.

Rob Lewis was arguing with one of the men of their company, gesturing to the bridge and pointing to the sky, as if to remind the older man of the time passing. "Too much, I suspect, considering the way they're arguing."

They went closer to listen to the argument. Rob's expression was set in granite. "Fifty cents a wagon is reasonable enough. The bridge is sturdy."

Win Price shook his head stubbornly. He was a grizzled widower, set in his ways and traveling with three married sons and two unmarried daughters and their combined life savings. "We can ford right over there without paying a penny. This is extortion, and I, for one, won't pay it."

"Take a look, Mr. Price." Mr. Lewis crossed his arms and stood implacably. Normally, Ros found this posture annoying. This time, she hoped it would intimidate Mr. Price into agreeing to the terms Captain Hellfire had set.

With a glance over his shoulder at the three Indians watching avidly, as if they were patrons at the finest show the London stage had to offer, Mr. Lewis added casually, "I think you'll find it's not as easy at it looks."

Price strode over to take a look at the river, and his already ruddy skin turned scarlet. "I don't believe it."

"What's the matter?" One of Price's supporters frowned and went to stand beside him.

Price turned, apparently noticing the crowd that had formed. He shouted heatedly, "They've felled two logs—the wagons'll never make it over them."

One of his daughters shouted back, "Let's pay the toll, then, Pa."

Ros hoped the argument would end now. She knew men well enough, had seen little disagreements like this lead to past fast friends cutting each other in public. She understood the dangers of splintering the group. From the way Mr. Lewis stood, his back to the Indians, his implacable gaze on Mr. Price, she suspected he knew it even better than she.

Unfortunately, Mr. Price didn't have an inclination to be reasonable. "I won't be tricked by the likes of these savages," Price declared. "Who's with me? We'll have to move them." Several men moved to volunteer, and a grumbling began among the crowd.

Still, he did not raise his voice, or show any anger at the man's foolish bullheadedness. "It will take you all afternoon to clear those logs," Mr. Lewis said reasonably. "We'll make better time if we pay the Indians for the use of the bridge."

"I won't let some backward—"

Without anger, Rob Lewis raised his hand to cut off the older man's tirade. "I'm not going to argue. Every moment of argument sets us behind. We'll pay for the use of the bridge—the price is fair."

"But—"

"There are more of these bridges ahead, Mr. Price. If you want to fight every time, you go right ahead, but don't expect me to sit around and wait for you. I'd rather pay and use the bridge—it's faster, and friendlier."

By now, the crowd had divided. Ros saw the teamster she had hired to drive her wagon among the men eager to move the logs.

"Mr. Barton!" she called.

He looked at her warily. He didn't like driving for a woman, she knew, but he had been respectful enough so far. "Please be so good as to drive my wagon up to the bridge. I'm happy to pay the toll."

His expression suggested he wanted to refuse. Ros said sharply, "It's my money, and you won't have to waste your time. Mr. Barton, surely you do not intend to refuse?"

Grudgingly, he moved toward her wagon. A few other men, recognizing the voice of common sense, even if it was female, went as well.

"Can you get them to go any lower, Mr. Lewis?" Bug Martin, Astrid's baby-faced husband, asked anxiously.

Bug's question was the one all the crowd really wanted to hear Captain Hellfire's answer to, Rob knew. "Fifty cents is fair," he reminded them. "Let me see if they'll take less."

As he turned toward the tallest Nemeha, White Crow, Rob saw Gwyneth at the edge of the crowd. She was watching him as if she thought he could lift his hand and all these men, women, children, and wagons would follow. Miss Fenster was watching him, as well. Her expression didn't reflect nearly as much faith in his abilities. He remembered now how he hated these little challenges; each one so small in itself, yet each holding the capacity to turn the journey toward disaster.

Rob turned to the Nemehas and spoke a few words in their language. At first, White Crow made a show of reluctance. As he turned to his sons and they exchanged a rapid-fire conversation he could not follow, Rob felt Gwyneth slip her hand in his.

"What are those?" She pointed to the moccasins laid out on the ground. There were twenty pairs of various sizes and designs.

"They're called moccasins," he explained.

"They look like slippers." She pointed to one pair in particular, with blue and green beads sewn across the top.

"They're leather. Indian shoes. Most likely White Crow's wife made them to sell to the emigrants crossing the bridge."

Wistfully, obviously aware that she would be impolite and impertinent to ask directly, Gwyneth said, "They're pretty. Maybe I'll get a pair for my birthday."

Rob felt a crawling panic close his throat. Her birthday. When was her birthday? Late May. Or was it the first of June? Would Miss Fenster know? He'd have to ask. He wouldn't want his daughter to know he couldn't remember the day she was born; he had a feeling she'd be hurt to know such a thing.

White Crow smiled at her. "You like?" He pointed to a pair of moccasins that looked to be the right size for Gwyn. "Five dollars." It was an outrageous price. White Crow reached down to pat her head. "Your daughter?"

Rob nodded and smiled down at Gwyn, who stood a little closer to him.

White Crow took the pair of moccasins Gwyneth had admired and laid them flat on his palm as he said to Rob, "Five dollars. Then forty cents each wagon."

Defeated, Rob couldn't help grinning, even though his pride was rubbed raw at the bargain he'd just made. Still, he'd made Gwyneth happy, and no doubt White Crow's wife as well. The concession in price would break the dam of reluctance among the emigrants, too.

He turned back to the crowd and shouted, "Forty

cents a wagon." Several men looked concerned and glanced pointedly over at the men still debating clearing the ford.

"Will they take flour?" Miss Fenster's cool English voice asked loudly. "Or perhaps another form of barter?"

Rob gazed at her a moment. She stared back, one cool brow raised as if she truly wanted an answer. He supposed he shouldn't be riled just because she'd shown herself to be a smart woman. Even if she did stand there with her arms across her chest as if she were better than all of them put together.

He turned back to White Crow. The Indian was looking at Miss Fenster in her bloomer skirts and her short-cropped hair with more than casual interest. Rob moved to block his view of the woman. White Crow turned his attention to Rob reluctantly, but there was a knowing look in his eye, especially when Gwyneth took her new moccasins and ran to Miss Fenster to show them off.

"Wife?"

"No." His words were infused with the horror of the thought.

White Crow said something over his shoulder to his sons, who laughed aloud. Before Rob could ask the question, the tall Nemeha said, "Forty cents, or handful of flour, beans, or rice each wagon cross."

They were happy enough to be paid in any currency. And equally delighted by Captain Hellfire's dilemma, which had no doubt added entertainment to their daily routine. He tried not to show his own annoyance that he hadn't thought of this solution first when he turned back to the silently waiting crowd and announced, "Forty center per wagon. They will also take a handful of flour, beans, or rice in barter instead."

"Robbery!" Mr. Price dug into his pockets for a

moment, but then set his chin. He and his family had ten wagons between them and every one of them, down to the two-year-old baby, had an appetite the size of a bear.

At last, with a disgusted growl, the old man turned his back on the procession of wagons going over the creaking but sturdy bridge. "I'm not fool enough to pay for what I can do myself for free."

Rob decided to say nothing at all to the men. He gestured to White Crow, a rather impolite assessment of Price, and the several men who joined their efforts, as fools. White Crow and his sons laughed, too amused by the spectacle they had witnessed—and fortified by the five-dollar moccasins Rob had purchased—to take offense.

Mr. Price and three other men went to the ford and set to work removing the logs without another word. White Crow sent one of his sons to observe, but overall the Nemehas seemed more amused than annoyed at the men, who were soon covered in mud and soaking wet.

The reaction among the emigrants was muted. Rob watched the faces, knowing that a leader could lose everything in a moment over what should have been a simple decision.

"Seems fair to pay a man for his hard work," Astrid Martin, who was standing close to Miss Fenster, said. He saw the look of encouragement she shot her young husband.

Bug echoed her sentiment as he nodded and smiled back at his wife. "Bridge seems sturdy to me. Saves a little time, too. I can stand the loss of a few beans to save me some time and sweat."

Feeling the momentum of the crowd shift, Rob took advantage by moving swiftly to Bug and slapping his back heartily. "Since you're the first to offer to pay, you can be the first to cross."

Bug, with the energy of youth, raced for his wagon. Astrid joined him, her skirts flying as she ran like the child she had been only a few years ago.

Relieved that others seemed to be following the young couple's lead, Rob walked over to where Gwyneth stood next to Ros, showing off her new moccasins while Ros held her discarded boots cradled in one arm. "I don't know if you did that couple a kindness. Maybe they should turn back if they can't afford the bridge tolls now, when we've just begun."

"They have money, but they'd like it to last. I just offered them an option. If they run low on food supplies, they can always replenish them at Fort Laramie. Gold's another matter altogether." Everyone knew the couple had saved a tiny precious stake for the future and were carefully guarding it.

"I'd rather starve than buy any more supplies than I need. I won't allow the Fort Laramie sutlers to rob me legally."

She smiled a little sadly as she glanced at the couple nestled side up side in the front of their wagon. "They'll manage. They have hope and youthful energy on their side. It'll take more than four months of hardship to wear it all away."

"Maybe so." He watched the couple. He'd taken them on reluctantly. Everything he knew pointed to trouble—they were young and traveling alone, they had scraped together barely enough money to make the journey, never mind to handle the disasters that often occurred on the trail. Yet, somehow, he didn't sense that they would bring trouble to the train.

But that didn't mean they'd keep their fresh-faced

enthusiasm—or that they'd even like each other by the time they got to California.

"I'm willing to wager on it." He remembered the stories he'd heard about her wild youth in London. Bug and Astrid might not be trouble. But Miss Fenster . . . she bore careful watching.

"I'm not a gambling man, Miss Fenster." Several more wagons lined up behind Bug, but men still stood stubbornly aside as well. From that crowd, there were dark looks when Bug drove his wagon over the bridge first, after happily paying the price in beans.

"I don't gamble anymore either, Mr. Lewis. Unless I think I can't lose." She smiled in challenge. He didn't know if she'd done them a favor, though. There'd be more bridges, more tolls, more places to spend money. He liked them both, but he had to wonder if the young couple was traveling with more hope than common sense.

"One thing I've learned in my years on this earth, Miss Fenster: Anyone can lose."

The folks who had been unsure got in line, one by one, to cross the bridge. One spot of trouble smoothed over. Rob wished he could take it as a good sign for the rest of the trip—all sixteen to eighteen weeks of it. But he knew better.

He didn't let himself rest easy until everyone was settled down for their evening meal. Even then he kept his ears and eyes open for trouble.

"Here, Papa." Gwyneth handed him his supper with a smile and a little bounce. He didn't know where she got the energy to bounce at the end of another long, hard day. "I gave you two biscuits."

Ophelia made a noise low in her throat, and Gwyneth suddenly looked like a child who'd forgotten her lesson in front of the whole class. His daughter threw her arms

around his neck, threatening the extra biscuit she'd
given him. "Thank you for the mocksins, Papa."

She continued to hang around his neck and he sat
there awkwardly, clutching his plate and trying not to
keel over into the fire, as he wondered what to do.

Miss Fenster bent down to whisk the plate from his
hand. "I think your daughter needs to hug you properly,
Mr. Lewis. I've never seen a child so pleased with a gift
before."

He put his arms, now free, around his daughter and
squeezed, worried that he might hurt her. But she only
burrowed closer in and squeezed him back without the
same concern for him.

Miss Fenster winked cheekily at him, expressing sympathy with the assault his daughter was making. She did
not, however, offer rescue for anything but his plate. It
was a good two minutes before he was released to eat
his supper.

As he ate, Rob tuned out his daughter's singsong
recitation of her day's highlights and listened instead
to the tenor of conversations around the smoky fires
scrounged out of chips. There seemed no difference to
it tonight, from last night. He strained his ears to hear
any hint of trouble, without giving his heightened attention away.

The murmurs of tired men and women who'd traveled hard all day were a constant hum amid the noise
of preparing and clearing away their welcome suppers.
Maybe a bit more laughter spiked through the hum—
the wait to cross the bridge had given them all a spell
of relief from the relentless travel.

He'd have to wander by his fire and talk to the men
to see if he had lost any of them today. Not that they
would tell him so in so many words. But he'd know
which ones would join another company. Which ones

would turn back. Those whose lack of faith would cause trouble.

Emigrants were a stubborn, headstrong bunch for the most part. If they took it in their heads to think they were smarter than the famous Captain Hellfire, they wouldn't follow him, no matter his reputation. And that could be deadly.

Reluctant to make his rounds, Rob told Gwyneth a longer story than he'd meant to, until she curled up by the fire, sound asleep, her prized moccasins still on her feet, his jacket covering her, keeping her warm.

He knew he should walk the camp, talk to the men. He knew it, but still he could not make himself leave the fire. A fire, he noted, that had been more wood than chips. He glanced at the other fires he could see. Smoky, all of them.

How had she . . . ? It took him only a moment to puzzle out the answer to that. He'd seen her, during the day, picking up the sticks and branches that other emigrant trains had considered too small to bother with. As a result of her industry, their fire burned bright and steady, much less smoky than the others.

"You have a talent for building a fire, Miss Fenster." He'd meant the compliment straightforwardly, but as soon as the words left his mouth, he realized that she could take it another way. His groin tightened involuntarily at the thought.

Many a woman in this camp might have thought his words were meant seductively. But he wasn't concerned that Rosaline Fenster would take them that way. Despite the fact that she had offered to warm his bed for the trip before they started, she hadn't flirted with him once since they began.

Watchful for trouble, he'd noticed that any man who had tried to flirt with her had been deftly diverted into a conversation about where to find the best game or how to build a good fire with such meager pickings. No, she wouldn't think he was flirting with her. But she might think he was angry that she had interfered this afternoon. He scanned her expression in the firelight but could not tell her thoughts.

*A talent for building a fire.* Did he mean it? Or did he still fear she'd cause trouble? Perhaps, she thought with a twinge of excitement low in her belly, he was trying to tell her that he wanted to accept the proposition she had made him before the trip. She couldn't tell from his expression in the firelight, although she thought he watched her rather warily for one who had just uttered a uncomplicated compliment.

"From you that is rampant flattery, Captain Hellfire." She laughed, as if she was not aware of the deeper meaning of his words. "But I confess it is more the responsibility of the wood I gathered today. I don't like a smoky fire if I can avoid one."

His expression was too hard to read from across the fire. She stood and lifted the coffeepot from the fire. "Have another cup of coffee."

"I should make my rounds." He made no move to do so, however.

"Of course you should. As soon as you have a warm drink to ease the chill of the evening." She poured for him and sat down beside him, resting the coffeepot on the ground. This close she could see his expression much more clearly. "Otherwise you'll look as if you're nervous that you've weakened the confidence of your company."

He stiffened beside her. "I am not aware that anyone in my company has anything but the utmost confidence in me."

"Perhaps I am too harsh in my judgment. But everyone knows that you lost your wife only a little more than a month ago. It's only natural to worry that the famous Captain Hellfire might not be as sharp after such a hard blow—and so recently, too."

"I am as sharp as ever. Caroline's death saddened me, but there is nothing I can do. I will not let it affect my judgment."

"No?" She continued to goad him. Did he blame her for her part in this afternoon's events? "I admit to having some concerns about the matter myself."

She thought he might admit his grief, his guilt to her. Instead, he turned to look into her eyes, his face inches from hers. "Have I lost your confidence?"

The bald question made her regret her attempt to get him to reveal himself with a verbal skirmish. Only force of will kept her from leaping to her feet to escape his proximity. "Indeed not," she confessed.

She leaned away from him, to throw several more of her precious supply of sticks upon the fire, even though there was no need for them. "I believe you've gained my confidence. I admire how well you handled the Nemeha—and Mr. Price."

Her words didn't seem to reassure him; he shifted restlessly beside her. "They forded without paying," he said darkly. "People will remember that."

Ros wondered if his worry was a result of his grief over Caroline's death, or whether his success was built upon a constant burning worry over such small incidents. "They spent half the day working in the mud to move the logs blocking the ford. Their first wagon forded the river the same time as the last one that crossed the bridge."

"True enough, but what each man chooses to remember is what they'll use to base the next decision upon."

"They'll remember—"

He interrupted. "How many will remember that he got across without paying and forget the work involved?"

Somehow he had turned the tables—he had gone from express confidence in his action to admitting his own vulnerability. She wanted to argue, but sitting this closely, she could see the assurance of experience in his eyes. Hadn't she seen the same kind of blindness to the truth back in Charleston? Yes, most slave owners treated their slaves well enough. But the ones who were inhumane had their transgressions overlooked by their peers, for the most part.

Like a man who beat his wife, an owner who beat or raped or killed his slaves might get a closed-lipped greeting from his neighbor's wife. But he'd be welcomed in church, and in the town hall, quickly enough.

His voice was calm, with just a hint of anger. "How many will think they might try that course next time? How much trouble will we be in if next time there might be a toll keeper who decides to take offense?"

# Chapter Thirteen

Ros tried once again to reconcile the careless wanderer she had thought Rob Lewis to be with this man, who watched out for his flock with the eyesight of a hawk. "Have you ever had the misfortune to be faced with mutiny?"

"Not yet."

"Well, then, why worry now?" she asked in her most reasonable tone. "Is this trip any different from any other you've undertaken?"

"Yes." There was a touch of dread etching the lines around his eyes into visibility. "This trip is different." His voice did not waver with any doubt.

"How? Caroline's—"

"No." He cut her off sharply, as if he didn't want to think about such things any longer. "I usually make it clear that if I say a toll is to be paid, there is to be no argument. I usually read out a list of Captain Hellfire's rules." He rubbed his jaw absently. "But this time, because of the delay, I didn't."

Impatient with his need to treat his emigrants like errant children, she asked, "Does it matter? Aren't we—with the exception of the children, and possibly Bug and Astrid Martin—aren't we all adults? Shouldn't we know what's right, and do it?"

At that, he smiled. A devastating smile that touched his eyes and lit his face. "I would accuse you of being naïve, but I think you might bite off my tongue if I did."

"Most definitely," Ros answered, hoping her words didn't sound as shaky as her insides felt. She had made a tactical error sitting this close to him. She had forgotten how powerfully his proximity affected her.

She wasn't sure she succeeded in keeping her attraction from him, because his eyes flared a moment, then narrowed, before he abruptly rose. "I'll gather everyone and read my rules to them first thing tomorrow morning. That will help." He looked down upon her with a reserved expression that hid his thoughts.

Did he pity her? Find her repellent because she had been bold enough—honest enough—to make him a straightforward offer rather than be coy? She didn't want to know. She didn't want him to know with any certainty that she had suffered a moment of weakness either. She stood and asked sharply, "Do you always worry this much?"

For a moment she thought he wouldn't answer. "No. But I don't have a good feeling about this trip."

"Because of me?" She didn't want him to agree. She wanted to hear him deny the idea.

The man, however, was damnably honest. "Maybe."

"I don't intend to cause trouble."

"Most trouble isn't caused by people who intend it. And that's the worst kind of trouble, too."

Ros understood that sentiment all too well. When she escorted slaves northward she could tell the ones who would need to be hog-tied and gagged to get them through a checkpoint without giving themselves, and everyone else, away. The few times she hadn't seen it coming, the trouble had always been ten times worse. "You can't catch everything, though. Not even the perfect Captain Hellfire can see every spot of trouble and every troublemaker. Even you can be wrong."

"I'm never wrong."

She made a little sound, a half-laugh, half-snort, at his confidence. Never wrong? Even she had never been foolish enough to say such a thing.

He shrugged. "Troublemakers are usually easy for me to spot. There are certain times, like when I read my rules, when they stand out. I don't let them in my company, or I part ways with them as soon as I see which way the wind blows."

"Do you really imagine you can prevent all trouble?"

"No. Just some of the worst of it." He shook his head, anger at himself vibrating from him. "I've put the whole company at risk because I was in a damn-fool hurry. And because—" He broke off.

Ros finished his thought for him. "And because you were distracted by a seven-year-old girl and a woman dressed like a man—two wild cards you hadn't wanted in your hand."

When he looked away she couldn't help smiling a little. She wouldn't have expected him to show the unnecessary chivalry of pretending she wasn't a giant thorn in his side. There wasn't anyone in the company who didn't know it. Even White Crow had seen the look he gave her and understood.

She did feel a touch responsible for his distraction, though. If she had been the nurturing, feminine type she'd have taken his concerns for Gwyneth right out of his hands. And she'd have worn skirts that wouldn't have raised eyebrows or gossip. But she wasn't that kind of female. Nor was she about to be, even if it made life easier for Captain Hellfire.

But there were a few things she could do instead. She touched his arm to draw his attention. "Don't worry that anyone in this company will forget watching Mr. Price and his cohorts go to all that trouble and then struggle over the branch at the same time as the last wagon."

He moved away from her touch abruptly. "I have no control over that."

She smiled. "I do. I'll tell the story far and wide, until it travels to the farthest company ahead of us to the newest starting out. Another legend for Captain Hellfire."

She would have expected him to be grateful, but instead he frowned. "I don't need another legend to my name."

His ungrateful—and uninsightful—response exasperated her. "I can say what I please."

"So can Win Price." He shook his head, as if to chase off an irritating insect. "The men were wet and covered with mud, but they seemed well enough pleased that they'd not had to pay out any of their goods to the Indians. And that's what they're saying tonight, mark my words."

What a hardheaded man he was. Ros said, "I do believe you look for trouble even when there's none in sight for miles, Mr. Lewis."

No trouble in sight. Rob Lewis wanted to laugh. For a man with his eyes open, there was always trouble in sight. And right now he was looking straight at her. He said sharply, "Any man who wants to lead a bunch of hopeful men and their families west had best look for trouble, Miss Fenster. Because it's surely going to find him whether he's looking for it or not."

She raised one elegant brow as if to dispute his words. "The trip so far has been uneventful."

Three days on the trail and she thought she knew more than he did? He was tempted to list the troubles ahead, but he knew better. He said flatly, "This has been the easy part."

She shook her head, a small smile bringing a dimple to her cheek. "I wouldn't call it easy. Walking over hilly ground twelve to fourteen hours a day. Making a meal on that," she said, pointing to the camp stove, which Ophelia had cleaned and oiled and set to dry by the fire.

He found the dimple surprisingly incongruous in her otherwise self-assured expression. Perhaps because of it, he couldn't seem to find the energy to be angry with her challenge to his experience. He satisfied himself with the truth. "You will swear this was a walk in the park compared to the rest of the trip—if you make it to San Francisco."

She frowned at him, her pride wounded. "Do I look as though I'm about to expire? Do you have doubts about my stamina, or my will?"

"Nope." He decided to give it to her straight. Both barrels. He had a funny feeling she was one woman who could take the truth, whether she liked it or not. "You don't look like you've done more than take a walk in the park, despite three days' hard travel. I don't doubt you could survive the next four months without a hitch in your step from a blister or bunion."

She seemed pleased by his backhanded compliment. A frown appeared, however, when he added, "But you make a good target for trouble, with your fancy foreign ways and those unnatural skirts of yours." He noticed the dimple appeared when she frowned deeply, too.

She glanced down at her bloomer skirts, which somehow accentuated the shape of her legs, and, he conceded, gave her a freedom of movement that had come in handy more than once since they began their travels. "Unnatural? These are no more unnatural than your trousers."

"Men and women—"

"Surely you are not going to call upon the Creator to settle this debate? I do believe we come into this world naked, do we not? After that, we dress to keep ourselves warm, and clean, and free from cuts and abrasions."

Naked. He didn't like the way she said the word. Didn't like what her voice conjured up when she did, either. He felt he'd traveled onto shaky ground and tried to jump to a firmer position. "Then why do you get stares from men and women alike when you dress like that? I don't get any in my trousers."

She lifted that regal brow and observed him. "You don't? Why, I imagine every woman in this company wishes you good day at least once a day."

The observation surprised him. It was something he would expect from another woman. But not from her. "Only being polite."

She shook her head firmly. "They watch you. They seek you out. And they don't seem to mind whether they have a husband or not."

He didn't like where this conversation was heading. With a normal woman it would be bad enough, but with Miss Fenster he had no idea where it might end up. "You sound like a jealous wife."

"Never." As he had hoped, his observation jarred

her. Unfortunately, it didn't shut her up. "I would never be a jealous wife."

"Why not?"

She took a deep breath to calm herself before she answered. "I thought I had made it clear to you already. I can see no purpose in a husband at all."

He remembered their conversation in the kitchen and threw it at her. "You offered to marry a stranger to travel with me once."

Her eyes narrowed. "I offered to provide comfort to you without benefit of marriage, as well. I am grateful that I had to resort to neither unappealing measure."

"Unappealing?" He snorted. "I saw the way you looked at me that day behind the house, when I was chopping the fence posts. You liked what you saw."

She smiled at him, her eyes glowing, as she nodded. "I certainly did, Mr. Lewis."

He felt himself react predictably and was caught between the desire to fight it and the desire to go with it.

Until she continued. "But now, as then, I really only wanted you on my terms—which doesn't include being indebted to you for either giving me your name, or your protection, for the right to sleep in my bed no matter whether I want you there or not."

"That's not the way the world works, Miss Fenster." On her terms? What chaos that would cause. "I don't think I'd ever be able to understand you, Miss Fenster. If I did, I'd have to beg for someone to put me down for madness." He hoped to leave that as a parting shot, something for her to chew on for the next few months.

"Nonsense. I'm easy as glass to see through."

He turned, unable to ignore that outlandish statement.

"That why you have been so successful at helping slaves run away? Because you're clear as a windowpane?"

Her eyes narrowed. "I thought you didn't want to know about my illegal activities."

"I don't. But I do want to point out that you haven't been caught. So don't go trying to claim you can't hide and dodge and pretend when you want to."

She turned away and began to pack the oven away. He was pleased. He'd gotten the last word with Rosaline Fenster. He hadn't been sure such a thing was possible.

*You haven't been caught.* His words still echoed in her mind a week after they were spoken. She knelt by the fire, glad that he was gone, getting the emigrants moving this not very fine morning. Every time she looked at him, a wave of guilt swept up her spine.

Not for wanting him only on her terms. No matter what he or any other man thought, that was how she liked things. But for not being honest with him about the runaways from the very beginning. It had been all she could do that night not to turn around and say just one word. *Yet.* A foolish urge, brought on by the firelight and the relative privacy and this sense of trust she had for him, despite what she knew about him. She'd been careful not to be alone with him again.

*Yet.* He'd put her out of his company without a second thought if he knew there was even a possibility that Jericho might know she was a woman. Might know her name. She couldn't blame him. Few men would put their trust in a woman to see to her own safety. There was no way she could think of to assure him that she'd die before she'd allow her foolishness to jeopardize the people of this train or to bring harm to Gwyneth.

Although she did wonder whether she had been wise to bring the child on this trip with her. Gwyneth hadn't complained about the hardship, but she had woken pale and coughing several mornings. It might have been the dampness. Or the chill in the air of a morning.

The lack of timber was irritating. Each evening they had to scrabble for something to burn to make the fire. It wasn't that the prairie land wasn't rich enough—it was the emigrants who'd been traveling the road for six straight years. They and their cattle had stripped the land of its bounty. Even her daily scrounging didn't bring enough for a fire some nights.

She had taken to paying the children for any sticks and branches they brought her. Unfortunately, her industry had not gone unnoticed by the rest of the families in her company, and there was stiff competition for the children's scavenged bundles of skinny twigs and slender branches.

Rob had said they'd likely find a little more wood when they had crossed Big Blue and reached Otter Creek. She would have liked it yesterday, when the rain made building a fire nearly impossible and they'd been forced to eat cold rice with a little milk.

This morning there'd been ice on the pans of water, and the dampness from the previous day's rain made what fires they built smoky enough to fog over the whole camp. She felt as if Jericho could appear from that fog, conjured simply by her churning thoughts.

Still, if Jericho were to come . . . Finally, as she stared into the smoky fire trying to get enough heat to bake a few pancakes to last them through breakfast and lunch, she made a vow to herself: If he were to find her, she'd take care of it without causing trouble. If she couldn't, she'd tell Rob Lewis then—and only then. She was certain she could handle it, although the thought that he knew she was a woman gave her just a twinge of doubt in her otherwise solid faith that she could escape detection.

Though she would prefer to be honest, it was simply too dangerous to tell Captain Hellfire until he had to know. Rob Lewis wasn't the kind of man to take a chance on her abilities. And Rosaline Fenster wasn't the kind to share her troubles. She had handled them herself up to now, and done a damn fine job of it.

She heard the noises of teams being harnessed and families preparing for the day's travel, although visibility was greatly reduced by the smoke, until she could only see Gwyneth neatly folding the pallets they'd laid upon in the wagon last night, to keep off the rain-soaked ground.

As she leaned over the fire, trying vainly to keep the flame alive, a shadow appeared above her. For a moment she was certain it was Jericho. But it was Moses.

She leaped to her feet, pancakes forgotten. "You're alive. Have you seen Ophelia? Do you need food?"

He held up his hand, which grasped a sack of food. "Fee gave me this. It's not safe for me to be here. Jericho be here somewhere."

She tried not to panic at the news. "Here?" She'd known it was possible. He wasn't a stupid man, even if he hadn't spotted them leaving Saint Joe.

"Not in this company yet, but soon." Moses looked at her as if he had too much to say and no idea how to put it in words. At last he said, "You got to be careful of that man."

"How is it that you're so certain where he is? Are you traveling with another company?"

He shook his head, scanning for any movement that might mean his imminent capture. "Seems like everyone knows I'm wanted."

"Then how are you—"

He held up his hand impatiently. "I'm traveling with

a band of Shoshone and they got ways to find out these things."

Ros couldn't help smiling at the thought that he'd made friends with a band of Shoshone and found a way to get information on Jericho as well. "Ophelia was afraid the Indians would scalp you."

"What would they want with this hairless head?" He laughed, but the laughter tailed off into a harsh cough that bent him nearly double.

"Are you ill?" Ros reached for his cheek to see if he were feverish.

Before she could touch him he melted backward into the fog with a whispered warning. "Got to go. Too dangerous."

"Who was that?"

Ros turned to see Rob Lewis by the fire. She thought about claiming to be speaking to herself, or Gwyn, but discarded the thought immediately. Moses's voice was deep, and Rob had undoubtedly heard it.

She bent over the pancakes again, careful not to look at him lest his observant gaze noted that she was lying. "One of the emigrants asking to use our fire."

As if he knew she was being evasive, he squatted next to her to better see her face. "Where did he go?"

She lifted a brow, as if she couldn't imagine why she should care where the emigrant had gone. "Off to find a better fire, I suppose. I told him ours wasn't hot enough for us." She looked down at the misshapen, nearly raw pancake. "I think we're in for cold rice and milk again."

He shook his head, looking off into the distance as if he might catch sight of Moses. "No. The clouds are lifting, though you can't tell it here because of the smoke from all these fires. Today will be a good day to travel."

"That's good news." She didn't know if she was looking forward to another rainy day of walking beside the wagons, in the cold and wet. She definitely would not choose to ride in the wagon, as Gwyneth and Ophelia had. She'd rather walk free and wet than bump around a tightly packed wagon. The thought alone brought a bitter taste of panic to her throat.

"I wanted to tell you that I'm sorry I doubted you. You were right about the road getting harder." They'd covered a great deal of territory in the last week.

Graciously, he did not gloat. "That's why I'm pushing everyone so hard now. The mountains and the desert are the most tiring part of the trip. We'll want to rest a while at Fort Laramie before we tackle it."

"I wondered why you were so eager to pass the Mission without visiting. I thought perhaps you did not want to be converted." They passed by but did not stop at the Presbyterian Iowa Sac and Fox Mission. Some of the Indians who had been converted by the missionaries and wore western clothing could be seen working in the fields. But the journey was too new and the emigrants eager enough to follow Captain Hellfire's advice to push on and shave a week or two off their travel time.

"No fear of that." Rob watched her carefully. She was hiding something, and he had a terrible feeling he knew what it was. The man he'd seen for half a second had not been one of his emigrants. He'd been big—and black as night against the fog. "How are Ophelia and the baby doing? I didn't see them yesterday."

"They stayed in the wagon, out of the rain, with Gwyneth." She was avoiding meeting his eyes. He didn't know whether it was a good sign that she felt guilty, or a very bad one.

"Are they traveling well?"

"Well enough." He thought she would keep her answers short, but suddenly she looked up and said,

"It's a little disconcerting. How do you do it every year? The days blend from one into another, everyone walking beside the wagons, listening to the creak of the wheels and the sound of the cattle being driven."

"Wilderness. You get used to it."

She nodded. "There is a sense of wilderness, an endless high rich prairie, and yet not. If I stand in the right place along the road, I can see companies of wagons stretching before me, and behind me as well. I fancy that the line might even stretch unbroken from Saint Joe to San Francisco."

"It almost does. But that's only an illusion of civilization. An illusion of safety."

# Chapter Fourteen

Miss Fenster smiled at him, a smile with a touch of scorn for his careful nature. "How can I not be aware of that? Every day I see wild wolves, Indians in their native dress riding their ponies—with spears that can be put to deadly use."

"They won't attack without reason, despite what you may have read before you embarked on this trip."

She nodded. "I know. I fear the other dangers more—the illness and accidents that have taken other travelers. The ones whose graves we pass."

He moved closer, as if he might touch her. "It's a long, hard journey. Not everyone makes it."

She backed away from him. "How can anyone forget their mortality when the children play with the bones of buffalo and the horns of elk?"

He realized that she was intentionally distracting him from discovering the secret she was hiding from him. "Who was that man you were talking to?"

"I told you."

He leaned in closer, as he had before. It seemed to rattle her. "I don't believe you."

"What am I to do about that?" She tried to back away from him, but he grasped her shoulders firmly and held her still.

"Tell me the truth or I'll have to leave you at Fort Kearny."

"That threat is getting tired," she answered sharply. "What would you do with Gwyn? Or would you happily leave her behind with me?"

"I'm not letting go of you until you tell me." He stared into her eyes. For a moment, he thought she would tell him. And then she leaned forward and placed her lips against his. She didn't kiss him. If she had kissed him, he'd have known what to do. But with just the soft press of her lips against his, he couldn't react for a moment. It was everything he could manage just to keep breathing.

Ros couldn't believe what she'd done. Worse, she'd expected him to either kiss her back or let her go, and he'd done neither. She twitched her lips, ready to laugh, and he jerked away with a harsh sound.

"Why did you do that?" His eyes blazed with fury and she could see with shocking clarity that he was not indifferent to her, no matter what he pretended by the campfire over supper.

*To make you let me go.* But she would never confess that to him. "Because I wanted to," she said instead.

"I will never understand you." With a look of fury, he turned and walked off. The fog swallowed him in an instant, and Ros felt safe enough that she didn't hide her shaking hands as she finished cooking the last of the soggy, unappetizing pancakes.

As he had promised, the day broke clear as soon as

they were away from camp. The feel of the sun on her face was a welcome change from the cloudy cool, rainy days that had gone before. "Looks like it will be a good day for a long walk," she joked with Ophelia, though she didn't truly feel lighthearted about another day of walking.

She had never walked so much in her life. She could, of course, have ridden, but there was no point—the wagons were not moving quickly, just steadily. Five, ten, sometimes as much as fifteen miles a day. And the land was hardly welcoming—the riverbanks and roadway were stripped bare of trees and bushes from the emigrants who had traveled before them.

Ophelia ignored her gloomy tone and beamed as she kissed Freedom's head. "He's alive, Miz Ros."

"I know." They didn't dare say too much. Ros had told Ophelia that Jericho was on their trail and they had to be careful not to be overheard. That was one thing she understood well—the danger of being turned in by others.

"Do you think his cough will kill him?"

"If the Indians haven't scalped him, and Jericho hasn't found him, what makes you think a little cough could bring him down?"

The thought seemed to cheer Ophelia through the next few days, despite the hardships that faced them. Fires were hard to make, and even theirs needed to be fed with chips. Ros gladly competed with the enterprising children as they foraged more widely for sticks and branches—and even a few pieces of broken furniture she had found that some emigrant had discarded beside a river fording.

That had brought a comment from Mr. Lewis. "Are you burning a table leg?"

"I am."

"Makes a nice blaze."

"It does indeed," she agreed calmly. All her reading hadn't really prepared her for this challenge. But with Rob Lewis's eyes upon her, she was utterly determined not to show her desire to take her fastest horse and leave this train and all these possessions behind. She understood completely why the emigrants who'd left the table behind had done so. The sheer weight of their possessions had made them feel they would never get where they were going.

They were all happy to reach the Platte River. The river meant water would be plentiful for the livestock for the next month, as they followed the meandering bank westward.

Fortunately, they would soon be stopping at Fort Kearny. Only a little more than two weeks into her journey and it felt like a lifetime of walking a dusty road, fording rivers—or taking bridges when there was one, always with a toll to pay.

She looked forward to seeing a semblance of civilization, being reminded that this life was not all there was. Not that she didn't enjoy seeing the things that, up until now, she'd only read about. She'd written to Jeanne, who'd made the journey to San Francisco by steamer. She'd informed the reporter that she must take the trail at least once or else she'd never know what kinds of stories she was missing.

She'd written to Caroline's parents, as well. No doubt, their grief still fresh from her last letter, they would read this one with sadness, but she tried to describe the journey their granddaughter was taking, so they would be better prepared to understand her state of mind when she finally arrived.

She'd post the letters at Fort Kearny to let everyone know that Gwyneth had become a good traveler. The child, indeed, was a better traveler than Ros. She bounced out of her pallet even on the most chill gray day with a smile. She had become fast friends with the daughter of one of the other families in the company and together they played games, gathered sticks, and pestered the adults in their parties for stories or food.

Most of the time, Gwyneth seemed happy with her new life, even though it was drastically different from her old one. The only time that Ros caught any hint of sadness was when a child was hurt and a mother came running to provide hugs and kisses—or sometimes, if the child had been hurt while taking a foolish risk—a scolding.

She knew she wasn't good at those motherly kinds of actions. But Ophelia had stepped in to fill the role adequately enough. And soon Gwyneth would be surrounded by her loving grandparents and aunts. How the child would react to having her father leave her, Ros didn't want to think about.

Whether Rob could bring himself to do so was another question. He was hardly equipped to keep her with him as he crisscrossed the country twice a year. But she had seen how much he loved his daughter and she was certain that any parting would be painful for both of them.

She stopped by the side of the Platte, to join the children who were tossing pebbles into the water. "Mine went farthest," she announced.

"No fair!" one of the boys complained loudly. "You're all grown up."

One of the others whispered, "But she's a girl, Henry."

They seemed to debate the issue for the space of a

moment and then shook their heads. "Nah. Ma says no real girl would wear those funny skirts."

Solemnly, the two informed her that her throws did not count. Ros accepted her defeat graciously.

As she started to turn from the riverbank, however, she caught sight of two pair of Indians skimming the river on a craft meant to travel fast. A canoe, she knew the craft was called.

She was tempted to call out and see if they might wish to trade her wagon for their canoe. She could easily imagine how pleasurable it would be to paddle with the current along the river rather than walk—or jolt along in the wagon.

One of the Indians lifted his hand in greeting, and she noticed that he was darker than the others. Much darker. Moses.

She lifted her hand in greeting, even as she quickly checked behind her to make certain that none of the rest of the company had seen him in the Indian canoe. The children were waving and jumping up and down, well used to the sight of Indians after almost two weeks on the trail. She heard nothing to indicate that they had noticed the strange dark Indian. Even Gwyneth seemed not to notice Moses.

She was grateful that none of the other adult emigrants were in sight. She turned back to wave again, and watched with a sigh of relief as the canoe slid quickly out of sight. If Mr. Lewis were to find out—she'd be left at Fort Kearny as quickly as he could manage it.

As she came over a rise, she saw a wagon that wasn't moving. Others made their way around it, but there were no extra hands to help, so they did not stop.

Walking briskly, Ros came upon the wagon in trouble. John Smith was trying to lift the wagon out of a muddy rut, despite the fact that the feat would have taken four good strong men his size.

She supposed it was his pretty wife, who sat at the wagon's helm, reins in hand, egging him on. "Can't you get us out? Everyone is going ahead."

John Smith studied the problem. "Give me a minute, Judith. The rut is deep." He had mud up to his knees and spatters on his face, but there was an expression of determination stamped on his features. Ros didn't think he'd ask for help anytime soon.

"It's been half an hour," Judith complained. "It's nearly time to stop for the evening. We'll never get a good spot by the river if we're stuck here any longer."

Ros came over and surveyed the situation for a moment. "Need a hand?"

"What can you do?" Judith Smith stared at her in frank astonishment.

John, however, said only, "Thank you for the offer, but I think it will take a hand a mite bigger than yours to help me out of this mess, Miss Fenster."

Judith said spitefully, "Why don't you go get your man to lend a hand—oh, I forgot. You don't have one." She laughed as if she'd made a joke.

Ros laughed with her. "And not looking for one either, I confess." She had become used to such attacks. She understood that Judith's unhappy nature made her work to sour the lives of those around her. There was nothing she would like less than to see Ros act as though she enjoyed the joke. "Which is probably why I've had to get my own wagon out of mud holes before. I can't promise brute strength, but maybe we can find another solution."

John said, with a hint of desperation, "I've tried about everything."

"Well, let's just try one or two ideas that have worked for me in the past before we give up."

"John, you are not going to let her waste our time, are you?"

The exhausted man wiped a trail of sweat off his forehead with his arm and then shrugged. "Can't hurt to try something—at least until the captain can send help."

Judith frowned, and Ros had a sinking feeling that Rob was not going to be pleased with her. No doubt he'd consider putting a frown on Judith Smith's face causing trouble.

Ros examined the hole. It wasn't wide, but it was deep. She grabbed a stick and dug out the side of the hole more, making a shallow incline for the wheel to climb.

"Put your shoulder into it," she ordered John as she went to the head of the team of horses to guide them slowly forward.

"Don't take so long about it," Judith said suddenly, when it became obvious that the wagon was moving, thanks to Ros's solution. Without warning, the woman slashed the whip down on the heads of her team and they broke into a startled run.

Ros fell backward, out of the way, but into a huge mud puddle. She watched the team begin to pick up speed with a cry of warning building in her throat.

Before anyone could make a sound, Rob Lewis rode up to cut the team off. He walked them back to the trail. "Hey!" He glanced at Ros sitting in the mud, but his attention was all for John Smith. "Are you trying to start a stampede?"

A stampede was a real worry here. Judith, a little too late to be useful, paled at the realization of what she had almost caused. "No. Our wheel was mired."

"Move slowly next time."

"We will." John and Judith both nodded solemnly, to show they understood the danger of what had happened.

The wagon master nodded in satisfaction and walked his horse over to where Ros was trying to pull herself out of the sucking mud hole.

"Need help?" He grinned down at her, holding out a hand and leaning toward her.

She thought for a moment of refusing, but instead she reached up with her muddy hands and gripped him tightly. He pulled her out at last, but not before she had made certain he was liberally splashed with mud.

"Thank you, Captain."

"You'll want to change those clothes," he ordered.

Judith, who had overheard, tittered. "Maybe you should make her put on decent skirts while she's about it, Captain."

"You could try," Ros muttered in a low voice.

"Is that a request for help, Miss Fenster?" His expression darkened for a moment, as if he was considering whether or not to take up her challenge.

Her blood pulsed more quickly in her veins as he stared down at her. "I was offering help when all this happened. I don't need any for myself."

"Or you didn't when you started." His grin flashed wide and mocking across his face. "That's what you get for helping when you don't know what you're doing."

"I knew what I was doing—it was Mrs. Smith who nearly got us all killed."

Rob felt the storm coming before he saw it. He ignored the puzzled glances as he sounded a command for the wagons to pull off the road. On horseback, he moved from one family to another, warning them of the coming storm.

He could see they didn't understand, but they did as he asked—slowly at first, but then, as the dust storm became visible in the distance, they moved with more speed. Mothers began calling children more frantically and children began running to answer their mothers calls.

He saw Gwyneth standing alone in the midst of the chaos and swept her up on the saddle with him. "What's happening, Papa?"

"A dust storm, Gwyneth. It'll be over soon. I'll bring you to the wagon."

"I want to go to Ophelia's wagon."

"Auntie Ros will be worried."

"Tell her that I wanted to stay with Freedom. Little babies get scared, and they need someone big and strong to show them not to be."

He suspected that another motive was his daughter's awareness that she'd get hugs and reassurances from Ophelia. He couldn't argue that it would be more likely that with Ros—or Rob himself—she'd get terse assurances that the storm would be over when it was over, and not much of a hug, if they thought to give her one at all.

When he rode up to Ophelia, she hugged the little girl at once. He saw that the wagon was nearly full—Ophelia, the baby, the twins who drove her wagon, and Miss Fenster's teamster all crowded inside.

"Where's Miss Fenster?" he asked.

"In her wagon," Ophelia answered. "She sent Mr. Barton to help the twins secure things around here and stayed behind to see to her goods."

So his biggest troublemaker was on her own in a dust storm? "I'd best check on her," Rob said. He peered inside the crowded wagon bed. "Should I take Gwyneth with me?"

The little girl clung tightly to the baby. "No. Freedom needs me, Papa."

Ophelia shook her head and took both children in her arms. "She can stay with me. Just tell Miz Ros, so she don't take a notion to go look for her in this storm."

Rob rode away, surprised and pleased at how quickly the camp had hunkered down, prepared to sit out the siege of the storm. He helped capture a canvas wagon cover that hadn't been tied properly for the strength of the wind and showed the frightened emigrants how to knot it down so it wouldn't let go again.

He scooped up two boys who seemed determined to see who'd be blown away first and restored them to their families and then went in search of Rosaline Fenster and her wagon. He hoped she'd managed to get everything tied tightly down, because the storm promised them a pitiless blasting.

She had tightened every rope, checked every knot, Ros thought with satisfaction. But where was Gwyn? Outside, the road was virtually deserted. She could see that most of the wagon flaps were being tied down in anticipation of the wind-driven dust.

There was no sign of Gwyneth. She could be with Ophelia. The wagons had gotten separated in the train today because the twins had to stop to repair a wheel. Ros wasn't certain how far back they'd fallen, but the thought of closing that flap, sealing herself in the bed of her wagon without knowing whether Gwyneth was safe was impossible.

She judged the storm would be on them in minutes or less, so she grabbed a heavy blanket and draped it over her head. It would protect her from the worst of the dust once the storm hit. She climbed out of the wagon and felt herself buffeted by the fierce gusts as the wind began to whip around her.

The storm was a howler. She'd never experienced anything like this in her life. She couldn't breathe, couldn't see. No rain, just wind. But somehow that relentless whining wind was worse than any storm of lightning, rain, and thunder Ros had ever known.

Dust rose in the air like a fog until Ros couldn't see her hand in front of her face. Dust whipped and choked and lodged in every nook and crevice it could find. She tightened the blanket around her head. She needed to find Gwyneth. Needed to know the child was safe.

From nowhere, two strong arms gripped her waist and tossed her back into the wagon. As she sprawled on her hands and knees, trying to untangle herself from the blanket, the wagon shifted with the weight of someone following her into the wagon. She pulled the heavy wool from her face just as the flap closed and darkness fell inside the wagon. The sound of the storm muted for a moment.

"I have to find someone." She turned, her hand wrapped around the hilt of her knife, prepared to fight her way out of the wagon if necessary.

"Gwyneth is safe in Ophelia's wagon, Miss Fenster." Rob Lewis's voice was roughened by the dust in his throat, but she recognized it well enough to realize she was not about to be assaulted. "You have no need to get yourself lost in a dust storm looking for her."

"You're certain?"

"I deposited her there myself."

"What about—"

"Ophelia and the baby are fine. The twins are fine. Even your teamster found shelter. There is no one else for you and me to see to but ourselves." He lifted the flap, letting in enough muted light that she could see his body coiled to leap out of the wagon. Before he could, however, the storm hit full force. Dust blew in and the wind rocked the wagon.

She didn't think twice as she watched him struggle to close the flap against the howling monster outside. She joined her efforts to his, and in a moment they had it tied tight enough to keep out the worst of the dust.

An eerie silence seemed to settle in under the monotonous sound of the wind. Ros found herself too aware of him in the close confines of the wagon, as they leaned against the tightly closed flap, breathing hard from their exertions.

She moved carefully along the narrow interior space, trying to find the lamp. "If you give me a moment, I can find the lamp and we can see again."

"Best to leave it off."

She tried not to panic at the thought of being closed in and in total darkness. "But I can't see."

He came up beside her and spoke into her ear so that she could hear him clearly over the storm. "If the wind were to turn over the wagon, the lamp might catch fire." He added softly, "Storm won't last long, Miss Fenster. Stretch out, shut your eyes, and wait it out."

# Chapter Fifteen

*Stretch out. Shut your eyes.* She could hear him following his own advice, but she couldn't do the same. The darkness made the close quarters unbearable.

She moved to the front flap and tried to open it just a little so that she wouldn't feel a suffocating sense of confinement, but the dust poured in and the wind nearly tore the whole flap out of her hands.

The wagon shifted as he came to help her secure it again. "Are you crazy? Can't you hear the wind whipping out there?"

"Yes." The sound made the darkness, the close space, even worse somehow. "I don't like to be closed in—not since I was a child and I was locked in a trunk by accident."

He put his arm around her and eased her back to a sitting position. One big warm hand massaged her arm while he rested his chin on her shoulder. "Just how did you get locked in a trunk by accident?"

There was a security in his size and heat that made her forget the close darkness. She turned into his chest, buried her face against his neck for a moment, and then lifted her chin to speak in his ear. "I was playing a joke on my twin sister. Only my older sister found the key to the trunk and locked it without knowing I was inside."

"How old were you?"

"About Gwyneth's age, I guess."

"Who found you?"

"Helena—my twin. She could sense that I was in trouble and made everyone turn the house upside down until they found me." Just remembering the hours of enforced darkness in a cramped space made Ros shiver.

He moved in the darkness, pulling her tighter against him. His hand reached for hers, grasping gently, so that she would not feel trapped. "How can I help?"

She closed her eyes, allowing herself to feel the comfort he offered. He was careful not to crowd her, and for that she was grateful. She did not know if she could face him without shame if she gave way to the panic she felt storming inside her. She forced herself to laugh. "Do you think you might make it stop?"

"I'm afraid I can't do that," he laughed. He was so close to her that she felt the rumble of his laughter along every point their bodies touched. His thumb stroked the inside of her wrist soothingly. "How about if we talk about something to take your mind off where we are?"

"I don't think that will work. All I seem to be able to think of is where I am." The way the darkness pressed against her on all sides. The smell of canvas and oil mingled with the scents of the rosemary and thyme hanging from the roof of the wagon. She buried her face in his neck again, inhaled the scent of him, and hung on to her composure with all her will.

"You're a mighty fine-looking woman. Whatever made you dress up like a man when you should have been wearing pretty dresses and learning how to keep a home?" His fingers worked up and down her spine, pressing and releasing.

"Are you trying to make me forget where I am by making me wish to throttle you, sir?"

"Is it working?"

She laughed, and felt her panic recede to a tolerable level. "I could do the things I pleased, then, without bringing shame on my family."

"Like gambling?"

"And riding. And moving about freely without a maid, or skirts to hold me back."

"Whenever your name came up with Caroline's family, they didn't know what to make of you. I was surprised when I met you to find you didn't have a pair of pistols on your hips and a deck of cards in your pocket."

"They've been good to me, like family. But I know they wish I'd settle down and marry. As if marriage is a cure for what I am."

"Marriage isn't a cure for anything—" He broke off, and she sensed that he wished he hadn't shared that with her. "Some folks just aren't cut out for marriage."

She nodded against his chest, knowing that he would feel it, just as she felt the beating of his heart. "I agree. Somehow, though, most of my sisters have made a success of it."

"Most?"

"My youngest sister, Kate, found that she had married an Irish rogue who only wanted her dowry."

"Caroline never told me that."

"I don't know that she ever knew. Kate's husband wooed her, married her, collected the dowry, and hasn't been seen again. The family simply never talks of it. She could have divorced him, but she's a stubborn thing."

"Like you?"

She pushed herself up against his rib cage in protest. "I'm not stubborn; I'm just sure of myself."

"Being sure of yourself is going to get you in trouble. Judith Watson is not the only one who'd rather you mind your own business."

"John Watson needed help." Ros felt curiously vulnerable to realize she was telling him things she hadn't confided to many people in her life. "I could help."

There was more than a hint of stern warning in his voice. "Stay away from him. He's married."

"I'm not in the least interested in him."

"I'm sure you're not. But he's young, and he's having wife troubles. Stay away from him."

"He's having wife troubles because his wife is a jealous shrew who doesn't recognize the worth of her own husband."

"I don't want trouble."

"I understand."

They were silent for so long, Ros began to feel she was alone. The darkness closed in around her and she fought the panic, made herself breathe shallow and even. His fingers trailed up and down her arm.

And then he said, softly, "Like I said, you are a damn fine-looking woman. Even in those bloomer skirts of yours. Why haven't you married?"

"I almost did, twice."

"Twice?" He shifted restlessly beneath her, and she moved away to give him room only to find that he didn't want room. He turned so that their bodies pressed tightly together again.

"The first one was just foolishness. He was a friend, and I wanted to help him out of some difficulty. I didn't love him. Fortunately my sister Helena did." Did he want . . . ? No. The quarters were small, that was all. He could have kissed her ten times over by now if he had the least desire to do so.

"The Marquis of Markingham? I met him once, but not his wife. Caroline said you looked eerily alike."

"We did then. I haven't seen her since she married Rand. She has long since forgiven me for coercing her into switching places with me at my wedding."

"She took your place at your first wedding? I'm surprised the marquis didn't refuse to marry either of you. Poor man."

"No, Helena is nothing at all like me, Mr. Lewis; you've no call to feel a jot of sympathy for the marquis. He's a rogue of great renown and is lucky to have my sister."

"I'll take your word for it, Miss Fenster. Although I shouldn't be surprised to discover that your first fiancé was a roguish marquess. What about the second man?"

"I loved him, but I found I couldn't marry him."

"Why not?"

"He wanted me to grow my hair long." It sounded like a petty reason spoken aloud.

Apparently, he agreed. "Sounds like a brute to me."

She laughed. "No. He was no brute. But he wasn't the right man for me. He is, I'm sure you'll be happy to know, married to a woman who suits him perfectly. They have a daughter upon whom he dotes."

"Never again?"

"Maybe. I'd like—" Ros broke off. Had she really nearly confessed that she wanted to know what it was like to share her life with someone who understood who she was and gave her the freedom to follow her own lead? "Truth is, no man is going to give me the independence I need."

"Maybe you only think you need independence."

"That's a marvelous irony, isn't it?" she said, angered. "You—the husband Caroline gave so much freedom that you only attended her funeral by chance."

"You don't understand."

"Maybe I understand too well," Ros said, feeling as if she did understand what had made them go wrong.

"I don't think you do," he argued. "We were young and foolish, but I took care of her. She wanted to stay in Missouri. She didn't want to follow me across the wilderness."

"She wanted you to be happy."

"At home in Missouri . . ."

"No," Ros said earnestly. "She wrote it in her diary. She said she hoped that you wouldn't let the differences between the two of you blind you to future happiness."

"I don't need to be happy. I tried to tell her that. I just need to do my job as best I can."

Whether he did so intentionally, or unintentionally, she would never know. One moment his hand was at her wrist, the next he had skimmed his fingers up her arm, past her shoulder, to the bare flesh of her neck. His thumb brushed her there, right under her jaw.

The moment passed in an instant from one of camaraderie to one of desire. She had never felt passion flame this intensely before. For the first time since the flap had been tied shut, her panic completely disappeared, engulfed by stronger emotions.

The intense desire to touch this man overcame her and she reached out for his face. At first her hand landed on his shoulder, but she traced upward with her fingers, as he had done for her. She ran her finger lightly along his freshly shaved jaw line.

"This probably isn't very wise, Miss Fenster." He reached up to grasp her wrist and stop her caress.

She wasn't interested in warnings. "This most definitely isn't wise, Mr. Lewis. But I am not in need of wisdom right now, only comfort."

She brushed her finger over his mouth and then lifted herself up to meet his lips with hers. He lay still beneath her as she kissed him. But one of her hands rested on his chest, and she could feel his heartbeat racing.

She touched her tongue to his lips and he shifted slightly, in order to bring both his hands up to cup her head and return her kiss.

Rob knew he shouldn't kiss her. He was courting trouble with a capital *T*. But he couldn't seem to stop himself. There was no room to escape, unless he wanted to go out into the storm. And she needed the distraction. He could still feel the tension that thrummed through her body at being confined in such close quarters.

When she first touched his lips with hers, he had toyed with the idea of remaining still and letting her distract herself with him. But once her tongue darted out to touch his lips, he could not be passive any longer.

He tried to pull her down to him, his hands on her shoulders gentle but demanding. She resisted with a little sound deep in her throat.

So he turned toward her, pulling at her hip to bring her hard against him. In a moment they lay pressed together from chest to groin, their legs entwined, and all he could remember was that she had offered to share his bed before the trip began. There was no reason for him to feel that he was taking advantage of the circumstances. No reason for him to hold back.

The storm outside intensified, rocking the wagon, rocking them against each other, and the storm inside Rob begged to be let loose. He'd just kiss her, he told himself. He whispered the words against her ear. "Just kissing, nothing more." He didn't know if it was a warning to himself or a promise to her.

She laughed, her mouth pressed against his neck, moving up to his ear. Her hands worked beneath his jacket, ran along the muscles of his abdomen. A little kissing couldn't hurt anything. She wasn't a dewy-eyed innocent—she'd been set to marry twice, after all. The howling wind sounded like mad laughter for a moment, but he took her mouth with his anyway.

As if to prove he was not dealing with an unwilling innocent, she rubbed her groin against his until he couldn't distinguish between the moan of the wind and the rush of the blood in his ears. He groaned against her mouth and moved his hands down to cup her bottom and press her tight against him. The idea of stopping with a few kisses deserted him. He didn't want to stop at all until he was buried inside her warmth, as deep as he could go.

Rolling over to cover her, he nudged himself between her legs and pulled her skirts up quickly—an advantage to short skirts, he realized muzzily. The trousers she wore under her skirts were what stopped him from total madness. He didn't know where the fastenings were. With a shred of sanity, he sat up and pushed away from her.

She didn't move, although he could feel her struggling to catch her breath. "What's the matter?"

"Those newfangled drawers of yours."

She moved in the darkness, and he had no doubt that she knew how to remove them. Temptation kept him still for a moment, but then he grabbed for her hands and held them quiet. "I said just kissing, Miss Fenster."

"I don't believe I agreed to your terms."

He laughed; he couldn't help it. She'd said she wasn't

stubborn, just sure of herself, but he didn't think that half covered it. "You haven't thought this through—you're off kilter—trying to forget you're tied into this tiny wagon with me."

"I could hardly forget you are here." She leaned against him and rubbed her cheek against his chest restlessly. "You fill up the space."

He pushed her away again. "If I fill up any more space right now, we're both going to regret it."

She climbed onto his lap and twined her fingers in his hair. She touched her lips to his. "What's there to regret? We're both full grown and we know what we're doing."

"What's that?"

"Riding out a storm." She rocked her hips against him, and he groaned.

"There's only one problem I know of with riding out a storm this way." With only a shred of willpower left, he lifted her away from him. "And I don't want you screaming out my name like a curse nine months from now."

She stilled, and he knew his words had reached her at last. She said softly, "Then just kisses, like you said at first."

Her mouth found his neck and moved up his jaw to his ear. He was more than tempted to agree. "I'm afraid I might not be able to stop at just kisses."

"I don't care." She pushed his shirt off his shoulders and lifted his undershirt to kiss his belly. "Don't stop." He felt her tongue tickling his navel. "If you stop, I'll know where I am." She pushed him backward and stretched out on top of him, every movement of her body against his an exquisite torture. "I don't want to know where I am."

He rolled over, trying to escape, but that was a mistake

in the tight confines of the wagon bed, because then she was beneath him, her hips moving. His hand was tangled in her shirt and then suddenly, warmly, against the bare skin of her breast. She threw herself against him, more in panic than passion. "I don't care about nine months from now. I don't care."

"Miss Fenster—" He moved his hand from her breast but found the enticing curve of her hip instead. "Rosaline—" His protest died when her hands traveled low and she stroked him through the denim of his trousers. He sprang into full arousal as she massaged along the length of him with both her hands.

He groaned and captured her mouth with his, unable for a moment to do more than surrender to the feeling of his tongue dancing with hers while his hips ground down on the powerful pleasure of her fingers working against him. "What are you doing?"

"Do you like it?"

"Very much," he whispered against her lips.

She laughed. "It is meant to bring a man to grace safely."

He moaned and moved against her with increased urgency. "Grace; is that what you call it."

His hands skimmed her breasts, her hips, grasped her to him. He didn't need to remove her bloomers to find the responsive spot between her legs.

"What are you doing?" she asked, going completely still as she squeezed his hand between her thighs.

"I thought you might require a little grace yourself."

"I've always provided my own," she said. He thought she would refuse him, but after a moment, when he put his mouth to her breast, she relented. His fingers found her heat and she moaned, moving against his hand with more and more urgency. "Harder," she demanded, her breath coming quick and rough against his neck. "Like that," she said, her hips twisting and bucking under his as he complied.

She fumbled to unfasten his trousers and he let out a harsh breath when she succeeded in freeing him and her fingers cupped his bare flesh. He drove himself against her, his lips, his fingers, his mouth, his hips. He knew she cried out; he could feel the sound in his bones, even though it was swallowed in the roar of the storm.

With every movement he could feel the storm inside her building. He closed his eyes against the darkness and saw a swirl of reds and greens and golds when she at last convulsed beneath him. Her fingers clenched around him and their hips ground together frantically until a sudden wash of passion and pleasure convulsed through him and he held her hips tightly and pressed against her belly with a groan.

They lay entwined and unmoving for some time, the only sound the moaning and the patter of dust against the canvas.

At last, still without moving, she said softly into the darkness, "Thank you. I didn't know grace could feel quite like that." Her voice was languid with spent passion. Her restless anxiety seemed to be gone.

"Grace. Odd name for something that could easily drive a man to madness," he whispered against her ear.

"The last man I nearly married thought we should stop with grace until after the ceremony." She stroked her fingers down his arm and entwined her fingers with his. "But he only spoke of his own grace." She brought his hand up to her mouth and kissed his fingers. "Not mine."

He reached up to kiss her mouth, not sure where it would lead, not even caring. Just then the wind lessened and began to die. In the silence, he could hear the camp stirring. Shouts of emigrants making sure that others had survived. Announcing their own survival with relief.

With a curse he sat up and fastened his trousers. He fumbled with the knots of the wagon flap. In a moment he had it untied and opened just enough to let a line of bright sunshine stream in. He'd have leaped out at once, but some time in their "just kissing" his jacket had come off and his shirt had come unfastened.

He hastily repaired the damage to his clothing and turned to remind her to do the same.

She lay as he had left her moments ago. But it was no longer dark. He could see her blouse, unfastened and half off her shoulder, her skirts up around her waist, the bloomers somehow almost more indecent than her bare legs would have been.

For a moment he was tempted to close the flap and—but that was pure trouble. And he was a man who avoided trouble whenever he could. He'd told her so.

"Never again. I give you my word, Miss Fenster. Never again." He leapt out of the wagon without looking back.

# Chapter Sixteen

*Never again.* For a moment, Ros thought, he had wanted to stay. There'd been a look in his eyes. Half wild, echoing the way she felt inside. But then common sense had returned—she had seen it clearly flooding into his eyes as he looked at her in the light.

She hadn't moved as he shoved his clothing back to rights. As if he wanted to hide what they had done. Hide it not only from the others, which she understood, but from himself as well.

There'd been a look of panic in his eyes right before he made his vow not to . . . to what? Kiss her? Touch her? Be alone with her? No matter; his words had been as clear as they needed to be. She supposed he deserved his turn at panic, seeing that it was her turn that had brought them to this pass.

The sound of the reawakening camp momentarily grew louder before the silence of the wagon pressed in on her again.

She sat for a moment, staring at the rim of sunlight that flashed where the flap gaped open. How had everything changed between them so quickly? Had it been an illusion? Next time she saw him, would she be able to put it behind her as easily as he seemed to do?

With a little shake, she pulled herself and her clothing together. The last thing she wanted was to give him an excuse to call her trouble. Being found like this would definitely qualify as such—no matter that he had played some part in their encounter.

"Auntie Ros." Gwyn's anxious call came three times, each time louder, until the flap opened again, streaming in full sunshine.

"Are you hurt?"

Ros laughed shakily and tied up the flap. She wanted the light, the fresh air. She needed it. "Of course not. I was safe in the wagon the whole storm."

"Were you scared?"

Ros looked at the child, wondering whether she wanted to hear that someone besides herself was scared, or whether she wanted to be reassured that some had not been scared by the ferocity of the storm. She decided on the truth. "I was more scared of being all closed in than of the wind. This wagon was made sturdily enough to withstand a little storm like this—just like Ophelia's."

"Good." The child's worried frown disappeared. "Did Papa tell you where I was? I knew Freedom would be scared, because he's just a baby. I wanted to show him how to be brave."

"Your papa told me," Ros answered, with her sense of reality shifting under her feet as she visualized him again, framed in the light, his shirt unfastened and gaping open, his undershirt shoved up his chest, exposing his flat-muscled abdomen. A ghostly remnant of the pleasure he gave her arched through her at the remembrance. *Never again.* Dare she hope he had spoken too hastily?

"Me and Ophelia told him to," the child confided. "We didn't want you to worry."

"Thank you for thinking of me." Ros closed her eyes, remembering the feel of his hands. His lips. "And you made the right decision, staying with Freedom. I can take care of myself." She wondered bleakly if that was true anymore. Something had twisted free inside her and she couldn't seem to shove it back into place.

Mr. Barton appeared. "Anything get damaged in here, Miz Fenster?"

"Not a thing," she assured him. "I had everything tied down tight." She didn't like the assessing look he gave her before he turned his attention to the team. She didn't like Mr. Barton. But she didn't think he was the kind of man for the idle gossip that the emigrants, often bored by the long, monotonous days of travel, engaged in. No doubt he preferred to be paid for his observations.

Idle gossip. For the first time she realized the kind of vicious talk that would spread if anyone in the company realized that she and Captain Hellfire had spent the hours of the storm alone together in her wagon. She sighed. More trouble to avoid. No doubt he'd blame her.

Gwyneth's adventure seemed to have exhausted her. She rattled on about her adventure in Ophelia's wagon, yawning more and more.

Ros, weary herself, tucked the tired child under her blankets and settled back down beside her. She made no move to leave the wagon when Mr. Barton climbed up on the seat and gave the order for the team to go.

She closed her eyes, feeling as if she'd lived three days in three hours' time. What had she been thinking?

To tell him she didn't care about consequences. She shuddered at the thought of what might have been if he had listened to her. But he hadn't.

She sat up abruptly. She couldn't hide forever. Without asking Mr. Barton to stop, she leapt down onto the hard-packed earth and resumed her walk beside the wagon. Astrid Martin slowed her normally brisk pace to allow Ros time to catch up to her.

As she drew near, Ros took a deep breath to clear her head of the unreality of the storm. "Did your goods survive intact?"

Astrid smiled, her eyes dancing with secret amusement, as she said, "Fine and dandy. In fact, I think sometimes a man and woman should be all alone in the middle of a storm."

Ros faltered a step, thinking that somehow Astrid knew. But then she recognized the glow. She'd seen it in the faces of her sisters often enough. Astrid and Bug had not wasted time worrying about the storm, or panicking in the confines of their wagon. "I take it you don't regret the stop." She couldn't help smiling at the other woman, whose pleasure with her husband just radiated from her.

"Not one bit," Astrid said. "In fact, I have to say my mother's advice was completely wrong—husbands do have some more uses than chopping wood and causing trouble."

Trouble. "I wouldn't know," Ros said. "Never having had a husband myself."

Astrid's smile dimmed. "I'm sorry. I didn't mean to speak out of turn."

For a moment she'd forgotten what a stigma it was for a woman not to be married at her age. Ros held up her hand to halt any more apologies. "Astrid, if I'd wanted a husband, I'd have had one by now. But I'm happy that you managed to confound your mother and find a good one."

"I didn't mean to be thoughtless. I know you say you don't mind being alone." Astrid looked like a child caught with a piece of candy too small to share. "But I don't know what I'd do without Bug."

"Have you told him so?"

"Do you think he doesn't know?"

"Trust me: Men never know. Even when you tell them, they forget."

The girl raised an eyebrow and replied cheekily, "How do you know all this, if you aren't married?"

"I'll have you know I've been engaged twice."

"Twice!" Astrid's eyes widened in shock.

"Yes. Twice. And never again." She shook her head. "I've been observing couples court and marry since before I came out in society."

Astrid said softly, "Goodness. I'd forgotten. Someone told me you'd been a London lady once."

"A long time ago. Anyone who knew me then would tell you that I did quite a bad job of it, too. I assure you, I don't regret turning my back on that life for a moment." Ros wondered who had known that. Mr. Lewis, of course. But she couldn't see him gossiping about her.

"Do you think that's why you haven't married? Because of all your observations?"

"Most likely," Ros conceded. "I've seen so many marriages bring unhappiness."

"My mother says the same thing." Astrid asked wistfully, "Haven't you ever seen a happy couple?"

"Many—at first. But I find it is the rare pair who don't succumb to the temptations of expecting too much of each other."

"Too much?"

"Do you expect Bug to spend his day making you happy?"

"No." Astrid said with a smile, "He has to drive the wagon sometimes."

"Some women—and men, too—look for their partner to provide happiness. That is a recipe for disaster, I promise you."

Astrid nodded. "My mother did that."

"So you know the damage that can be done by such foolishness. Perhaps, being forewarned, you'll avoid the temptation if you find yourself wanting more than Bug can give you." She realized that her lecture was more for herself than for Astrid. Before Rob Lewis entered her life, she had been sure she knew how to avoid such a foolish temptation.

She sighed. *Never again.* The tension that had been boiling inside her flowed away. Rob Lewis had been right all along. The panic had made her blind to the consequences of her actions. She wasn't cut out to make a man happy—except perhaps in the most fleeting of ways. Blushing child brides and grooms aside, men and women were destined to rub each other wrong for eternity.

Thankfully, their indiscretion hadn't been observed. From now on, she'd make certain to ensure she did not get caught alone with him. Men, being the creatures they were, he'd probably blame her for any difficulties that sudden flare of passion might have caused them.

Ros took a small measure of comfort in the fact that he hadn't told her before he leapt out of her wagon today that she'd caused too much trouble and he was banishing her at Fort Kearny. No doubt he realized that he wasn't blameless. She couldn't deny that she had indeed thrown herself at him shamelessly, though he hadn't refused her anything, but . . . she couldn't help smiling as she remembered . . . having her cursing his name in nine months' time.

She'd have to thank Captain Hellfire at supper. He'd saved them both a tremendous headache.

*Never again.* He'd meant it when he said the words. So why did he see her, undressed and sprawled in the light, every time he closed his eyes? Why did his heart start to race when he thought of supper by the fire— Gwyn asleep, Ophelia off tending the baby—watching *her* in the firelight? Why did his imagination take him into her tent, as if curious eyes wouldn't see him?

He lingered past the usual suppertime, checking wagons and livestock. The company's unrelenting push to get the first leg of the journey done quickly had been hard on emigrants and wagons alike.

He thought it likely they could make it to Fort Kearny without undue hardship, but everywhere he stopped, he heard that the emigrants were tired and wanted a day to rest. A day to wash out their dusty clothing and repack their wagons, now that they truly understood what life on the road meant.

He stopped climbing in the wagons to inspect them. The smell, the shadows, all reminded him of how she had felt tight against him in the dark, close space. At last, when nearly everyone in camp had eaten and cleared away their dishes, he decided it would be cowardly to ignore his daughter. He would not disappoint Gwyn just because he was afraid he couldn't control himself.

But he had no need to stay at the fire. No need to play with whatever fire flared between the unorthodox English lady and Captain Hellfire. No. He would tell Gwyneth her nightly story and leave without betraying his desire to change his definitive "never again" to "right here, right now." After all, the legendary Captain Hellfire had a will of iron. One English enigma couldn't break his will—unless he let her.

Before they saw him, he heard Gwyneth ask plaintively, "Why do you think Papa didn't come to supper, Auntie Ros?"

Her answer was steady. He saw no sign that she felt any qualms at all about what she'd done with him—to him—earlier. "I suppose he's helping fix any damage the storm might have caused." That guiltless patrician voice, oddly enough, set his gut twisting with anger. He'd rather she had shame. Regret. She shared the burden of what they'd done; why shouldn't she share the guilt that would keep them from repeating the mistake?

Gwyneth nodded, as if that excuse was a reasonable one to her. But his daughter had her mother's nurturing heart. "I don't want him to go hungry."

"He won't go hungry," Miss Fenster said briskly. "He's welcome to eat at the other emigrant's campfires, you know that."

Gwyneth was still not quite satisfied. "Maybe we should save him some stew?"

"I don't know . . ." At that moment, Rosaline Fenster looked his way and caught sight of him. Whatever she'd been about to say died on her lips. For a moment there was a flare of panic in her eyes. *Good,* he thought. She wasn't as shameless as she had seemed a moment ago. But then she smiled down at Gwyn, turned the little girl his way, and said in an unmistakable challenge, "I'm sure he'd be pleased if you did."

Gwyneth rushed to take his hand and lead him to the fire. She dished out a plate of stew for him and sat and watched him eat every bite. Fortunately, Miss Fenster busied herself by the river, cleaning up the supper dishes, despite Ophelia's rather vehement statement that she needed no help.

When Gwyneth curled at his feet by the fire, he told her the shortest story he knew. The women had not returned yet. Good. He bent to kiss his daughter on the forehead. "I have work to do, now. I'll see you tomorrow morning."

She hugged him. "Sweet dreams, Papa."

He'd prefer no dreams at all, if the truth be told. The way his mind had wandered when he was awake, he didn't like the thought of being held captive by his imagination in his sleep. He thought he'd escaped, until a sharp voice called out to him. "Just a moment, Mr. Lewis."

He stopped—out of earshot of any curious onlookers, he judged. "Did you need something, Miss Fenster?"

She had the coffeepot in her hand and she held it out, as if to show him something. Her words were low enough not to carry far. "I believe we can rest easy that we were not observed. I've heard no gossip."

Gossip? He nearly reassured her that no one, man or woman, had given him even so much as a knowing look. He didn't, though, preferring that she worry a little longer—at least until he could trust himself again. "I didn't think you cared about your reputation, Miss Fenster, considering your choice of costume."

She pressed her lips together tightly for a moment, but her voice remained neutral when she replied, "It wasn't my reputation I worried about, but yours."

His reputation? "I'm a man—no one here would fault me for taking what you offered."

"You're not a man—" she began, and he had the strongest urge to lean down and kiss her just to prove her wrong. Until she finished, "—you're a legend. I'd hate to tarnish Captain Hellfire's name."

*A legend.* Right now, near enough to reach out and touch her if he wished, he didn't even have to close his eyes to remember how she tasted. A legend? He'd never known the full irony in it until this moment. He suppressed his laughter so that it was only a rumble in his throat. "Tarnish? Knowing the stalwart wagon master had taken the bloomer lady on the ride of her life might just polish it to a shine."

Her face smoothed of all expression and he regretted his words instantly. He'd meant to hold her off, not hurt her pride.

"No one knows. No one will ever know," he offered in apology before he turned away.

"Mr. Lewis."

"Yes, Miss Fenster?" He turned back toward her, only halfway, reluctant to give her that much. Would she take a shot at his pride as he had at hers?

She met his eyes squarely and held out her hand. "Thank you."

Did she expect him to shake hands with a woman? With her? For what, exactly? The ride of her life? "There is no need to thank me."

She didn't flinch away from his gaze. "Another man might have taken advantage of my weakness this afternoon and I'd have more to worry about than a little blot on my reputation—which, as you were so kind to remind me, I've never worried much about."

He guessed he did deserve thanks for that little breath of sanity in an otherwise crazy encounter. He shook her hand once, firmly. "Only a man who couldn't see the trouble ahead, Miss Fenster."

Without even a hint of amusement, she murmured, "For once, Mr. Lewis, I am exceedingly grateful that you are always on the lookout for trouble."

She turned back to the camp, and he was caught by

the sway of her hips as she moved away from him. He hissed out a breath in frustration and made himself walk away. Truth be told, in her case, he was afraid he might be looking for trouble, instead of looking out for it.

When the next day dawned cool and rainy, Rob thought briefly about pushing on toward the fort in spite of the weather. On a good day, the journey would be two days. But they wouldn't make as much progress in the mud and rain. Travel would be more tiring, as well, for man and animal alike.

He couldn't ignore the lack of enthusiasm when the travelers woke to discover the weather. Perhaps he had been driving them too hard. "Wilson!" he called to one of his men.

"Yes, sir?"

"Let the company know that we'll stay put today. It's time to get some of those repairs done before we head into the fort."

Wilson, who'd been with him on his last trip and knew how generous he was being, grinned from ear to ear. "They'll be happy to hear that, sir."

"As long as they know I'll not do this every other day," he answered grouchily. His sleep had been troubled by the pleasant dreams Gwyneth had sweetly wished him, though he couldn't remember exactly what he had dreamed. He suspected the cause but didn't want to dwell on it. He'd just try to stay out of her way as much as he could, and no doubt things would be back to normal soon enough.

Rob ate a cold breakfast, alone, and began surveying the company to ensure that whatever needed to be done got seen to today. He didn't intend to rest here more than that, no matter what the weather. He crushed any wandering thoughts with an unrelenting attention to his work. He acted as blacksmith, as engineer, as stevedore.

Whatever needed doing. He didn't want to waste a minute when he could be useful.

When suppertime came, he ate two cold oatcakes—alone—and kept right on working until he dropped onto his bedroll too exhausted to dream.

The day had dawned bright and beautiful. The smell of the grass underfoot seemed fresher and sweeter scented from yesterday's rain. Ros took her shotgun with her as she walked—farther from the trail this time, because game had become scarce as the plague of emigrants rolled endlessly along. They hadn't had fresh meat in a while and she was restless. His words echoed in her ears during the day and haunted her dreams at night. *The ride of her life.*

He'd been intentionally crude, but he hadn't meant to tear at her quite so cruelly. She'd told him many things during the dust storm, but she hadn't told him everything. She hadn't told anyone everything. Even Helena, her own twin, didn't know for certain whether Ros had ever slept with a man or not.

She'd always felt a perverse delight in her closely held secret. She wanted no one complacent enough to believe they knew just how bold she was willing to be. Which, as it happened, was not quite as bold as many would have guessed.

Despite her experience with her second fiancé, she hadn't yet made love to a man. No matter that it was an annoying fact that women could not make free with their affections without consequences, she was not so foolish as to deny a hard truth: For every woman, unlike for most men, there was a price to be paid for the pleasure. No matter that she'd wanted to, and nearly succumbed once or twice, she'd always held back. Always heard that warning voice in her head. The one that said the price might not be worth the experience.

She hadn't heard that warning voice with Rob Lewis. Not a single whisper. The realization chilled her at one moment and sent a lightning bolt of pure heat through her center the next. If he hadn't had the sense to stop them . . . Then she might have had the ride of her life, instead of just a taste of what it would be like.

# Chapter Seventeen

A rabbit jumped a field's length away, and she aimed and shot from long-honed instinct. The creature went from graceful leap to ungainly flop in an instant. She headed toward where it had fallen. They would have meat for dinner. And she would not forget again the dangers of being too close to a man who was half legend and half flesh and blood.

When she neared where the wagons had stopped to camp, she found Bug Martin and John Smith, their own shotguns on their shoulders, just heading out.

"Any luck?" Bug called.

"I managed to bag a half dozen rabbits, but I had to go over a mile off the trail. There's not much out there today."

The men nodded and took her word for it. She wanted to smile but didn't. At the start of the journey they would have looked at her haul and been certain they could do ten times as well as any woman. After the deer and two dozen smaller creatures she'd brought into camp, they knew better.

"Glad to hear it, though Astrid will be disappointed," Bug replied, wiping a weary hand over his face.

"I'm bound to try anyway," John said morosely. He looked tired from a long day of struggling to get his wagon across the plains. There'd been three fordings today, always a chore, no matter how small. "Judith swears she won't cook another pot of beans until she has some fresh meat to throw in it."

"Take two of mine," Ros offered. "Both of you."

The men protested politely, but she insisted. "We'll only use two ourselves."

Bug had a hungry light in his eye. "I will if you let me pay you for it."

His pride had made him make the offer, but Ros's wouldn't let her take advantage of him that way. She didn't need his money. "What about a loaf of Astrid's bread? She makes the best in camp."

"One loaf for each rabbit."

"Agreed." She glanced at John Smith. "Mr. Smith?"

"Judith still hasn't forgiven me for that incident with the wagon. She'd skin me alive and toss me into the stew, bones and all, if she knew I'd taken anything from you." He didn't look happy about the fact, just resigned.

Ros didn't say a word, just tossed a canvas bundle to him. He reached out and plucked it from the air instinctively. When he gave her a puzzled glance, she smiled. "Now you can tell her you caught them yourself."

A smile broke through the weariness etched into his face for a moment. "You are one clever woman, Miss Fenster."

Bug grinned as they all headed back to the wagons

and tents, looking forward to the evening meal. "Not to mention the best shot in camp."

"What can I do in return?"

Ros didn't have any work she couldn't handle herself. But she didn't want to offend the man. "There's a board coming loose in my wagon. You could fix that for me."

"That's not much."

"It's all I need right now."

"Then I'll do it first thing tomorrow. Don't know whether to wish there were more women like you or be glad there aren't," John teased. "A man likes to feel needed."

"Women will always need men, Mr. Smith, I assure you. Otherwise life would be much too serene." Ros's words held a bite of acerbity as she thought of Rob Lewis. It was incomprehensible to her how she could still be attracted to him. But if she closed her eyes, she could see him as she had seen him after the storm— half dressed, half tempted to ignore his duties and make love to her. Worse, she could feel the desire rise in her to see him that way again. "Who else but a man can drive a woman to distraction and then blame her for reaching that unhappy state?"

As she headed to where Ophelia and Gwyneth had set up their tent, she shook her head at her own foolishness. She could keep herself fed and think quickly enough to extract herself from most trouble. She didn't need a man. Any man. Not even Rob Lewis. She only wanted him.

"Rabbit meat. I know just what to do with it." Ophelia took charge with a cluck of delight. She enlisted Gwyneth's help and the two of them soon went off to fetch water and whatever else was required from the wagon.

Ros sat by the cooking fire and set about cleaning her shotgun, wondering if the wagon master would come to supper tonight or not. And whether she'd rather he did or he didn't.

Perhaps she should have realized that someone would tell Judith Smith that John's rabbits had come from her efforts. They'd been near enough the camp when they made the exchange; anyone could have seen them.

Until the woman appeared, however—face red, holding a bloody canvas sack—Ros hadn't given the matter much thought. "Mrs. Smith." She rose warily, sorry that her shotgun was in pieces as she took in the other woman's total fury.

"We don't need nothing from you." Judith Smith dropped the bloody sack at Ros's feet. "You keep your free-love hands off my husband." She had noted with amazement the way trivial but potentially explosive information passed through the camp as if it were a spark heading up a line of black powder. Very much the way London society had been when she'd been in it. She supposed for both the company and the upper crust it came of having relatively little to do during the day but gossip.

"I have no intention of putting my hands, or anything else, on your husband." Ros picked up the bag. "Would anyone else want some fresh rabbit meat? Mrs. Smith is content with her beans and has declined my offer." No one came forward, although no one left either. They smelled blood in the air, and it wasn't from the rabbit meat.

John ran up behind his wife, his face flaring red. "Judith. Miss Fenster just offered what any good neighbor might. She gave two rabbits to Bug Martin as well."

Judith was not to be appeased, however. "Bug promised her two loaves of bread for his rabbits, John. What did you promise her? A visit to her wagon when no one was looking?"

"Judith!" John's face paled at the accusation. Ros wanted to slap him. Why did he have to look guilty? She'd asked him to fix a board in the wagon, not invited him for a quick tryst. "That's ridiculous. I was just going to fix a loose board for her." But his voice was weak and wouldn't have convinced her if she hadn't known the truth firsthand.

Apparently Judith had made a shot in the dark with her accusation this time because her fury tripled as he spoke. "Is it? Do you think I don't know what women like her believe? That other women's husbands are fair game for their naughty games."

"Judith—"

"I've seen you look at her, don't think I haven't."

Ros didn't know whether she wanted to rescue the hapless John Watson or strangle his wife. Either way, she needed to stop this before it escalated into what Captain Hellfire would call trouble. "I am not after your husband, Mrs. Smith."

"Liar! You've been after him since we started. Why else would you have helped him when our wagon was stuck?"

"I thought I could help—"

"You pretend you aren't a woman, but I know what you want. Wearing those clothes. You say they're more comfortable, but the truth is you know they make the men look at you. But they're laughing at you, and not one of them will have you, either."

Ros knew she shouldn't, but she couldn't prevent herself from pointing out the inconsistency in that statement. "If I am laughably unattractive to men, then why would you worry that I can steal your husband away from you—even for a brief encounter in my wagon?"

There was a titter of laughter from those closest, and Judith stood still, her eyes blazing hatred solely at Ros.

"I know what you are. Stay away from my husband or you'll have to deal with me." An angel of vengeance, Judith launched herself at Ros, her hands outstretched, prepared to pull at her hair and scratch at her face.

Ros, trained in fencing and in boxing, neatly sidestepped her onrushing attacker. As Judith rounded for another chance, Ros knocked her down with one clip to the jaw. John Smith let out a muffled moan, but he didn't move forward to help his wife, who lay sprawled in the dirt, dazed and gasping for breath enough to shriek some new insult.

There wasn't a pair of eyes not turned on Ros. Not a pair that weren't opened wide in shock. Ros turned to walk away and ran full against Rob Lewis. She'd have bounced off his chest and fallen onto her backside if he hadn't reached out to grab her shoulders and steady her.

He didn't look at her, but at the others, when he asked, "What just happened here?"

John Smith lied, more convincingly than he'd told the truth to his wife earlier. "Judith had an accident, Mr. Lewis."

Ros twisted away from his grasp to look at the people surrounding them. Everyone knew Captain Hellfire's rules: At any sign of trouble, you'd have to leave the company. There wasn't a man here fool enough to think two women fighting over a man wasn't trouble.

Unfortunately, Rob Lewis wasn't inclined to let the lie stand. "An accident? Or a little trouble with Miss Fenster?"

Fully prepared to defend herself, Ros said, "I did nothing—"

He interrupted her. "Of course you didn't. You merely offered her a cup of coffee and she tripped and fell."

"She hit me," Judith moaned as she sat up.

"Judith was being unreasonable," John offered. "Miss Fenster was only defending herself."

The wagon master glared at him. "Tend to your wife, John. Leave me to tend to my business." He glared at Ros, and she glared back.

As her husband helped her up, Judith Smith regained her senses—and her anger. If her husband hadn't held her back, she would have flown at Ros again. "Put her off at Fort Kearny, Mr. Lewis. She's not a decent woman. She doesn't belong here."

Ros was not comforted by his harsh answer. "That's for me to decide, Mrs. Smith."

For some reason, Judith ignored the warning implicit in his tone. "What are you waiting for? The hussy to share her body with every man in camp?"

Ros went cold with the accusation. Would he believe that he had been only one in a string of conquests? She couldn't tell when he said icily to the angry woman, "You have no proof of that, Mrs. Smith."

Judith Smith's mouth curled up in a pleased smirk. "I know she's been alone indecently with one man here already."

"I beg your pardon?" That couldn't be true. The woman had to be making up a story that just happened to fall close to the truth. "You are mistaken."

"I saw her." Judith turned toward Rob Lewis. "During the storm."

Rob fought his urge to glance at Rosaline Fenster. She could offer him no help. He studied Judith Smith, not liking the look in her eyes as she stared back, angry as a rattler with a foot on its tail. His voice was low and lethal as he asked, "And how do you know that?"

"I saw him leave her wagon." There was a triumphant gleam in her eyes.

*She'd seen them.* Rob was struck dumb. He'd been sure he hadn't been spotted. Could she be lying? But she didn't look like a woman who had any doubts. In fact, her voice vibrated with confidence when she asked, "Do you want me to name him?"

Before he could answer, Ros said sharply, "That won't be necessary, Mrs. Smith."

There was a little sigh from the onlookers. Most of them would consider her intervention confirmation of her own transgression. Which it was, he supposed. No doubt she thought she was protecting him.

He tried to shake Judith Smith's confidence. After all, if she'd seen him, then she might be swayed by a little persuasion. "I don't suppose it has occurred to you that what you saw might have been innocent?"

"The man's shirt was half unbuttoned. And he definitely looked like a man who'd been doing something he shouldn't."

A flush crawled up his neck. He *had* been a man doing something he shouldn't. But he didn't want the whole camp to know about it.

The corners of her mouth turned up with pleasure. "I saw him. It was—"

Her husband clapped a hand over her mouth. "Judith, if you say anything more, I'll turn around and bring you back to your mother."

She glared at him and bit his hand. When he let go with a wince she said, "John Smith—"

There was no way to know if she'd have spilled his name in public or not then. She never got the chance. A murmur of astonishment went through the crowd when John, an incredibly mild-mannered man, slung his wife bodily over his shoulder and turned to glance at Ros. "I'm sorry, Miss Fenster, Captain. I'm afraid my wife is just out of sorts today."

As he walked away, Judith shrieked, "You fight like a man, Rosaline Fenster. What man in his right mind would want you?"

Rob struggled to deal with the way his world had tilted right and then left. John Smith was a brave man. But it wouldn't be long before the entire company had been informed of the name of the man who had been seen coming out of Miss Fenster's wagon half undressed. No one would dare face him about it. As he had told her, the legend of Captain Hellfire wouldn't suffer. If he got rid of her now. If not, there would be jokes, sly innuendo, and worse. Four months of that would erode his leadership and his peace of mind.

"Miss Fenster." He glared at her. There was only one way to keep his authority from shredding into so much kindling. She wasn't all to blame for what had happened between them in the wagon, but she was responsible for everything else. "You're leaving this company as soon as we hit Fort Kearny, tomorrow."

"This trouble wasn't entirely my fault," she argued, her cheeks bright with anger and embarrassment.

"But it will end if you leave the company." He added almost apologetically, "I'm sure you see that I have to do what's best for everyone. An unmarried woman, without the benefit of a man to guide her, is bound to cause trouble."

She said cynically, "And all trouble has to be nipped in the bud?"

"I'm afraid so."

"Surely no one would criticize you if you considered the matter a bit longer and allowed me a bit of grace." Her flush deepened. "I mean—"

*Grace.* That was the last thing he needed to give her. He shook his head, and there was no uncertainty. "You're not going any farther than Fort Kearny with my company. I should have trusted my instincts and refused to take you at all." As soon as the words were out of his mouth, he wanted them back.

She looked as though he had struck her. "Perhaps you should have." Her fury was quiet and palpable. Once word spread that he'd been in her wagon, they'd all think he'd meant those words in an entirely different way. . . . "But you didn't."

"Fort Kearny, Miss Fenster."

Her jaw set and her steady gaze challenged him. He'd never seen the streak of pure aristocratic arrogance surface so strongly as when she said regally, "I guess that allows me a day to convince you to reconsider your decision, then, Captain Hellfire."

*Time to reconsider his decision.* Like hell he would. He wouldn't even give her the chance to try to change his mind.

Gwyneth came up from the river and ran toward him. "We're having rabbit stew for supper, Papa. Auntie Ros bagged them for us."

He patted her head blindly, needing to get away. "I'll have to miss supper tonight. I've got work to do." He didn't look at Rosaline Fenster before he strode away. He didn't need to see her face to know she thought he had betrayed her.

In the morning he found the camp was divided. Half agreed with him. Half agreed with her. Unfortunately, it was the female half agreeing with him and the male half siding with her.

A good round of gossip might change that. John Watson had prevented his name from being spread about. So far. It was a wagon master's worst nightmare come to life.

He couldn't deny that he shared the blame for what had happened. He couldn't deny, either, that once she was gone, the trouble she caused would vanish, too. The only way to keep her with him and keep discipline would not be one either of them would like—he'd have to offer her the dubious protection of being his paramour.

He didn't care how much he wanted to change his mind. His reasons were all suspect, having to do with something south of his belt buckle and not his common sense. Rosaline Fenster might not mean to cause any trouble, but she was a lightning rod for it nevertheless.

Unfortunately, that left him a huge problem and one day to solve it—what would he do with Gwyneth when Rosaline Fenster and her party left the company?

All day he made an effort to seek out the women he thought might take Gwyneth under a wing. There were surprisingly few, when it came right down to it.

Mrs. Barton shook her head firmly. "I'm sorry. I have enough with my five. I wish I could help you, but—" She glanced away. "What about Mrs. Calhoun?"

Rob had already tried Mrs. Calhoun. "She says young 'uns give her a headache."

Mrs. Barton nodded in sympathy. "They do take some folk like that. Have you asked that young thing? Mrs. Martin? She hasn't any of her own, so she might be more agreeable."

"Not yet." Astrid Martin would have agreed, he knew. Except that she was part of the camp rooting for him to change his mind. She was a loyal young woman and she had taken a shine to Rosaline Fenster. He'd have to ask—hell, he'd have to beg her, though, if no one else agreed. He wouldn't leave Gwyneth behind.

Come late in the afternoon, though, he found himself riding up to the Martin wagon. They both stared at him with hope in their eyes that dimmed when they saw his expression.

Bug asked, "Is that Fort Kearny?" The young man

seemed disappointed, despite the bustle that was evident around the fort.

Looking at the collection of ramshackle sod huts, Rob couldn't blame him. Not much better than some of the Indian villages he'd seen—and a sight less pleasant to stay in.

"They don't have a wall," Astrid said, her tone a little stiff, no doubt because she didn't approve of his actions toward her friend. "How do they keep out the Indians?"

"They don't bother," Rob explained. "The Indians don't like the place any better than most emigrants."

"But what if there's a war?"

"Then they'll stand their ground and fight, I guess." Rob shrugged.

"Without a wall?" She couldn't seem to get past the idea that the government wouldn't have built a wall to protect their investment. "The government says it's too expensive to build one," Rob explained.

A ragtag unit from the fort approached on swayback nags. One gestured to Rob.

Astrid murmured, "Is it too expensive to provide decent uniforms to the soldiers, as well?"

He looked at the way some of the soldiers—half day's growths of beard and hair that hadn't seen shears in months—were staring at the young woman. He said quickly to Bug, "Best keep her in sight. I wouldn't trust these men farther than I can throw them."

Bug nodded, his eyes narrowed as he stared at the patched uniforms and unkempt, obviously inebriated men. "Don't worry. I can take care of my wife. It's Miss Fenster's welfare I'm concerned for, now that I see where you intend to abandon her."

Abandon her. Why did it feel like he was? Of all the women he'd ever known, he had a feeling she could take care of herself. Even in a hellhole like Fort Kearny.

"Got any whiskey for sale?" one soldier called out before they reached him.

Rob shook his head. "No whiskey, gentlemen. Just a company of emigrants heading for California and glad to have made it this far."

He exchanged greetings with the men, accepted an invitation to dine with the fort commander in the evening, and hastened them away from the company when one man made a forward comment on Astrid Martin's blond braids. Fortunately, the fool had spoken out of Bug's hearing.

# Chapter Eighteen

Rob drove the company a half mile away before giving the signal to make camp. Maybe that would be far enough away to avoid trouble—if no one provided the soldiers with whiskey.

Of course, he was leaving the fort commander even more trouble than he already had, in the form of Rosaline Fenster. For the first time he wondered which of the two he should feel the most sorry for.

"What we going to do, Miz Ros?" Ophelia was beside herself with worry, and her worry made Freedom fussy.

"If I can't convince him to reconsider, then I suppose we'll find another company to join." She closed her eyes. He hadn't joined them for supper last night. "Not everyone is as unreasonable as Mr. Lewis."

"What about Moses?"

"He'll find us. I suspect we'll be easy enough to spot, no matter which company we're in."

"I guess so," Ophelia said slowly. "Maybe we should just go back home where we belong."

"What?" Ros felt as if her life were shattering apart in her hands. And now Ophelia was having doubts?

"Seems like this has been a big mistake. Me walking and walking and walking and never getting nowhere. Moses out with the Indians, any moment fit to be scalped. We don't has to bring the child to her grandparents no more. Her pa'll do that. Maybe we be best just to give up."

"Nonsense. We've done well so far, and we've done a third of the journey." The easy third, according to Rob Lewis, but Ros didn't share that with Ophelia.

"I'm awful tired."

"But you're free."

"Free ain't all it cracked up to be." Ophelia had evidently thought about the subject considerably, because she quickly added, "I'm not ungrateful for your help, Miz Ros, but maybe this is a sign from God." She gazed down at her son's face. "Maybe he don't want this boy's grave marker on the side of the road for folks to gawk at."

"He's been healthy so far." But she knew that argument wouldn't sway Ophelia. They'd both seen too many graves along the road to doubt that anyone in the company could be the next to go—from illness or accident. Some folks had even brought wood for coffins with them in their wagons.

"Moses is wanted for murder, Ophelia. He can't ever go back. No matter what."

That argument stopped the girl. "He didn't kill no one."

"Do you think anyone will believe that except you and me?"

The girl shook her head, her eyes welling with tears.

Ros said, "Let us see if Mr. Barton gains us acceptance to another company. Then we can decide for certain what we'll do." She hoped the man returned soon, with good news. She hadn't liked the looks of Fort Kearny when they passed by.

"Will you take me with you, Auntie Ros?" Ros wasn't happy to see Gwyneth watching her with big frightened eyes. The child was upset at the unexpected turn of events, despite all attempts to console her.

To her surprise, Rob Lewis stood beside his daughter. She hadn't expected to see the coward again. He didn't even have the decency to don the most insincerely apologetic expression.

She tried not to glare at him as she answered the child. "That depends on your father, Gwyneth. You are welcome to travel with me. However, if he wants to take you to San Francisco, I can't stop him. He is your father, after all."

He said stiffly, "I'd appreciate it if you'd ask Astrid Martin to watch over Gwyneth after you leave."

"Me?" A brief flash of fury touched her but vanished. She didn't want the child to be cut adrift from her father. "Of course I will. If you haven't reconsidered by then."

"I assure you I won't have."

"Papa—"

He said, "Gwyneth."

The single word was enough to silence her. But not enough to erase her worried expression as she stared at Ros. "What will you do?"

Ros tried not to show how much she'd miss not having Gwyneth nearby. She didn't want the child to worry about her. She had enough to worry about with a father like Rob Lewis. She raised an eyebrow as if she had no concern at all about her future. "Goodness, child, I won't be too far away."

Gwyneth smiled brightly and then frowned in puzzlement. "You won't?"

Ros shook her head. "Of course not. Haven't we seen companies traveling ahead of us—and behind, as well?"

Gwyn nodded.

"I'll be in one of those." If Mr. Barton managed to arrange it. "Unless your father reconsiders my transgression and allows me to remain with this company."

He was quick to answer his daughter's hopeful glance. "Don't count on it."

Ros answered, pained by Gwyneth's dejection. "I wouldn't dream of counting on you, Mr. Lewis." She knew she struck a low blow. She hoped it hurt like hell.

"Sensible of you." His expression didn't change as he added, "I hope you'll see fit to continue being sensible."

"Why? Have you something new in mind for my life?"

"I do indeed."

"What?"

He stood up and tipped his hat. "Get washed and into your finest, Miss Fenster. We have a dinner appointment with the fort commander in two hours."

For a brief moment she considered refusing outright.

"Thinking of causing more trouble?" His expression suggested that he could read her mind.

"What possible difference could it make to you— you've made up your mind and have no intention of changing it."

"I guess you're right about that." He left without another word.

Ophelia and Gwyneth watched her carefully when she didn't move to do as he had ordered. *Ordered.* How dare he throw her out of his company and then order her to attend dinner with him?

Ophelia asked timidly, "Are you going to pitch a fit and refuse to go, Miz Ros?"

"Have I ever pitched a fit in your presence before?"

Ophelia shook her head. "No. But when Miz Ada get crossed—"

Ros shook her head. "I'm not your former mistress, Ophelia, thank heavens." Did they really think she'd lost her mind? "I don't pitch fits." She smile as a thought struck her. "Although I'm willing enough to engage in warfare for what matters to me."

"Warfare?"

"Only the most civilized kind—no bloodshed." Or not much, anyway.

"So you're going?"

"Oh, yes." Ros stood. "The fort commander could prove to be a friend."

Unfortunately, the fort commander proved to be a drunkard with the commanding presence of a ground-hog. His quarters, while slightly better than the filthy garrison his men were quartered in, offered almost none of the amenities she had expected, with one exception: There was a fine dining table and chairs, and two magnificent candelabra.

"Left behind by some emigrants who wanted to lighten their wagon load," the commander volunteered in a loud whisper when he saw her wipe one finger across the unfortunately grimy mahogany surface.

In fact, every comment he made to Ros was issued in that same loud whisper, as if he thought it necessary to speak to a lady in such a manner. "I hear you're to join us for a while, Miss Fenster."

"The legendary Captain Hellfire has decided I'm to leave his company because I am unmarried. He believes unmarried, unchaperoned women can only cause trouble." And because he got caught with his fingers in the cream and wanted that matter forgotten as quickly as possible.

The commander smiled broadly. "He does have a point."

"Does he?" She remembered to smooth the sharp tone of her voice just in time. After all, this man could be an ally. "The incident was not entirely my fault, I assure you, Commander." She extended her open palm toward him, in a gesture of helplessness she had seen other women use.

"Of course not." He patted her hand, as if expecting more, but she had exhausted her ability to flirt with that one gesture.

One of the commander's top men asked, "If your unmarried state is a problem, then why not simply marry?"

The legend, who had added nothing to the conversation since they arrived, erupted in laughter, and Ros was tempted to kick him, as he was seated directly across from her.

Happily, his laughter stuttered to a halt when he saw that the rest of the men at table had not joined him. "Are you seriously suggesting that Miss Fenster take a husband? She's been quite clear on that subject. She doesn't need a husband. She doesn't need a man."

The eager officer smiled at her indulgently before he answered. "But we, as men of the world, know that is absurd."

"Do we?" He glanced at her, as if wondering why she hadn't put the young man in his place.

"Of course we do. So why not suggest she marry to satisfy your objections? Surely there are unmarried men who would be pleased to have her travel with them and ease their days . . . and nights." He smiled with all the sincerity of a snake. "A woman needs a husband to keep her in line, as you have so rightly pointed out, Mr. Lewis."

"Marry a stranger?" Ros would have rejected the idea outright. But his indignation made her hold her tongue. Mr. Barton had come back right before she left for dinner. No other company had room for an unmarried woman and her party. Her stay at Fort Kearny might be longer than expected if she didn't find some way to change his mind.

Perhaps, if he thought she would do such a foolish thing, he might relent. He might allow her to continue with his company, unmarried, unhindered. "Even if I concede that point to you, sir, I'm afraid I don't know any gentleman nearby very well. How might you suggest I choose a husband?"

Another junior officer offered, "We decide things by shooting contests around here."

"Indeed?"

"Yes, ma'am. Line up fourteen tin plates. Whoever hits the most, wins."

He was furious. "What if more than one man manages to hit all fourteen? Does she marry both men and have them take turns?"

The young man ignored his sarcasm and answered as if the question had been seriously meant. "Then the one hits the most plates closest to center wins."

Ros encouraged the conversation, trying to increase his dismay. "What if you haven't enough plates for the contestants?"

He beamed at her. "Always have enough, ma'am— it's one of the first things emigrants tend to throw out to save space and weight."

The sour expression on Rob Lewis's face made up her mind. "Please arrange matters as promptly as you can, then, sir."

"Miss Fenster, you can't be serious."

"Why not, Mr. Lewis? I'm not foolish enough to believe in marrying for love. Why not make the practical choice?"

"Practical?" He wouldn't allow her to marry in such a foolish fashion, she was certain. Surely he'd see that he must agree the best course of action would be for her to continue with the company.

She hoped he would. For the commander and his men were surprisingly enthusiastic. "This'll be better than our regular Sunday shooting match."

"Why's that?" he asked, one brow raised.

"Best prize is always on Sunday—a pint of whiskey. Shooting for a woman's even better than for drink—and it's bound to be more entertaining. Any hidden liquor will come out to celebrate a wedding."

Ros felt a twinge of worry. "Indeed?"

"Not, begging your pardon, ma'am, that I'm fool enough to participate. But I'll be happy to bet on the winner. And drink a toast to the happy couple."

The rest of the dinner was spent with the men planning the event for ten in the morning the next day. All the men with the exception, of course, of the one who listened to the nonsense with growing unease until the last of the meal was cleared. Then he grabbed her arm and said unceremoniously, "Let's go."

As they rode back to the camp, Rob wondered whether to say anything or not. She wasn't inclined to hear his opinion on anything to do with her right now. But the fort commander wouldn't stop the nonsense, and his men actually seemed to think it a fine idea.

That convinced him to try one last time. "What do you think you're doing?"

"Finding a way to make a stubborn man change his mind."

So that was it. She thought she'd force his hand. He supposed it was the gambler in her. "I won't."

"No?" Her look was pure challenge. For a moment he felt like he'd been trapped with her in a small space once again.

"No." He'd survived being alone in the dark with her once, he told himself. He could do it again—especially when their clothes weren't about to come off.

"Very well." For a minute he thought she'd changed her mind. But her question was harsh. "You claim I'm trouble without a husband?"

"Haven't you proven it?"

She hissed like a jar of preserves opened for the first time. "Judith Smith was the troublemaker, not I."

"She may have started the fight, but she was right about what she saw."

"No, she wasn't." But some of the conviction had left her voice. "What happened between us was the result of an unforeseen set of circumstances, not any predilection for free love on my part."

That he could grant her. But she hadn't looked forward for trouble potential, like he had. "What if it had been John Smith, or Bug Martin in the wagon with you?"

"Then nothing would have happened."

He wanted to believe that. But he remembered her panic. "Can you honestly tell me that you wouldn't have torn the clothes off any man in those circumstances?"

"Of course not! If you hadn't been there, I would have put a blanket over my head and gone to huddle under the wagon."

"What made me so special, then, that you—?" He shouldn't have asked that question. He knew it as soon as he asked.

Maybe she knew it, too, because she didn't answer right away. But then she said quickly, "Because I knew you wouldn't make more of it than it was."

That wasn't the answer he'd been expecting. "What?"

Reluctantly, she added, "Another man might have thought he'd have to ask me to marry him."

If she was trying to make him feel guilty enough to change his mind, she was doing a good job of it. "I've made that mistake once, Miss Fenster." He didn't know if she'd appreciate his honesty, but he felt he owed it to her. "I don't intend to make it again."

The intensity of her answer carried to him even through the darkness. "Don't you see? I understand that." Her voice grew low and fierce. "I approve of your attitude. I didn't want an offer. I wanted you to do as you have done. Gone on about your business. Left me to mine."

He had to admit she'd only once tried to make him squirm—when he'd used that unfortunate choice of words to tell her that she would be left behind at Fort Kearny. *I wish I hadn't taken you.* But that still didn't answer the real question. "What if I tell you that I'll refuse to take you along, married or not?"

"Then I challenge you to explain such a wildly unfair decision to your company. Surely some of them will see that I've done my best to comply with your restrictions. What will they think of your refusal? Especially once Judith Smith tells everyone you were the man with me during the storm."

There wouldn't be a person left who'd respect him at all. "Are you threatening to tear my company apart?"

"No. I am asking you to agree that I accompany you to San Francisco. It is only fair, after all. I will allow you to decide whether I do so with or without a husband."

He laughed. "I don't believe you're as foolish as you want me to think you are."

"Determined, Mr. Lewis." They reached the outlying edge of the company and she dismounted as if the conversation were over.

"Hardheaded is a better word if you intend to go through with this damn-fool stunt tomorrow." If the men weren't too drunk to remember what they'd planned tonight at dinner. He wouldn't mention that possibility to her. She might take a notion to get over there early and remind them.

She tossed her reins to one of those keeping watch over the livestock and walked away from him. "That is entirely up to you, sir."

He followed, reluctant to leave the matter unsettled. "You could join another company."

She turned around, and the stark expression on her face caught him by surprise. "Unfortunately, Mr. Barton has made inquiries of all the wagon masters within a day's ride. They have declined to allow me to join their companies, to a man, because I am not married."

He hadn't expected that. He wondered if Barton had told her the truth. The man hadn't made a secret of the fact that he'd rather go home to Missouri than make the trek across the mountains again. "There are new companies going through every day. Eventually you'll find one. Unless you decide to go home instead."

"I am going to San Francisco with or without you, Mr. Lewis. If acquiring a husband is all that is required for me to travel with you, I am happy to do so." Her voice vibrated with determination.

For a moment . . . No. She just wanted him to think

she would. He snorted a rude laugh. "You're going to look foolish when you don't go through with it."

Ros lifted her rifle. The time had come for the contest. There was an unsettling number of people about. Many of the soldiers at the fort. Emigrants from her company. And emigrants she didn't recognize from the other companies camped nearby.

She'd waited for him to send word that he'd recognized she was right. That he didn't expect her to take a husband to continue traveling with his company. But he hadn't. She'd waited at camp as long as she could.

She'd ridden to the fort hoping that the men had consumed enough alcohol to erase the memory of the whole evening. Unfortunately, the officer who'd suggested the contest remembered every detail. He had added a few embellishments of his own, too—a dingy white lace curtain hung over the porch where the preacher sat in a Hepplewhite chair.

And now, here she was, going through with this ridiculous farce, without a single protest from Rob Lewis. Indeed, he seemed to be betting on the outcome of the match with one of the soldiers. She hoped he lost.

There was a line of men willing to take their chance. Some of them she wouldn't have been willing to speak to, much less marry. Fortunately, most of those were sodden with drink and not likely to be good shots.

"I just have a few terms for my husband-to-be," she announced, hoping to whittle down the line to only a few men. "I won't vow to obey. I will dress as I see fit. I won't grow my hair long for any man. And, unless we find we suit very well, I'll be getting a divorce once I reach San Francisco."

One of the men started to weave his way out of line,

before he stopped to grumble loudly, "What *will* you do?"

A woman from another company of emigrants in the crowd answered loudly, "According to the gossip I hear, everything else."

There were cheers.

"Don't believe all the gossip you hear." Ros refused to blush at the crude comments that ensued. She wasn't here to be treated respectfully. She was here to bring a man to his knees. Figuratively, anyway.

There were still too many men willing to take a chance on winning her hand. "I have one more requirement." She didn't want to have the contest won by a man too drunk to be reasonable. She already had one unreasonable man to deal with; she didn't need two.

"Get on with it!" called the man who'd nearly left the line before.

She lifted her shotgun in the air and let go with a blast that made the rowdy crowd quiet. "I won't marry a man who can't shoot almost as well as I can."

"What man can't shoot as well as a woman?" one soldier jeered as he lifted a bottle to his lips.

"I guess we'll find out today." Ros lifted Rosebud, her favorite shotgun, and carefully shot all fourteen plates, one at a time. By the time the last plate had spun its way to stillness on the ground, there was dead silence.

One of the soldiers gathered all the plates. He went through the stack once, and then again. "All fourteen— hit near to dead center as can be." Several onlookers shouted out their doubts that he was sober enough to judge. But when he held them up, one by one, there could be no doubt.

Several of the men dropped out of the line and there were a flurry of new bets made.

She waited a moment, hoping that she had made her

point. But the one man who could stop this whole farce cold said nothing. He stood, arms folded, watching as if he had no interest in the outcome at all.

# Chapter Nineteen

Unnerved by his lack of concern, Ros decided to make certain he could not claim later that he hadn't understood her terms. A direct challenge would be necessary. "Mr. Lewis."

He smiled and reached up to tip his hat to her. "Changed your mind, Miss Fenster? Ready to go home where you belong?"

The crowd booed and hissed at him. He hadn't expected that, apparently, because he gave a startled glance around.

She waited for him to turn his attention back to her before she spoke. "I just want to make certain we are agreed."

He looked at her as if she were a rattlesnake about to strike. "Agreed on what?"

"That you will allow me to continue traveling with you as long as I have a husband."

He seemed to be considering the matter, and her

pulse quickened. Would he refuse? At last he said slowly, "On one condition."

"What condition?" Would it be something ridiculous, she wondered, and then caught herself. How much more absurd was it possible to be?

"I'll let you travel with us as long as your new husband travels along with you." He tipped his hat again. "Just to keep you out of trouble, you understand."

She smiled, as if he had been the voice of reason. "I accept your condition. Which means I will be traveling in your company, Mr. Lewis. Because I intend to have a husband shortly." To her relief, several more soldiers stepped out of line.

She waited another long moment for him to relent. But he leaned back against the fence post behind him and smiled at her. "I'll believe that when I see it, Miss Fenster. Which won't be today, the rate you're going."

Overconfident man. She straightened. "Now's your chance. Any man willing to marry me,"—she added with a glance at the unkempt soldiers—"and head west in Mr. Lewis's company, take your shot. I'll take the best man to the altar, just to please our beloved Captain Hellfire."

The first man stepped up. Ros waited for reprieve, but none came.

She looked at the prospects. Not the best men. Those from the company she respected well enough. The soldiers were wild cards, even though none of them were sober. She glanced at the estimable Captain Hellfire. He seemed to have closed his eyes for a short nap.

Damn the man. If he would just be reasonable—Ros spun toward Bug Martin, who had agreed to be a judge. "What are you waiting for? Begin." Bug nodded, though he looked more as if he wished to halt the proceedings.

As she had suspected, most of the men couldn't match

her shooting. Very few of the fort's men hit any of the plates dead center. She questioned whether two of them—unless they were too inebriated to recognize the targets—pulled their shots on purpose, for which she could only be grateful.

Two candidates came close. Both were from her company. One, an older man who was heading for the gold fields, seemed eager to have a wife to help in the work. Fortunately, Emerson Packer—strong, healthy, fairly good-looking, and young enough to be reasoned with—was the winner. Bug, with a reluctant gait, crossed to shake his hand.

With one last hope, Ros surveyed the crowd. "Anyone else?" She didn't think anyone would outshoot Emerson, but she wanted to give Mr. Lewis one last chance to stop the proceedings.

"You look a little nervous, Miss Fenster. Maybe you're not as eager to be a wife as you first thought."

Ros looked him in the eye. The key to a successful bluff was not to flinch. Even knowing that any minute would bring about her utter humiliation, she smiled as if she had every intention of marrying Emerson. "I am a woman of my word, Mr. Lewis. Just as I trust you are a man of yours."

"And if no one else wishes to compete, I believe we should move on to the wedding." She smiled at Emerson, who blushed bright red. For a moment she couldn't breathe. The poor boy *wanted* to marry her. He didn't have any idea that she was playing a game meant to bluff Rob Lewis into changing his stubborn, unreasonable mind.

Suddenly she wasn't sure what to do. She disliked anyone—man or woman—who didn't keep his word. And she would be one of those dishonorable souls if she backed out of the wedding now that he'd won the contest fair and square. Unless Rob Lewis relented in the next few seconds.

Bug looked miserable. "Maybe we should wait until tomorrow."

*He wasn't going to speak up.* As the blood began to beat in her ears, she felt a reckless desire to show him that she would not be bested. Maybe she'd even go though with it. A husband. She, who had avoided marriage for this long, marrying the winner of a shooting match. Ridiculous. Jeanne would make her a legend to rival the great Captain Hellfire if she ever got wind of this foolishness.

"Nonsense. Everyone is gathered and waiting. Why make them wait?" If the man wouldn't speak now, he wasn't likely to speak at all. The wagon master stared at her in disbelief, as if, for the first time, he thought she might actually go through with the marriage.

She didn't blame him. Even she didn't know if she was bluffing any longer or not. "Where is the preacher?"

She'd run her bluff all the way to the end and now, at the last minute, she was too hardheaded to admit it hadn't worked. Rob knew he should walk away. Let her suffer the consequences of her actions.

But she wasn't just going to hurt herself; she was going to break a boy's heart. Emerson Packer didn't deserve her. No man deserved her—a wife who'd choose a husband in a shooting match.

For one moment, he considered giving in, allowing her to remain in the company. But he couldn't, not with the rift she'd caused. The half who wanted to see her go would lose faith in him. The other half would think he was weak and take advantage of him.

He'd have to hope she didn't go ahead and marry Emerson . . . unless . . .

He grinned. She thought she'd called his bluff—and she almost had. But he had one card up his sleeve she couldn't possibly have counted on.

As the preacher stood up, he said sharply, "Wait."

All eyes focused on him. Emerson seemed ready to challenge him to a fight, while Bug looked as though he might hug him.

He most enjoyed the burgeoning look of triumph on Rosaline Fenster's face, though. He let her think she'd won. And then he said, "I haven't had my shot yet."

"Your shot?"

"Anyone can enter the contest, right?"

"That's absurd; you're the reason I'm doing this in the first place. . . ." Her protest drifted off, but her mouth pressed tight in dismay.

"I feel like shooting. Haven't got anything better to do. You don't think I'll win, do you?" He grinned.

"Then be quick about it," she snapped.

Feeling like a fool but focused on the thought of how her expression would change when she wasn't looking at marrying a green boy, but a man she couldn't bluff, Rob clipped each of the targets in rapid succession.

Bug grinned broadly. "Fourteen, dead center."

She looked at him warily, as if she understood what he had done but couldn't believe it. "You don't mean this."

He grinned. It felt good to outbluff a master at the game. "I'm as dead set on marrying as you are."

He enjoyed watching her expression as it dawned on her that he was calling her bluff in the only way he could. Several emotions crossed her face in rapid succession. Shock. Admiration. And, most frightening of all—the expression of a gamester willing to bluff to the bitter end. To his shock, she smiled up at him and shrugged. "Very well."

The preacher, impatient to be out of the sun, started the ceremony, reading in a rapid monotone.

She was daring him to break his word. Daring him when she smiled and repeated her vows—omitting obey, of course. Daring him when she said, "I do." Her voice was so rich with mockery that there was a ripple of laughter from the crowd. No doubt they knew when she said "I do" she really meant she wouldn't.

He had forced himself to say the vows, but he couldn't . . . he wouldn't say "I do." He stood, stubborn and silent for a moment, knowing that he would, in the end, be the one to break. He wouldn't make the same mistake twice.

"Wait!" Gwyneth's childish shout was unexpected. For a moment he thought salvation would come in the form of his daughter. He could claim he changed his mind for her sake.

She ran toward them, and he crouched down to let her run full tilt into his arms. "How did you get here?" She wasn't supposed to know about this foolishness.

"I'm not a baby. I rode my pony. I wanted to be here when you won the contest."

"What contest?" He cursed the way gossip traveled in a company.

"The one to marry Auntie Ros, of course."

She held up a wreath made of tiny flowers. "I knew you'd win, Papa."

She turned to the woman who had caused this fiasco and held out the wreath to her. "Bend down, Auntie Ros. I made this for your hair."

"If this upsets you, Gwyneth, I understand," he said, feeling his salvation slipping away.

"Mama always said that a woman like Auntie Ros

needed a man like you. She said your tempramints were perfectly suited."

He glanced up at Rosaline Fenster. What he saw on her face echoed the panic inside him. They'd carried this foolishness too far. They'd bluffed each other into a marriage that neither of them wanted. He couldn't help wondering if Caroline was somewhere, laughing at them as she watched. Temperaments suited like hell.

The preacher snapped his book shut sharply and wiped a bead of sweat from his forehead. "Well, sir, do you or do you not? I haven't got all day."

He stood. "I do," Rob said, taking no pleasure in his bride's sudden pallor.

Those around them didn't seem to realize that neither the bride nor groom believed there was a cause for celebration. Bets were paid off eagerly or grudgingly, cheers went up to their long life together. Toasts were called for.

"I need to get back," he said tersely.

She just nodded, as if she were too overcome to speak, and turned toward her horse.

"Wait." Gwyneth again.

"You are coming with me," he said. "This is no place for a child."

"But you have to kiss her first."

Kiss her. In front of all these people. What he'd rather do was throttle her.

The look of horror she stifled quickly before Gwyneth took notice was small comfort. Neither of them were happy about this foolishness. But the onlookers weren't ambivalent. They hooted and cheered. "Kiss her," chanted the crowd.

She didn't move toward him, but he could see her shoulders relax and her mouth curve softly as she gave in to the will of the masses. "I suppose I owe you that much."

He closed the space between them, infuriated further by her amusement. With a ferocity that brought a gasp from her, he clasped his arms around her waist and pulled her full against him. "You owe me that—and more."

She didn't pretend to misunderstand. Unfortunately, she didn't look the least bit unsettled. In fact, her eyes lit with an unholy delight. "Don't worry, Mr. Lewis. I honor all my debts."

He closed his eyes against the sight of her, so confident she could handle anything he could throw at her. Why didn't she cry, like a normal woman? She hadn't wanted this any more than he had. Had she? He looked at her, hard, then. "Just remember, you brought this on yourself."

"So I did." She tilted her chin up until all it would take was for him to lower his head a few inches and their mouths would meet. The bystanders' chant grew more insistent.

Rob wanted to kiss her. He wanted to do more than kiss her. But he couldn't. Not here.

She leaned up against him, smiled up at him so that he could see her curiosity, her willingness. "You're disappointing your people, Mr. Lewis. Do you need a howling wind and complete darkness before you can kiss me?"

Damn the woman. For such an unfeminine creature she knew how to make a man burn. Deliberately, he bent to kiss her forehead.

"I told you," a soldier crowed. "He doesn't know what to do with her."

One of the losing contestants—one of his own emigrants, unfortunately—called out. "Give her to me, Captain Hellfire. I know what to do with her."

The threat of unpleasantness, of a crowd turning ugly, was the only reason he forced himself to laugh as he looked down into his bride's face. "Believe me, gentlemen, I know what to do with her. And I intend to do it as soon as we get back to camp."

There were shouts of laughter and the threat retreated as quickly as it had appeared. But it would return, fueled by boredom and liquor, if he didn't do something about it.

He turned to the crowd, keeping one arm tightly locked around her waist just in case she took a notion to run. "I'm sure you'll all excuse us if we'd rather head back to our tent than celebrate with you."

"If you need any help, give us a shout," the fort commander called out.

Rob forced himself to laugh again, as if he'd found the commander's ribbing amusing. Revealing his true feelings would only cause trouble. He had enough of that already.

It was time to get out of there. Rob took his bride by one hand and scooped up Gwyneth in his other arm and moved swiftly to escape before things took a turn for the ugly.

He wasn't even sure she understood what she had forced upon him until they had mounted their horses and begun the ride home. With a backward glance at the boisterous celebration behind them, she said, "You should have agreed to let me stay in the company without a husband. Now that you've married me, they're going to expect you to put me back in skirts."

Aware of Gwyneth listening to every word they spoke, he said tersely, "Putting you into skirts is the farthest thing from my mind right now. But maybe it would be a start."

"Surely you don't—" She broke off, with a glance at Gwyneth. "Why don't we just go on as we have been? Nothing needs to change."

"Everything has changed," he said, slowing his horse so that he could meet her eyes. He didn't want her to think he didn't mean what he said. "I warned you. I'm a man who does his best to avoid trouble. But when it comes, I'm not afraid to handle it."

She would have argued the whole ride home; he could see it in her expression. He turned to Gwyneth. "I'll race you," he challenged. They spurred their mounts and left her and her less capable horse in the dust.

Within a minute or two, Gwyneth reined in her pony. "Papa, Auntie Ros's horse can't go so fast."

"She'll catch up soon enough," Rob said. Too soon, for that matter.

"What if the Indians come steal her?"

"Your Auntie Ros can take care of herself, Gwyn." She'd just proven that.

"Aren't you happy to be married, Papa?"

"Of course I am," he lied. Damn. He didn't want to look back. And, for once, he didn't want to look ahead, either. He'd married her. Worse—he thought he might have wanted to. Or, at the very least, he hadn't wanted to let anyone else marry her. How had she gotten him to this point? She didn't flirt. She didn't offer the usual feminine flattery of agreeing with a man just to stroke his ego. She didn't even smell soft and sweet like a woman; her scent had a dangerous tang to it. The woman had ripped off his clothes once, in a blind panic. And now he couldn't seem to get her off his mind.

He glanced back surreptitiously to see that the infernal woman wasn't even hurrying her nag to try to keep up with his. No doubt she thought she could handle any trouble that came her way on the ride back to camp. Worse, he thought just maybe she could—leaving trouble for others to clean up in her wake.

Why did the thought make him want to smile, as angry as he was? As angry as he had every right to be. He didn't know. He didn't know anything right now except that he wanted to finish what they had begun in that wagon.

And there was nothing to stop him from doing it now. She was his wife. What had he been thinking? But he knew. He'd been thinking about how those infernal bloomer trousers of hers unfastened. Not that he was about to compound the foolishness of marrying her by making love to her.

No matter how tempted he might be by the idea.


"He rode off and left you behind? And you his new bride?" Ophelia clucked her tongue against the roof of her mouth in dismay. "Freedom, you hear that?" She cradled the baby and shook her finger at him. "What's that man thinking?"

Most certainly not the same things that were flooding through his new wife's mind, given the way he'd pecked her on the forehead and looked as if he wanted to strangle her. "I can't really blame him. Everything went so much farther than I had intended—"

What had she been thinking? To give up her freedom to a man like Rob Lewis? But then, she knew what she'd been thinking. About him with his shirt half off, his hands on her warm and strong and sure. About making love to a man without paying the price. As if marriage wasn't a steep price. "I'm a fool—"

Ophelia waved away her explanations. "At least you

has a husband and we can stay with the company. Moses don't have to go looking for us."

Didn't the girl understand what had happened? "If Mr. Lewis has his way, Moses may not recognize me, even if I do remain in this company." As her husband, he had that right.

"He going to beat you till your face swell up with bruises, like Master done Miz Ada sometimes?" There was a touch of sympathy in the girl's voice.

Ros shook her head. "I'm afraid he's going to do something infinitely worse—I can survive a beating better than being told what to do. What to wear. Who I must sleep with."

"Oh." Ophelia broke out in a wide smile. "Sometimes I forget you don't know everything, Miz Ros, since you acts like you do." She lowered her voice, adding wistfully, "A man in your bed ain't a bad thing. You get so you miss it when he's not."

"I'm willing to have him in my bed, Ophelia." Eager, curious, and unnerved, as well, but Ophelia didn't need to know that. "It's only fair, since he married me, whether he meant to or not. But he seems to feel that he must also dictate my dress—no doubt my life—to prove his leadership to the company."

"The things a man'll do for his pride." Ophelia shook her head. "What you going to do?"

At last, a question she could answer with confidence. "I'm going to ask him for a divorce." She hadn't decided whether she'd ask before or after the wedding night. After all this trouble, she'd be truly frustrated to end up with a man too honorable—or angry with her— to make love to her.

"Divorce!" Ophelia seemed shocked. "You be a scarlet lady."

"Maybe. But I'll be a free scarlet woman."

The girl's eyes narrowed, as if she wasn't sure whether Ros was teasing her or not. "You ain't no slave."

"No, I'm not. And I'm not really a wife."

"Mr. Lewis know that?"

"Of course he does." She ignored the tiny worrying thought that he could exact more revenge as her husband than he could if he allowed her to divorce him without argument once they reached San Francisco. Ultimately, he was a sensible man.

# Chapter Twenty

A hissing noise distracted her from any doubt about Rob Lewis's intentions. "Do you hear that?"

"What?"

"That sound. Like a snake?"

Ophelia lifted her skirts and glanced nervously down at her feet. "Is it?" They both searched the ground for anything moving sinuously. Ros didn't see anything suspicious at first. Still, she followed the sound, knowing there were poisonous varieties to be found in the area.

"Oh, lordy!" Ophelia exclaimed, stepping away from the back of the wagon.

For a moment, Ros thought Gwyneth had hidden herself in the wagon bed as a prank. Then she saw that Moses was concealed in the shadowy recesses. The first thing she noticed was the weight he'd lost. The feverish cast to his eyes.

She looked over her shoulder, relieved to see no one had noticed Ophelia's startled movement or exclamation. For once the company's willingness to treat the girl as if she didn't exist had benefited them. "What's the matter?"

He bent over, wracked by a cough for a moment, and then gasped out, "Jericho's on his way here. You got to get Ophelia and the baby hid quick."

"Jericho?" How had he found them? Or had he? "How do you know?"

Moses shook his head and said in a harsh and raspy voice, "Don't have time to waste with questions, Miz Ros. If you can't hide them, I'll take them with me."

"No. We'll stay here," Ophelia said quickly. "Them savages might eat the baby."

"Then hide, Fee." He was so gaunt that Ophelia backed away from him in fear at the fierce expression in his dark eyes. "Hide quick."

"I'll tell the twins," Ros said, turning toward the area where the livestock were grazing.

Moses shook his head. "The twins is coming with me. They don't want to hide in camp."

Ros nodded as a pang of understanding shot though her. She wouldn't want to be cooped up inside the hidden compartment either. "Take good care of them."

"Leave my wagon. Jericho will want it. Maybe it will appease him."

Nothing would appease the bounty hunter except Moses in chains. "Nonsense," Ros said. "Everyone thinks it's my wagon anyway. I'll hire another driver to get it safely to California for you."

"You're a good woman, Miz Ros."

"I owe you," she said honestly. "You've saved my skin more times than I can name. Don't worry."

"Keep them safe, Miz Ros," he whispered in that strange hoarse voice, before he disappeared from sight.

Ophelia returned with a sack of food and some blankets in one arm and the baby in another. "How long you think it be until Jericho is gone?"

"I hope it won't be long."

"If it is?"

He could follow them for months; they both knew it. Ros didn't really see the point in saying so aloud. "Then we'll manage, won't we?"

Ophelia looked down at her son. "Freedom ain't going to be able to be quiet in there for long."

She was right. If the baby cried when Jericho was near, they would all be found out. "Give him to me, then."

Ophelia seemed reluctant. "Maybe I can—"

Ros interrupted, her mind made up. "Jericho's not going to look twice at a baby—I'll keep him bundled up and hidden in the wagon."

"But—"

Impatiently, she asked, "How hard can one little baby be to look after? Honestly, Ophelia, you'd think I was incapable of the job."

"No, ma'am. I didn't mean to say that." Ophelia kissed the baby on the head and handed her precious bundle to Ros.

She opened the door to the secret compartment. "Get in there and don't worry about the baby. I'll let you know when Jericho's gone."

Ophelia climbed inside and inched her way into the farthest recesses of the hiding place. She whispered, "If Jericho finds me, you don't let him get the baby, Miz Ros."

Ros cradled the squirming baby firmly against her and promised, "I won't let Jericho near him. I promise you that. Now keep still and we'll all be safe soon."

Freedom began to cry, as if he knew his mother was out of his reach. Ros jiggled him a little against her hip and he quieted. His big brown eyes stared up at her out of a face that was the exact same shade as milky coffee. He seemed to be asking wordlessly if she was worthy of his trust.

She rubbed his cheek with her finger, as she had seen Ophelia and Gwyneth do when they talked to the baby. "What are we going to do with each other, Freedom?" He smiled back at her, wide and joyous, his round little cheeks plumping with the effort. Ros had never been so scared of anything in her life.

It occurred to her that she would be better off to avoid meeting Jericho face-to-face. After all, he had seen her in her male costume and already suspected she was a woman. Would the bounty hunter recognize her easily, or had he seen too little of her face as he chased her? Unless he had somehow unearthed her real name . . . A bolt of lightning went through her chest. Her maiden name. She was Mrs. Lewis now, not Miss Fenster.

Mrs. Lewis. Would that be enough to fool the man, if he had learned her name from Jackson, Moses's old master and Ros's nemesis? "What do you think, Freedom?" she asked the baby. "Are we safe from that mean old Jericho now that we're Mrs. Lewis instead of Miss Fenster?"

The baby began to cry. Ros jiggled him again, which made him cry louder. She put him on her shoulder and patted his back. His tiny face turned red and his cheeks puffed out with the force of his cry.

This was not at all wise, standing here in open camp with a crying baby. If she didn't get him quieted soon, she'd bring everyone's attention to the fact that Ophelia was nowhere around. That would offer more gossip for Jericho to feed upon when he arrived. If the baby stayed with her, she'd lead Jericho right to him.

With a sense of relief, she realized the baby was better

off in someone else's care—experienced care, to be sure—until she knew exactly what Jericho had discovered about her. To be on the safe side, she asked Astrid Martin to watch over the child.

She had a story prepared, in case the girl had questions, but Astrid had only smiled and taken the child willingly. Which was fortunate. The one question she'd asked had been hard enough to answer. "What shall I feed him?"

"I don't know. Ophelia usually—"

Astrid waved her hand. "I'll boil some goat's milk for him, then, if he gets hungry."

Ros stared at the girl, suddenly seeing her in a new light. "Wherever did you learn so much about taking care of infants?"

Astrid's mouth twisted into a mock grimace. "I was the eldest of twelve."

"Twelve." Ros remembered then that Astrid's mother hadn't found men good for much more than splitting wood. Apparently her husband—or husbands—had been good at least one other task—making babies. "No wonder you act like an experienced mother. You are one."

"Experienced sister, not mother. Not yet. One day." Astrid smiled down at the baby wistfully. Blissfully unaware of the effect of her next question, the girl beamed up at Ros—"Do you hope that you and Mr. Lewis will be blessed with a family soon?"

He'd have to sleep with her. They'd expect that. After all, he'd willingly entered the contest. He'd said the vows in front of them all. But sleeping in her tent didn't mean making love to her. He would avoid that. He wasn't sure how. He could have Gwyneth share their tent—but then he wouldn't be able to tell her exactly what he thought of her.

Not in front of his daughter. She liked her Auntie Ros. His shoulder blade started to itch and he closed his eyes. What now?

One of the emigrants on watch rode up. "We've got a guest riding in."

He wondered, briefly, if one of the soldiers would tell him that it had all been a huge practical joke. That the preacher hadn't really been a preacher, and he was not a married man. But he wasn't that lucky. When he saw who it was, Rob rode out a short way from his company to greet him. The rider wasn't a soldier. He was a man bearing bad news. Very bad news that could be laid at the feet of Miss . . . his wife.

The man nodded gravely. "Lewis."

Rob nodded back. "Jericho."

There was only one reason for the man to be here. But Rob waited for him to say it aloud. "I'm looking for some runaways I think are in your company."

The man was a bounty hunter and his methods questionable, so Rob felt no guilt in being evasive. "I don't know of any runaways in any of my families."

The man unrolled sketches from his pack and handed them over to Rob.

He didn't want to look at them. But he had no choice. Ophelia. The twins. A fourth one was of the murderer on a WANTED poster Rob had in his pack.

He was glad to be able to be totally honest about that one.

"I've seen these three. Not him." He handed the sketches back. He didn't need them. He'd been living with these people.

"He's married to the girl. They have a baby with

them, too." Jericho rolled up the sketches and put them away.

"Married to her?" He'd assumed Ophelia was married to one of the twins. Ros had to have known. "The girl has a baby with her, but I haven't seen the man. He's wanted for murder. If I'd come across the man, I'd have arrested him and turned him over to the fort commander."

"Arrested? Hanging's what that one needs." Jericho turned his head away and spat out onto the prairie. "Where are the girl, the baby, and the twins, then?"

"I'll turn them in to the fort commander."

The bounty hunter shrugged. "Suit yourself about the others. I got a letter from the owner. He wants me to fetch the girl and the baby home to him."

Rob led him though the camp, to the wagon. He watched for her. His wife. But she did not appear. His expression must have been truly awful—one suited to a legend like Captain Hellfire, not a mortal like Rob Lewis—because no one in the company dared even greet him.

What had she done to him? His journey had barely begun and already he had all he could do to keep it from turning into a disaster.

Jericho dismounted from his horse and crawled all over the abandoned wagon. "Is this some kind of joke? You said they were here this morning. Where are they now?"

"I was at the fort most of the day," Rob said. Bluffing himself right into a damn-fool marriage. But Jericho didn't need to know that.

"I can have you arrested for aiding—"

Rob interrupted him. Jericho was a bounty hunter; Rob was a Pinkerton agent. The two didn't always get along. "I have no intention of aiding any criminal activity, Jericho."

"Then where are they?"

Rob shrugged. Almost certain they weren't, he offered, "Maybe they're gathering firewood, or doing laundry down by the river."

As he had expected, a thorough search of the entire camp turned up none of them. Someone must have warned them. He knew who was most likely. But he didn't see the point in telling Jericho. He'd handle her himself.

The man was like a hound dog following a scent—relentless. "Where's the colored girl?" He must have asked the question a dozen times before he happened upon Astrid Martin.

Her blue eyes guileless and her blond braids as neat as a pin, Astrid offered earnestly, "She and the twins took some horses and rode away this afternoon." She shifted the blanketed baby she held to her shoulder as naturally as if it were her own. "Why? Aren't they back yet?"

Jericho leaned down from his saddle. If he'd been a hound dog, Rob would have said he caught a strong scent. But it was the wrong one. "Which way did they go?"

Astrid pointed northward. "That way, I think."

"Thank you, ma'am."

"Not at all." She smiled at him in her usual friendly manner, but not with her usual carefree smile.

Jericho didn't seem to notice anything amiss, except her age. "She's awful young; do you think she's a reliable witness?"

Rob glanced back at the woman, who cradled the baby tight against her chest. "Good as anyone else." Rob shrugged. What did Jericho expect him to say?

"The women see a lot while they're walking. Nothing better to do than gossip."

"So you'd trust her information?"

"I would." Rob wouldn't have advised the bounty hunter to do so, but that wasn't the question he'd been asked.

Jericho looked northward reluctantly. "I think I'll check the companies ahead on the road, first."

"Sounds like a wise thing to do. I'll keep a lookout in case they come back here."

The bounty hunter might have gone then, if he hadn't caught sight of something. "That woman—is she wearing those bloomer skirts?"

"She is." She was standing by the river's edge, throwing pebbles into the water with the children.

"She in your company?"

Unfortunately. "She is."

The bounty hunter's eyes narrowed lasciviously. "That true what they say about free love?"

"I wouldn't know," Rob said, for once able to be entirely honest with him.

"Who is she?"

He didn't want to answer, for many reasons. But anyone in the company would do so gladly. "My wife." The words sounded unnatural and yet perfectly comfortable at the same time, once he'd said them. He hoped Jericho hadn't noticed his initial hesitation.

"Wife? I thought she was a schoolteacher who didn't travel with you."

Rob felt a chill of alarm. Just how much did Jericho know about him and his family?

"My second wife." Newly minted and not even consummated. His first wife dead little more than a month. The shame of that flamed inside him suddenly. He felt as if he'd never known Caroline at all, despite the fact of Gwyneth. Of his daughter. But that was his problem and he didn't intend to share it. "She and my daughter are with me this trip." If Jericho hadn't heard about the shooting match at the fort, maybe he wouldn't until Rob and his company were long gone.

Already he was calculating how long it would take them to pull out. If he could get rid of Jericho, he could get the word out and they could leave as early as tomorrow morning. If he could get rid of Jericho.

"Quite a costume."

"She's partial to the bloomer skirts. Says they're more comfortable, especially on the trail."

"It's a rare woman who can wear those without shame. I heard tell of one back where I'm from—"

"Shouldn't you be heading north, Jericho? You wouldn't want the trail to grow cold now, would you?"

"No, sir, that I wouldn't. Thank you for your help. I'll make sure to write Mr. Pinkerton special to tell him how much you helped me."

"Much obliged. Mr. Pinkerton's quite the skinflint; maybe your letter will induce him to give me a raise at last."

"A raise?" Jericho laughed. "Could be."

Rob watched the man ride off northward, his shoulder itching like the devil. He didn't know if it was Jericho or Rosaline Fenster . . . Lewis. He let out a groan that startled his mount.

As he looked on, she walked to a spot where she could easily watch Jericho ride away. So she hadn't been down by the river by accident. She had been hiding, hoping to avoid meeting the man who was hunting her runaways.

He couldn't blame her for helping Ophelia and the twins. But a murderer? What had she been doing helping a murderer escape from justice? That didn't fit with the woman he'd come to know. The woman he'd married. He shook his head. How could he say that? He'd only known her a little more than a month.

One part of him wanted to call her to account right now. Another part suggested he'd be much wiser to wait until they arrived safely in San Francisco.

He'd brought the man right to the wagon. Thank God Moses had warned them or Jericho would have had them all—except Moses himself. The man had found nothing. No one. She had watched him ride away. Would he be back?

Ros went to the wagon and crouched down near the secret door. "Jericho's gone."

Ophelia whispered back quickly, "He didn't find Moses or the twins, did he?"

"No. He went off in the wrong direction completely." She didn't know why, but she was grateful for how providence had misdirected him.

She helped the girl out of the secret compartment and watched in silent sympathy as Ophelia stretched her numbed limbs and tried to walk without falling.

"You can stay out for a little while, but keep out of sight." Ros didn't know how well the girl would like her next words. "I want you to stay in here tonight. I think it might be safer, in case Jericho comes back." In case Captain Hellfire thought it was his job to turn her in.

Ophelia didn't look happy, but she didn't argue. "Okay. But I got to have the baby with me. He needs me."

"I'll get him." There was little doubt Freedom needed his mother. The baby hadn't taken to the goat milk Astrid had tried to feed him. But Ros had to wonder if Ophelia didn't need the baby, too. Sometimes a warm body in the darkness could ease the most looming of fears.

Dismay plain on her face, Ophelia demanded, "Where he been, if not with you?"

Ros held her hands out in a gesture meant to calm her agitation. "With Astrid."

"That girl? She ain't no more than a baby herself."

Ros shook her head. "She's the eldest of twelve and much better with infants than I am."

Ophelia had a doubtful expression. "You bring him quick. He probably hungry."

Astrid and Bug were sitting by their campfire, leaning against each other and gazing at the baby, when she arrived.

She took the baby from where he slept in Astrid's arms. "Thank you for watching him."

Astrid smiled. "We enjoyed it."

Bug nodded. "Good practice for when we have a dozen of our own."

"Two," Astrid corrected firmly.

"Six?"

Ros laughed. "One is more than I know what to do with."

"You'll learn easy enough when you have to." She grinned at Ros's rueful head shake. And then, with a quick glance to make certain there was no one to overhear her, the girl confided, "I told that nasty man Ophelia and the twins had headed north."

Ros, startled, laughed aloud. "Are you sure you're only sixteen?"

"I'll be seventeen by the time we reach California," Astrid said, with a small self-satisfied grin.

"Thank you for helping with the baby—and with Jericho. But don't do anything else." She glanced at Bug, who didn't seem to think his wife had done anything dangerous. "I couldn't bear the look on your husband's face if you found yourself in difficulty for helping us."

Astrid frowned. "Bug better not try to tell me who I can and can't help."

He grinned, as if the thought had never crossed his mind.

Astrid shook her head, smart enough not to trust the innocent look on her husband's face. "I married him for better or worse, but I didn't leave my conscience at the altar."

# Chapter Twenty-One

Ros hoped that Jericho, with the word of innocent Astrid, might be following the wrong trail for good. Still, at supper she had no choice but to explain matters to Gwyneth, when she asked where Ophelia and the baby were.

"Why do they have to hide?"

"Because if they don't, Jericho can take them back home where they came from. Even though they don't want to go."

"It's not fair."

"No. But we have to change the laws of the country before we can make it fair."

"Like Grandpapa does?"

Ros nodded. "Senators help make laws. I'm quite certain that your grandfather will help make sure that Moses and Ophelia are one day free in every state. But you and I can do our part now to keep them free here."

"Why can't we just buy them and set them free?"

"I wish we could. But their master doesn't want to sell them."

"Not even if we offered lots and lots of pure gold? It's on the ground in California. I could pick it up and give it to him."

"Not even then."

"Is Freedom scared?"

"No, honey, he's safe with his mother tonight, and he'll be with Bug and Astrid tomorrow during the day. But you mustn't tell anyone."

"I won't even tell Betsy Anne. Can I go whisper good night to them? I won't let anyone see."

"After supper. If there's time. Now you have to help me make supper." She handed the girl a small bucket. "I need this filled with water."

"I'll make sure it's filled to the tippy-top. Papa will come to supper tonight, for sure, now that he's married to you." Gwyn happily went off to fetch water.

Ros felt a buzz of shock pass through her. Married. She'd almost forgotten. Why hadn't he come? He'd talked to the bounty hunter. Shown him the wagon Ophelia and the twins had been traveling in. Why hadn't he come? Had he told Jericho about her? No. The bounty hunter wouldn't have gone off without her if he knew who she was.

He didn't arrive for supper and Ros's stomach began to knot anxiously. If he'd thought she was trouble before, he'd *know* she was now. Had Jericho's untimely visit convinced him to leave her—and the troubles she brought him—behind at the fort? He had to be angry. Damn the man, why didn't face her?

Well, if he wouldn't come to her, she'd go to him. She had just resolved to put Gwyneth to bed and search him out when the child called out happily, "Papa, you missed dinner."

"I had things to tend to," he said, swinging her up into his arms and giving her a quick, hard hug. The gaze he turned on Ros was anything but warm. "We're pulling out tomorrow."

"Tomorrow?" Jericho's visit was the reason for the rush. She chose her words carefully, wanting to make her question clear to him and not Gwyneth. "All of us?"

"We'll have to talk about that." He twitched one of his daughter's braids. "Gwyneth."

"Yes, Papa?"

"Mrs. Martin is going to watch you tonight, because Ophelia had to go away—"

"I know, Papa—but you'll help us keep her safe, won't you?"

He glanced at Ros, and she sensed another black mark going against her name. "Mrs. Martin's waiting."

Ros watched as Gwyneth grabbed her pack and pallet and carried them off to the Martins' tent. She waited until the little girl was safely inside before she said, "I know you want to throttle me, and you have good reason—"

"Inside."

He pushed her toward the tent with little ceremony.

She dug her heels into the ground and resisted him. The look in his eye made her stomach twist. He growled low in his throat. "Do you have any idea how many pairs of eyes are on us right now?"

She glanced around, as if she had lost something. Though not one of the people tending to their business was overtly rude about their curiosity, she could see he was right. They were being watched. A flush of humiliation spread through her. "They think it's our wedding night."

"It *is* our wedding night. And I don't want anyone to guess there's anything wrong between us." He cradled her up against him, his arm tight around her waist, his chin on her neck. Anyone watching might have thought he had done it affectionately. But his voice was tight with the anger he held in check. "Come into the tent."

"I want a divorce." She didn't know she was going to say it until she did.

"Gladly—if we make it to San Francisco alive." Impatiently, he lifted her feet off the ground and half carried, half propelled her into the tent.

"I'm sorry about Jericho. I'll take care—"

"You'll take care of nothing. Nothing. You'll do nothing. This is my problem now."

She didn't like the closed look in his eyes. "How can you say that?"

"I didn't. The law did. A man is responsible for his wife."

"We're not really married."

"No? I seem to recall that I tried to call your bluff and you called mine fair and square, right in front of the preacher."

"Neither of us meant it to go this far."

"True. But it did."

"Why didn't you just say that you would give me a second chance?"

"I thought about it, but I didn't think you'd like the terms."

"You could have halted things with a joke." She shook her head wearily. "I'm already a source of amusement to many for the way I dress."

"Maybe I could have. But I didn't. We're married and your troubles are mine. Where is Ophelia?"

"If I tell you, will you promise to keep her safe?"

"No."

"You don't understand—"

"I'm afraid you don't understand." He lit the lantern and unrolled his pack. Inside, she saw a sheaf of posters rolled up, and her stomach began to ache.

Without a word, he took the top poster and unrolled it. Moses's face stared up at her. WANTED was printed in large letters over his likeness. "Jericho has similar ones for Ophelia and the twins."

"What are you doing with this? What do you care about Jericho? He's just a bounty hunter—someone who hunts down slaves like they were animals."

His face could have been chiseled out of granite. "And I'm a Pinkerton detective. A man who catches bank robbers—and murderers."

"You? Captain Hellfire? You must be joking. When would you have time to chase runaways while you're escorting a company of wagons across the wilderness?"

"Pinkerton recruited me because of what I do. A wagon master sees everything. It's not just the law-abiding who head for California and gold mines."

"So you chase runaways." There was a world of contempt in her voice.

"I chase criminals. That man's a murderer."

"How do you know?"

"The poster says so."

"What if the poster is wrong?"

"Ros—what do you know about this man?"

"Nothing."

"Tell me the truth."

"Why?"

"Because he's Ophelia's husband, and if you've helped him, Jericho can make big trouble for you."

Her face paled when she realized how much he knew,

but her stubborn resolve didn't break. "I'm willing to take the risk."

"I'm not."

"What does it matter to you if I—"

"As of that ceremony today, your business is mine. Who do you think will believe I was sleeping with you and didn't know what you were up to?"

"You weren't sleeping with me."

"You and I know that. But who in this company would believe it after what we've done?"

"You don't understand. He doesn't deserve to be hunted like this. He's a good man—"

"Do you know where he is?"

"No. And I wouldn't tell you if I did."

"He's a murderer."

"No. He's not."

"Do you have any idea what you've done to me?"

"Yes. I've found a way to tarnish your reputation." She bit her lip, but her eyes were fiercely unapologetic. "I'll find a way to fix it."

"There is no way to fix it." He shucked off his jacket.

"What are you doing?"

"We've a wedding night to see to." He began to unbutton his shirt. "Remember?"

"You can't be serious."

His eyes were stark and shadowed as he said harshly, "Do you think they'll follow any captain who wins a wife and then doesn't sleep with her?" He finished unbuttoning his shirt, revealing the undershirt below.

Ros shook her head. "If you think I'll let you touch me now—"

"Why not?" He was tempted to tell her that her virtue, whatever was left of it, was safe with him tonight. Instead, he decided to exact a measure of revenge. "You were planning to sleep with Emerson if you married him."

"I thought you'd stop the contest."

"You thought I would, but you weren't a hundred percent sure. So tell me, honestly, if I were Emerson, would you be arguing with me now?"

"Emerson freely entered that contest. He *wanted* me."

He shrugged out of his shirt and pulled the undershirt off his body in a single fluid motion. His gaze pinned her. "What makes you think I don't?"

She became perfectly still at his words. Like a mouse that had seen a cat ready to pounce.

He raised his hand and laid his palm flat against her cheek. His eyes were dark with emotion. "You owe me this." He took her hands in his and dropped to his knees, pulling her down to him.

She could have resisted easily enough. But she didn't. "Not like this. Not in anger." But she fell against him, slid down his body, held on to his waist.

He held her tight to his naked chest. She turned her face into his chest, rubbed her cheek against his skin. Her face was cool against the heat of his skin.

He inhaled the spicy, dangerous, familiar scent of her for a moment as he held her there against him. His hands moved over her back, her hips, her bottom. He pulled her to him and then released her with a harsh exhalation.

She reached her hands up to cup his face. "You're angry with me. Is this wise?"

His breath blew out in a sigh over her ear. "Nothing I do with you is wise." He rested his hands on her shoulders, using his thumbs to stroke her neck. "Why should this be any different?"

She reached up to stroke her hands through the hair that curled at his nape. As she moved, the lamplit shadows shifted eerily within the tent. Their silhouettes must be clearly outlined on the canvas covering of the tent.

He remembered what he was doing, then: putting on a show. Were the watchers still watching?

As if she, too, understood that their shadowy figures were clear to the watchers, she reached to turn out the light. He stopped her. "No. Leave it on."

He kissed her on the mouth, his lips hard against hers. Her lips fell open beneath his, but he did not take advantage of what she offered.

Instead, he moved his hard, tight mouth down against her jaw, her neck. Brushed his unyielding lips against her shoulder for a moment. The weight of his head rested on her shoulder briefly as he fought the urge to do more than satisfy his pride. His hunger for her gnawed in his belly, but he ignored it.

She pulled back to look at his face, and a flash of surprise, perhaps a touch of hurt, moved through her eyes. What did she see in his face? Grim determination? She brushed her fingertips across the lines deepening his forehead. "You don't want to do this."

*I do.* But he wouldn't. He captured her hands with his and moved them away from his face. He touched his lips to her ear and whispered, "Want means nothing. I *have* to do this."

He bore her down to the pallet, pinning her to the ground as he reached his arm to turn out the lantern. Cruel or not, he wanted her to understand. "And everyone has to know I have."

The darkness fell around them, and Rob regretted turning out the light. But he couldn't keep up the show for much longer. He was too angry. He lay over her, unwilling to do more, unwilling to move away.

She stiffened beneath him. "All of that was for show?"

"I wouldn't want anyone to know I have no intention of sleeping with my wife."

"No intention . . ." Her breath was warm against his neck. "I thought you said you wanted me."

He closed his eyes against the images her words conjured. Heat and tight, wet depths. "Oh, I do." He gave in to the powerful urge convulsing through him and ground himself against her once. "I don't think there's anything I want more right now than to be inside you."

She sucked in a breath and tensed under him. His body begged him to move against her again. Move inside her. Ruthlessly, he ignored his instincts and lay still above her. "But I've learned that not everything I want is good for me. And you definitely fall on that side of the fence, Miss . . . No. Miz Lewis."

Knowing that his night would be sheer torture, he rolled over to his side and wrapped his arm around her waist, spooning her stiff body into his. He couldn't take the chance she'd run away in the night.

Rob Lewis. Captain Hellfire. A Pinkerton detective. A man of a thousand faces, and she had shackled herself to him like an ankle chain.

She slept, fitfully. Waking now and again to find his arm resting on her hip, in the curve of her waist, his hand warm on her thigh. This wasn't how she'd imagined sleeping with a man would be. She'd finally gotten everything arranged so that she could find out what all the fuss between men and women was about. Unfortunately, she'd chosen a man who made his living pursuing criminals when he wasn't shepherding emigrants west.

She turned onto her other side. His mouth was close enough to kiss, but she knew better than to start the excitement spiraling low in her belly. All too soon it would be twisting out of control. Like her life. How could something so simple as saving her friends become so complex that she had a devil's choice between Rob Lewis's reputation and honor and the freedom of her friends?

Poor man. She'd made a true muddle of his life this last month. Of course, if he'd told her what he was—a Pinkerton, for heaven's sake—at Caroline's, she would have known to avoid traveling with Captain Hellfire, legend or no.

She sighed. No excuses. There was only one thing she could do to fix the mess she'd made for all of them and still keep everyone safe.

Her only regret was that she'd never get to know what it felt like to make love to a man. This man. His breath fanned warm against her face and she closed her eyes, remembering being held by him in the wagon. The feel of his fingers pressing against her, making her breath hot and hard in her throat.

She covered the large warm hand resting on her hip with her own. Gently, lingeringly, she traced the long, callused fingers that had given her surprisingly more pleasure than her own ever had.

The hand under hers flexed and shifted. His breathing hitched and then resumed an even pace. He wasn't asleep, but he wanted her to think he was. She sat up, to test her instinct, and was pleased to see she was right when he turned over swiftly and pinned her back down to the ground. For a moment she thought he might kiss her. And more.

But all he said was, "You need to rest."

No. She didn't need to rest. She needed to . . . But not like this. Not when he wanted to keep her prisoner. To endanger the people she'd tried so hard to help. "Are you going to take me with you when the company leaves tomorrow?"

He didn't answer for so long, she thought he might

have fallen asleep. At last, his voice thin with resignation, he said, "What choice do I have?"

"You could leave me here." She could find another company to join. "After all, I'm not an unmarried woman anymore. Surely being married to a legend should count for something with another wagon master—who doesn't have a second job chasing criminals."

"I have already abandoned one wife, Miss . . . Rosaline. I'm not proud of it—and I don't intend to make the same mistake twice. Whatever trouble you're fixing to cause, I want to be there to stop it, if I can."

"I won't be causing any more trouble for you . . . Rob, I assure you. I appreciate your kindness." She wouldn't be continuing with him much longer, either. Moses and Ophelia were going to California sooner than the rest of these emigrants. It wasn't safe for them to linger here any longer. But she had no idea how to contact Moses to make the arrangements. She'd have to wait until he contacted her.

"Not kindness—self-preservation. And I have a feeling you're not going to appreciate it for very long." He pulled her close to him, spooning warmly against her. "Go to sleep. Busy day tomorrow."

She didn't think she slept at all, but when dawn came, he was gone. She could hear the sounds of the camp packing up to move on. Surreptitiously, she visited Ophelia, bringing the girl food and water. She took Freedom again, without telling the girl about the events of the last day. No point giving her more to worry about, cooped up as she was. Astrid and Gwyneth were delighted to look after the baby again.

He rode up to her. With everyone looking on, he dismounted and gave her a tight-lipped kiss. She felt a wicked temptation to tickle him with her tongue, but she managed to control it. "I've asked some men to help pack you up, since Ophelia and the twins are no longer with us. Gwyneth is with Astrid Martin again."

She was proud to be able to say, "I'm all packed and ready; you can have your men help someone else."

She thought everything would be all right, then. They would leave the fort and head away. Away from the East, where men could be owned like beasts of burden, and away from Jericho, who cherished his pieces of silver.

She was certain she'd thought of everything. Until he said tersely, as if he expected an argument and was not prepared to listen to reason, "We'll have to leave the wagon the twins drove behind."

The wagon Ophelia was hidden in? All of Moses's goods? "I won't leave it behind. I'll find someone to drive it." The idea was daunting, though. There were so few men who weren't already in charge of their own wagons. Young boys of thirteen and fourteen were too slight for the task.

"There's no time to waste. We're leaving as soon as we're packed up." He wasn't in the mood to be even slightly conciliatory, and she couldn't tell him about Ophelia and Freedom.

She wouldn't leave them. They wouldn't be safe, not even this close to Fort Kearny. Jericho or some other bounty hunter would find them within the week. "If I can't find a driver, I'll drive it myself."

"You'd do okay for about an hour. But you're not going to manage a whole day of driving. Leave it behind."

She wished he wasn't right, but he was. She couldn't manage weeks driving the wagon. "I can't leave it behind."

"You don't have a choice."

She wouldn't accept that. "I'll hire someone."

"Who are you going to hire out here?"

"I'd be happy to drive it for you, Miz Lewis."

Ros turned, wondering which of the emigrants had spoken. But it wasn't an emigrant. It was Jericho.

# Chapter Twenty-two

The bounty hunter was back. "I beg your pardon." She tamped all the panic she felt down into a tiny corner and raised an eyebrow, as if at an impudent student. She wasn't supposed to know who he was, but that didn't mean she had to pretend to like him.

His eyes narrowed, as if he was trying to remember where he might have seen her before. "I'm going your way for a while. I wouldn't mind making a few extra dollars driving a wagon."

She'd be drawn and quartered first. But she smiled with frozen civility. "No, thank you."

"Don't be too hasty, honey." Rob put his hand on her arm. "I think you're looking at the answer to a prayer."

She put every ounce of fury she felt into making her words drive like particles of sleet into his skin. "This is *my* wagon and I don't wish to hire this person to drive it."

His grin was narrow, almost dangerous. "You're my wife. Everything you own is mine. And I'm happy to let Jericho drive *my* wagon."

"You can't be serious." But he was. And he was legally in the right, as well.

"Completely."

"Mr. Lewis—" She had to change his mind. He didn't understand what was at stake . . . and she couldn't tell him.

"Make up your mind, Mrs. Lewis. We leave the wagon, or we hire him."

"Fine." She nodded stiffly to the bounty hunter. "You may drive the wagon."

The odious man squinted at her as if he were reconsidering the offer. "How much you going to pay me?"

Rob squeezed her arm in warning before she could reply with any of the scathing remarks that came to her. "A dollar a week."

"You're paying your other teamster two."

"Two, then." How had he known what she paid Mr. Barton?

As he walked away she muttered angrily, "How could you do such a thing? That man—in the company?"

He raised an eyebrow and pulled her close to him to whisper intimately in her ear. "You know what they say? Keep your friends close, and your enemies closer."

Ros didn't think they said that when there was a runaway hidden in the wagon the enemy was driving. Unfortunately, she couldn't point that out to him.

The days began to blur in her mind. Day after day of having Gwyneth or Astrid or Bug distract Jericho so that she could sneak food and water to Ophelia. Bring the baby to her to feed. Find a chance to let the girl out to feel fresh air, if not sunlight.

It was a miracle that Jericho had not found them out. But she didn't know how long the miracle could hold out. Maybe she should send the girl away alone, not wait for Moses at all. She could not envision Ophelia alone on the long journey west. She needed her husband. Where was he?

Ros scanned the horizon but saw nothing—not even any game. Her eyes were bleary with exhaustion and she thought for a moment she saw a dark shadow moving along the ridge. But no. There was nothing. Nothing.

Perhaps if her nights were not so tormented she would not feel such a draining pessimism when she thought about keeping Ophelia safe. But Rob followed the same routine every night—a fervent, lantern-lit pretense at making love. And then a restless night, the two of them tossing and turning . . . and burning.

Needless folly. Neither one of them could afford to be less than sharp. She was going to put a stop to his torment of them both. Tonight.

She needed a good night's rest in order to decide what to do about Ophelia and Freedom. And she knew how to get it. No matter how hard he resisted, Captain Hellfire was about to find out just how determined his wife could be.

Rob tucked Gwyneth into her little tent and the sleeping girl curled up with a sigh of contentment. He looked at his tent. Rosaline was already inside, waiting for him. Damn, it felt like he was going to his execution instead of his bed. Two weeks of this torment. He didn't have a clue where the runaways were and he was near dead on his feet. He'd almost missed heading off a stampede today when that excitable white-spotted ox stepped on a snake.

She didn't turn when he entered the tent. She had lit the lantern and was undressed, her looming shadow on the tent wall magnifying her motions. He swallowed. Every night became more difficult. Tonight she wore only—damn! She wore only his shirt. No wonder his pack had seemed lighter this morning.

He scuffed off his boots by the entrance of the tent. "Isn't that my shirt?"

She glanced over her shoulder, as if she hadn't realized he'd come inside. "Yes." Somehow he was sure it was only a pretense. The itch under his shoulder blade sprang to life.

"I don't recall you asking to borrow it."

"Take it back, then." She swung away from him and folded her clothes neatly, ready for the next day.

He quickly stripped down to his drawers, ignoring her challenge. He wasn't in the mood for games today. He'd pushed his emigrants hard. They could see Chimney Rock ahead, and it seemed to give them a new spark of determination. They hadn't reached it today, but they'd reach it tomorrow, and he'd let them rest a day.

Rosaline played with her clothing, smoothing at an imaginary wrinkle, pretending she didn't know what he wanted. Impatient, he demanded, "Come here. I'm tired and I want to go to bed."

She hesitated a moment and then came to stand before him. His shirt was only half fastened. He could see both the shadow between her breasts and that she was wearing nothing else but the long cotton shirt, which fell almost to her knees. Her legs stretched long and slim and bare. He had been wrong—the trousers of her bloomer costume were not as indecent as her bare legs. Not by far. He closed his eyes and dropped to his knees, pulling her down with him.

Unexpectedly, she resisted, bending slightly, so that they ended with him kneeling before her, she bent down at the waist over him. He opened his eyes to see the tail of his shirt fanning out from her legs, touching their joined hands. Inches from his nose, the open top half of the shirt fell away, revealing the round curves of her breasts. He glimpsed one pink nipple and a jolt of lust ran through him in an instant.

"What game are you playing now?" He tugged at her, tried to bear her down to the pallet as he had done for the last two weeks, but she shifted her weight so that he lay beneath her and she knelt above him.

"If you're going to give them a show, Captain Hellfire, then give them a show."

She reached up to completely unfasten her shirt— his shirt—exaggerating the movement for any curious eyes that might be focused on their shadowy figures.

"Let them think you're a lover, not a rutting beast who doesn't even take his wife's clothes off."

She took his hands and pressed his palms against her breasts. He curled his fingers around the softness before he pulled them away.

He sat up and kissed her, without heat. "You're going to get yourself into a heap of trouble playing around with a man like this, Rosaline."

She touched him lightly. Ran a hand along his jaw. "I want you, Captain Hellfire, though I'm not sure that you're a wise thing to want."

He reached up to grasp her hand and hold it still. She flattened her palm against his cheek gently, and he turned his head slowly and kissed her wrist. "I'm not so sure you're not a dangerous thing for any man to want, Miz Lewis."

"Thank you." She ran her hand lightly down his chest, across his stomach.

He nearly swore. He nearly backed away. He hadn't counted on this. The blood pounded inside him with the insistent beat of native drums.

"Give me one solid reason why this is a good idea." The only one he could think of was throbbing for attention between his legs.

"If we don't, I'm going to have another sleepless night. And so are you." She turned out the lantern. Her voice vibrated warmly in the darkness. "You want them to think you make love to me. What difference can it possibly make if you truly do?"

"How many reasons do you need besides the obvious one? I don't want to get you pregnant."

As if she'd been prepared for his argument, she ran her hand up his arm. "What about a little grace?"

"There's no such thing as a little grace." He sighed and reached out for her in the darkness. Slipped off the shirt she'd stolen from him and put his lips to the bare skin of her shoulder. She tasted like sin. He closed his eyes and moved his hands to her hips and his mouth over the swell of her breast.

She made a sound of surprise. Or delight. Maybe both.

He closed his eyes. She wanted grace. He'd give her grace. And take a little for himself in the bargain. He pulled at her elbow so that she tumbled into his lap like a silken bundle. It would be good to sleep soundly again. After.

He skimmed her body with his hands, warm flesh, secret curves and hollows. She gave a husky murmur and reached her hands behind his head, pulling him down into a long, drugging kiss. She shifted restlessly, so that she straddled him. He took advantage of the position to explore the secrets of her body—a light touch of his thumb made her shiver, one finger made her plunge away from him in surprise, three made her plunge toward him and moan low against his shoulder.

He cataloged further reactions—when he added the sensation of his teeth lightly grazing her nipple she sucked in a quick breath of air; when his tongue explored her navel, she shivered. From head to toe she reacted to his touch, telling him with all of her what she liked. "I'm going to fall apart," she whispered into his mouth, pushing against his fingers urgently, her hips twisting against the intimate pressure of his hand until she shuddered and moaned softly into his neck, bearing him all the way down to the bedroll.

Before he could regain his senses, she shifted position. She was on top of him, straddling him, pressed against him. He was poised at her entrance, the thin wool of his drawers seeming a flimsy barrier against what his body wanted. What he wanted. One hot surge away from everything he needed.

"We should stop this." But he didn't think he could. With a force of will he didn't know he possessed, he rolled her onto her back and straddled her, using his legs to push hers tightly together so that temptation was not so dangerously near. He had to hold on to his sanity. He had to.

He pressed his face into her belly, nuzzling his way up to rest his mouth between her breasts. His shaft squeezed into the tight hollow between her thighs, no longer at risk of betraying them both.

She slid her fingers between their bodies, under the thin wool, and gripped him. He put his hands to either side of her head and braced himself to give her access. He pushed himself into her hand, against the silken glide of her fingers.

As if she knew what he needed without his having to ask, she squeezed him, gently at first and then harder as he gasped against her breast. He reached down to take her mouth with his, plunging his tongue against hers, rocking against the tormenting tension and wet slide of her touch until he burst with it.

The ferocity of their encounter left him shaken and spent. He reached for her, covered her against the night chill. "Next time I'll be more gentle. Take more time."

She snuggled back against him, warm bare flesh against warm bare flesh. "What makes you think I'll let you do this to me again?" He felt the rumble of amusement vibrate through her.

"Are you laughing at me?" he asked with a touch of amazement. He'd known she wasn't a prim-and-proper miss. But what amusement was there in what they had done? Need alone had driven them.

"You say next time so smugly—as if it were your idea entirely. If I'd been foolish enough to leave matters in your hands, there wouldn't have been a first time."

"A second time." He stroked his hand down between her breasts, over her belly, letting it come to rest warm between her knees. "Have you forgotten the storm?"

"I'm heartened to hear that you haven't. Pleasant dreams, Mr. Lewis."

Dreams. He didn't need them. He'd settle for a whole night's sleep. He needed all his wits about him. Because he didn't know what he thought he was doing holding a warm-blooded woman against him all night long without expecting all hell to break loose—even if she was his wife, for a little while longer.

They followed the Platte until they reached Fort Laramie. Now they stood at the gateway to the mountains.

Though she heard the complaints about mountain prices—prices much higher than in civilization, back in Saint Joe—Ros looked toward the mountains and felt her heart race.

If only they could get rid of Jericho here. Otherwise he'd make the whole trip over the mountains with them. She didn't want that.

"Where do you suppose he's got to?" Ophelia's voice was muffled by the floor of the wagon. Ros had to listen carefully to make out what she was saying.

"He's just being extra cautious. He'll seek me out soon." She walked far from the trail, in order to give him the opportunity. But so far Moses hadn't taken it. Nearly four weeks without a sight of him.

They had stopped at Fort Laramie to give the animals a rest before beginning the rough climb over the Rocky Mountains. Still he hadn't made contact with her. Though she would never confide such a thing to Ophelia, she was beginning to think he might have died— of illness, hunger, or accident she couldn't guess.

She hadn't planned on being with the company for a month, keeping the girl locked up. Slavery had to be better than a closed wagon bumping over a rough trail. Safer, anyway.

Twice this week alone, she'd had to hurry to distract Jericho and release Ophelia before a particularly deep river ford. Their luck seemed to be running out. Where was Moses? Should she wait for him?

"He looked poorly last time we saw him. What if—"

"Hush." Ros rustled about in the wagon as Mr. Barton drew near. "Can I help you find something, Miz Lewis?"

"No thank you, Mr. Barton." She held up the blue ribbon Ophelia had bought in Saint Joe what seemed like a lifetime ago. "I've found it."

He frowned. "Never seen you wear ribbon before."

"It's not for me, it's for Gwyneth."

He nodded but didn't move on. She didn't have much time before Jericho came back.

"Good day, Mr. Barton." She smoothed the ribbon through her fingers, pretending a particular interest in one stubborn wrinkle.

Reluctantly, he moved on.

She whispered, her mouth against the wood separating her from Ophelia, "I'll be back as soon as I can."

Jericho found him inspecting a broken wagon axle. The bounty hunter's expression was sly. "I've seen the murderer."

"Where?"

"Couple miles away." Jericho spat. "He got away before I could catch up with him. But I know how to get him. As long as you keep your wife from interfering."

"Rosaline will not be a hindrance to you." Rob was determined to see to that, if nothing else, despite what it would undoubtedly cost him.

Jericho looked skeptical. "Come with me, then, to see to it. If I'm right, we'll have the murderer and his wife come morning."

Ophelia? Was she with Moses? He'd thought Rosaline had left her back at Fort Kearny. Maybe the girl had followed her husband alone? But no. Rosaline wouldn't have abandoned her anymore than he would abandon his company of emigrants. She would never forgive him for this. And he didn't blame her. But he had to follow the law.

When they arrived at the wagon, Rosaline was just climbing out. She smiled at him, a slow kindling of heat that reminded him how they spent their nights. And then she saw Jericho and the smile turned frigid enough to freeze a man's drawers.

"Afternoon, missus."

"Afternoon," she answered grudgingly. He wanted to sweep her up, away from here, before everything she'd worked for fell in ashes at her feet. But he couldn't.

Jericho frowned, glancing between them—two people whose faces he couldn't read. "Got a favor to ask you."

She stood like a trapped animal, looking at Rob while she spoke to the bounty hunter. "I can't imagine there's anything I could do for you, Jericho."

"Yes, ma'am, there is. You could open up that secret compartment in your wagon."

Secret compartment? Surely she hadn't dragged Ophelia along with them for a month right under his nose? But she had. He knew, as soon as he saw her expression. And she didn't intend to give up the girl easily.

He didn't know if anyone else could read her bluff. But he knew it too well, despite the icy disdain in her voice when she said, "I beg your pardon? Secret compartment?"

"You heard me." But Jericho wasn't in the mood to play bluffing games. "Open it or I'll smash the wagon. I'd hate to do it; might hurt the girl and she's worth money, long as she's got that baby."

"I have no—"

"Do as he says, Ros." Rob held her arm tightly. He didn't loosen his grip when she winced. She'd risked everything he'd fought for to carry the girl this far. But he couldn't let her do it anymore.

She tried again to bluff him. Him. As if she might ever do that again after what had happened at Fort Kearny. "I don't know what he's talking about."

Jericho took an ax and hefted it.

Rob said hoarsely, "Please."

Ros stood, fighting the inevitable. Jericho's ax came down on the wagon and it shuddered under his assault. He knew. How could he know? What had she done to betray Ophelia? Freedom. "How did you find out?"

He brought the ax down against the wagon again, and a splinter of wood flew through the air. "The little girl. She likes to take her dolly and whisper up against the side of the wagon."

Gwyneth made a little gurgling sound in her throat. Rob picked her up in his arms and turned her face away from what was happening. She wanted to appeal to him to help her. But she knew better. His face was unyielding. Ophelia was a runaway. She was a threat to his company.

She'd go back for her. She wouldn't let Jackson have her. Not now. "Wait!" she called out as his ax raised again. Frantic thoughts raced in a circle around her mind as Ros unlocked the secret door. When Jericho reached in to roughly haul the girl out, she found her knife in her hand—pressed against his throat.

"You going to kill me?" He looked for a moment as though he'd relish it. "You'll hang for it."

She prodded him away from the wagon. "Let the girl get out on her own." She put the knife away once Ophelia stood blinking in the sunlight. From the look on her face, she'd heard everything. There was an expression of resignation on her face.

Jericho pushed past her and bent to look into the secret compartment. He turned like an angry bull. "Where's the baby? She ain't no good to me without the baby."

No one spoke. Jericho looked toward Astrid, who was attempting to slip backward through the gathered crowd, Freedom bundled in her arms. But it was too late. A gleam of understanding grew in the bounty hunter's eyes. "Give me the baby, Mrs. Martin."

Astrid looked stricken and shook her head, but he only said, "You've got skin the color of milk and your husband is pale as a ghost. Too much coffee in that baby's skin for him to be yours." There was no answer to the truth of that. Ros suddenly wished she had used the knife on him, whether she hanged or not.

"He belongs with his mother." She took the baby from Astrid and placed him gently in Ophelia's arms. She whispered, "I'm sorry, Ophelia. I'll think of something. Be brave." The girl clutched the infant to her but didn't look at Ros.

She, on the other hand, couldn't stop looking at Rob. How could he let this happen? But a voice whispered inside her: How could he not? She knew well enough she should have gotten Ophelia away. Had she stayed only for the selfish need to spend the nights in his arms? Had she risked everything for that?

# Chapter Twenty-three

Jericho would have staked them both out in the sun to lure Moses in, but Rob refused to allow the inhumane treatment. "While you're in my camp, you'll treat all human beings with basic decency."

Thwarted, Jericho took a short chain and hitched Ophelia to the back of the wagon that was to have been her freedom. And then he climbed into the wagon, a shotgun in one hand. "Hand me the baby," he ordered her. With a look of terror, she obeyed. He smiled. "I think I'll keep him with me. Don't want anyone getting any bright ideas on rescue tonight." Gwyneth tightened her arms around her father's neck. Her face was pale. "I'm sorry, Papa. I didn't know it was bad to talk to Ophelia when she was in the wagon."

He wanted to be angry with Rosaline. Wanted to say something to make Gwyneth know that it was all her fault. But seeing Ophelia chained like an animal, her son kept from her, he couldn't bring himself to believe it.

He kissed his daughter's smooth braid. "Sometimes bad things happen, Gwyneth, even when we don't want them to. We just have to do our best to make it right when we make a mistake." If there was a way to make it right.

He gave the child to Astrid. "Watch out for her tonight."

"I will," she answered him shortly. "And you watch out for your wife."

Rosaline. What was she planning? If he felt as if he should snap Ophelia's chains and carry her off to safety despite the laws, what must Ros feel?

She had not protested. She had, in fact, done nothing but stare starkly away from him since handing the baby to Ophelia. But there was a set to her shoulders he had come to recognize. She wouldn't let Jericho win easily. And he wouldn't let her break the law.

"There's nothing we can do," he told her. Told himself. He put his arm around her, but she shook it off and moved away.

Her expression was bitter with disappointment. "I shouldn't have let this happen. I should have left."

Left. Left him, she meant, before he could lead Jericho to Ophelia. "Ros, I did what I had to. The law is clear—"

She looked at him as if his words made no sense to her and then she shook her head wearily. "I don't blame you. You did what you had to. But I didn't. I let myself believe I could play wife without paying too steep a price. I thought I only risked my heart. What a fool I've been."

"You've done the best you could to save them. You're

going to have to let the law handle it from here. I can ask my father to help."

A light of hope burned bright for a moment in her eyes and then died. "Ask whomever you wish, Mr. Lewis. It won't change the hard truth that Ophelia will sleep chained tonight—bait to catch her husband so that he can be hanged as a murderer, while his wife and son are bought and sold as property." She turned away from him, all the fight draining from her.

"It could take several nights—"

She bent her head and spoke so low he could barely hear her. "No. He'll come tonight. He won't let her be treated like this. If he's still alive."

Despite her appearance of resignation, he kept his arm tight around her. He told himself it was only to prevent her from warning the murderer of the trap set for him.

But she said nothing at all when she saw the runaway come creeping in under cover of darkness to free his wife and son.

Jericho stepped out of the shadows, into the moonlight, as the big man reached his wife's side. "Moses."

The big man tensed, and Rob wondered if he'd run. But when he caught sight of the bounty hunter, he froze. "Jericho."

"That's *Mister* Jericho to you." The man held a pistol in one hand. But what he held in the other was what kept the runaway from taking his chances—a sleeping baby.

Moses said nothing. He moved not a muscle, caught in a paralyzing quandary—save himself and sacrifice his wife and son or let himself be captured and most certainly hanged.

Jericho smiled. "Guess you'll be coming along quiet like, then."

"Guess I will."

"You gonna let us take him, right, Pinkerton man? Even if it don't make your wife happy?"

Rob tightened his arm around Rosaline, who stared at the bounty hunter with an expression that promised retribution. But she made no movement beside him. There was nothing he could do. "Got the law behind you." He wondered, were she to look at him, if her expression would hold the same contempt for him that it did for the bounty hunter.

Jericho chained the gaunt, unresisting runaway to the back of the wagon. "Much obliged to you, Captain. We'll be off in the morning." The man set his bedroll out of reach of either of the runaways and lay down to sleep, as if there was nothing bothering his conscience at all.

"Let's go," said Rob.

"Where?"

"To the tent."

"So that we can be comfortable when they're not? You go. I'll stay here."

He could have carried her bodily back to the tent, but he didn't. They sat on the cold hard ground, waiting for dawn.

Come morning, the whole camp came out to goggle at the two runaway slaves. Jericho checked the wagon over for damage. His ax had not broken anything necessary for travel. Once he satisfied himself of that, he kicked at the runaways, who lay huddled together on the ground.

Moses put himself between the bounty hunter and his wife, using his body to protect her as they rose stiffly. Freedom began to wail. Jericho plucked the baby out of his mother's hold. "We'll have to teach him not to cry." Ophelia moaned softly. Moses's eyes were fixed with hatred on Jericho. Rob had no trouble believing this man a murderer. Only his chains prevented him from committing another.

Ros tensed beside him, and Rob gripped her arm, afraid she meant to do something unwise.

Astrid Martin, pale-faced and red-eyed. stood watching. "Be careful with that baby, Mr. Jericho."

"He's a right valuable piece of property, ma'am, don't you worry none. He just needs to learn his place. His master won't want him to be like his momma and daddy—ungrateful runaways." He swung the baby by the arms. "He'll learn to stop crying; he'll be out in the fields by the time he can walk."

"My son won't be no slave."

Jericho laughed. "No?" And then he looked at the baby more closely, at Ophelia and then, again, with an insolent leer. "Well, lookie here. I guess you're right. *Your* son ain't going to be no slave. This boy's too light to be *your* get. No wonder your master says he don't want the girl without the baby."

Rob felt a shock of recognition as the truth of what Jericho said hit him. Moses couldn't be the baby's father. Moses's rough bellow of outrage was scant warning for the laughing man. With a rough, tearing sound, the huge runaway ripped his chain from the wooden post and rushed Jericho.

Rob tightened his hold on Rosaline, afraid she would join the fray, but she didn't move. No one did, paralyzed by the sudden violence of the next few moments.

If the runaway had been careful not to hurt the baby, he wouldn't have succeeded. But he knocked the baby from Jericho's arms with a fierce growl, not stopping to see the small body bounce hard on the ground, a scream of infant outrage cut off dead at the second bounce.

Moses was a madman and Jericho was his target as

he twisted the chain around the bounty hunter's neck and tried to strangle him.

Ros twisted in Rob's grip, but he held on until she turned to glare at him with fierce contempt. He released her, and she went to the baby. At the same time Astrid gestured to Bug, who was near the baby's still body. He scooped it up and brought the limp child to Astrid. Ros touched the baby, held him. Astrid began to cry, and the three of them collapsed against each other in despair.

Rob wanted to go to his wife. But as he moved, she glanced toward him, and her look of betrayal and heartbreak stopped him.

Moses was too weak from privation and hardship to prevail once others had joined with Jericho to subdue him. The bounty hunter's rage was palpable as he saw the tragic expression on Astrid Martin's face as she held the limp bundle in her arms.

He kicked the huge runaway, hard. "That boy was good money for me. Your master won't pay for the girl without the baby."

"You should have thought about that before you killed him." Astrid's eyes were red-rimmed, but her voice was steady and full of outrage.

"*He* killed him," the bounty hunter argued in disgust. "He's a murderer; what do you expect? A father's love? From the likes of him? He ain't even the father." Jericho sneered, though it must have pained him, seeing that his lip was split and bleeding.

"Why you kill him?" Ophelia's broken question hung in the air.

Moses stood bloody and bowed for a moment and then, straightening painfully, he said with conviction, "Freedom better off dead than back where they're taking us."

Jericho kicked him again. "Shut up, you murdering dog."

Moses looked toward where Astrid and Ros stood, holding the body of his son. "Let his bones lay here. Halfway to freedom."

He didn't protest when Jericho chained him to the back of the wagon and put two large iron chains on his ankles. He stood without flinching, shackled to the wagon that had held all his hopes and dreams for a free life for his son.

Jericho moved to climb in the wagon. Drive away, leaving the company in shambles. Rob wanted to prevent him, but the bounty hunter had the right of law behind him.

"Wait," Bug called out.

"What?" Jericho seemed irritable, a sign that Moses had done him some harm during the battle.

"You say her master doesn't want her without the baby. Let me buy the girl."

Rob was struck dumb by the boy's generous heart.

"I don't know." Jericho appeared to think about it and then shrugged. His glance at the big runaway suggested he thought separating them might be one more torture for the man to bear before he was hanged for murder. "One less mouth to feed on the way back."

He named a sum, which was no doubt the entire savings of the young couple, but Bug didn't blink. He went to his wagon and came back with the money. Ophelia was unhitched from the wagon, her expression one of confusion and grief. She wasted no time in going where her son, his tiny face covered, lay.

Without a glance at her husband, Astrid Martin announced, "You're no longer a slave, Ophelia. We free you." It wasn't exactly a formal manumission, but Rob didn't argue. The gesture seemed right. Astrid placed the limp body in her arms and Ros put her arms around the runaway—no, freed woman now. "I'm sorry, Ophelia."

Tears fell down the girl's face as she held her son. She crumpled to the ground, cradling the still little form in her arms.

"Free. What a waste of good stock." Jericho spat on the ground, as if to dare any of the angry, shocked onlookers to do anything about the injustice of the morning. He climbed into the wagon and rode away, Moses stumbling behind in his chains. Not a soul moved from their watchful stillness until he was out of sight over a rise.

Rob moved stiffly to stand before Ophelia. "We'll give him a decent burial, preacher and all. I promise you that."

Astrid looked up at him, her eyes shining with tears. It took him a moment to realize that she was smiling. "There's no need for that, Mr. Lewis."

"He's got to have a decent burial, Astrid." He'd seen this reaction before. Grief could queer a mind for weeks sometimes.

"No. You don't understand." She glanced at Jericho's wagon, still visible in the distance. She whispered. "He's alive."

Ophelia unfolded the blanket that covered the infant's face, revealing a miraculously unharmed Freedom staring up placidly at the foolish, tearful adults looking down upon him.

Rob felt a jolt of joy rush through him and glanced at Ros. But her gaze was focused on the spot where the wagon had disappeared in the distance.

\* \* \*

The company began moving again, as if eager to put the events of the past day behind them quickly. But Ros couldn't do that. Not until she had made everything right. Ophelia was safe now, thanks to Bug and Astrid. Freedom was alive—thanks to a power higher than them all. But she had not been able to save Moses from the bounty hunter. She had failed him, despite her promise. The failure burned inside her until she wanted to scream.

Rob watched her from a distance without speaking. His expression was wary. No doubt he thought she hated him for what he'd done. She wished she could, a little. But the blame was hers. She'd let herself get distracted and Moses had paid the price.

At last, around noon, he rode up to her and dismounted to walk by her side. "You have no more obligation to him now, Rosaline. You've seen his wife and son safe. He's a murderer, Ros. He has to face justice."

"Justice?" The word tasted bitter to her. "There'll never be justice for him."

"One man can't kill another—not even if he's hurt because his wife bore another man's child."

She wanted him to know—to understand exactly what injustice had been done today. "Moses *is* the baby's father."

"How can that be? He's much too light—"

"Ophelia's not his natural mother. Though she is ten times better than the unnatural woman who bore him."

He struggled to comprehend what she was telling him. "But she nursed him."

"She had a stillborn baby the night before Freedom was born. Freedom's mother is . . . was . . . Jackson's wife, Ada."

Shock wrenched a gasp out of him. "His master's wife?" Rob's face grew grimly serious—the face of Captain Hellfire. "So he's not only a murderer but a rapist, and you helped him escape?"

She couldn't blame him for jumping to such a conclusion. There wasn't a man alive who wouldn't—unless they knew the true circumstances. "She wasn't the one raped. He was."

He swept her with a chillingly disappointed gaze, as if she were a surprisingly naïve child. "A man can't be taken against his will. Not a man the size of Moses. He lied to you."

"What makes you so certain?"

"I'm a man, Rosaline. You may have seduced me, but do you think you could have forced me to touch you?"

"True. You are a man. And you are not a slave. Perhaps you should not be so quick to assume that no man, not even a slave dependent on his owners for his very breath, could find himself forced by circumstance to share his mistress' bed, in order to keep even more trouble at bay?"

Doubt came into his eyes at last. But he rejected the parallel. "He could have said no. I said no."

"Did you?"

"That's not fair." He put his head in his hands and said through the muffling wall of his fingers, "I took care not to get a child on you."

"What if I had asked you to?"

"Never." He shook his head. She wasn't sure either of them believed he spoke the truth.

"But then, I don't own you. And only your pride was at stake—not your life."

"No one would have killed him for saying no."

"He thought that himself," she agreed. "He did refuse. Once. She sold his sister to a brothel owner in New Orleans."

"He could have run away, then. Before."

"Even slavery can't take a man's pride if he doesn't let it. He had a wife. He was saving to buy her freedom—and his own—so that no man could ever question it again. Tell me, Rob, would you have run?"

He didn't answer.

"She knew he was helping slaves. She knew I was. And others, as well. She threatened to expose us all. Would you have run, knowing the lives you risked?"

She answered for him. "You didn't run away from me, a woman you hardly wanted for a wife. You slept with me to keep your emigrants' confidence in your leadership. How can you fault Moses for making the same decision?"

He held her to him, his hands warm and strong and gentle on her shoulders. He looked into her eyes, his dark silver with his conviction. "He killed her."

She shook her head. "He didn't."

"How do you know that?"

She rested her cheek against the rough fabric of his shirt. "She was alive when we left that night. I saw her myself. She was furious because Jackson had told her that she'd gone too far and he was sending her away to a convent in New Orleans."

# Chapter Twenty-four

Rob shook his head. It wasn't possible. He couldn't imagine such an outrageous thing. "You only have his word for it."

She smiled bitterly. "No. He never told me. Ada told me herself. She was proud of what she had done. She thought she would pay Jackson back for his behavior with the slave women on their plantation."

He wondered if this might be a bluff. But no; her breath was harsh in her throat and her cheeks were flushed with emotion. The woman must have been crazy to think she could deal her husband such a blow— giving birth to—

It was easy enough to imagine what had happened once he'd found out. Easy enough to understand why Moses had to run. A wife, a baby to protect. What man wouldn't, slave or not? There was nothing left to say.

Astrid Martin hailed them, a worried frown creasing her brow. "Have you seen Gwyneth?"

"Not since last night." When Jericho had all but thanked his daughter for her childish whispers to a not-so-empty wagon.

"She disappeared last night. I thought she had come back to be with you. She was so sad about what happened to Ophelia."

Ros said sharply, "So you haven't seen her since then?"

"No."

"We need to find her." Could the child be feeling guilty? Had she hidden away? "I'm certain she's fine. We'll find her shortly." But, after today, he wasn't certain of anything, and he saw by her expression that his conviction did not ring true with her any more than it did with him.

The child was not with Ophelia. She was not playing with another child. Was not anywhere to be found in the entire company—despite the fact that he rode to each and every wagon, each and every family, asking after her. Calling her name.

Gwyneth had disappeared. She hadn't been seen since Jericho's wagon pulled out, a blue ribbon trailing on the ground behind it.

Rob rode after the bounty hunter, certain he could catch the heavily laden wagon in a few hours, but within the hour he spotted a lone horse with two riders in the distance. The larger rider was dark and tall. As they neared, he saw Gwyneth perched on the horse ahead of the runaway. She was smiling, as if she wasn't being held by a murderer. But then he remembered that Moses wasn't a murderer. Or, at least, he hadn't been. Where was Jericho?

Moses' eyes were lifeless, but there was no anger in his greeting. "Mr. Lewis."

"Moses."

"I made everything right again, Papa." Gwyneth smiled at him. "I helped him escape the bad man."

"Did you?" He wondered if Jericho lay dead. Surely Gwyneth wouldn't be smiling then.

Moses said impassively, "He got a leg broke when the little miss unlocked my chains." One big dark hand rubbed Gwyneth's head gently. "He meant to beat her for helping me. I didn't see no sense in letting another child die." The man continued dully, "I ain't going to go back. You can shoot me, if you want." He lifted Gwyneth and handed her to Rob as he spoke.

Rob said curtly, "I'm going to go help Jericho. Come with me. Tell the truth."

"The truth? No one believe the truth."

"I believe it."

"Miz Ros made you believe it. But she can't change the whole world, no matter how hard she tries."

"You have to tell—"

"Why? Who do it matter to? Ophelia knows. I know. Miz Ros knows. And now you. My word against Master Jackson. Who going to believe me? A man who killed his own baby."

No one. The truth wouldn't change a thing. That was stark reality. But one truth mattered. "Your son is alive and well."

A spark of life ignited in the dead eyes. "And free?"

"And free. But you're not. I won't take you in. I can't, knowing the truth, knowing—but there'll be ten men after you tomorrow."

"Let them catch me, then. Tell Fee to take good care of him. I'll find her if I can. If it's safe." Moses turned and cantered away without another word.

Gwyneth waved good-bye to Moses's back. "Do we have to go help that nasty man, Papa? I don't care if he has a broken leg or not. He hurt Freedom. He tried to hurt Ophelia."

"He was just doing his job, Gwyneth. Can't leave a man to die for that." Even if you wanted to.

"Thank you for letting him go free." Her voice carried across the darkness of the night, magnified by the water of the hot spring in which they were bathing.

"I don't capture innocent men, Ros. Only guilty ones." Like Jericho—an angry man with a badly broken leg. He'd been delirious when Rob had left him at the fort. He didn't know if the man would survive and he didn't care. He'd done his duty by getting the man to safety. That was all he needed to worry about.

She splashed him playfully. "And women?" Moses's freedom—questionable though it was—had taken a weight off her shoulders.

He ran an exploratory hand up her thigh. "You're no innocent. Look how quickly you abandoned your clothing to frolic in this pool with me."

"You are my husband, after all."

She scooped a handful of warm water and poured it on his chest. "I'm glad he knows about Freedom."

"Not that it does him much good—he's a wanted man, and even if Jericho's broken leg puts him off the trail, there's bound to be others right behind. He's likely to wander with no home and no place safe to rest his head."

"Maybe he'll become a legend. Like you, Captain Hellfire. Two parts myth and one part man." She moved down his belly, her light kisses growing more and more serious as her head dipped beneath the water and disappeared.

He sucked in a startled breath when her mouth found

him and he could see nothing but moonlight on the unbroken water and feel nothing but the spread of heat her lips and tongue and fingers offered.

Her head broke the water and she gasped for air a moment before she kissed him full and deep.

"New tricks?"

"Astrid mentioned—"

He laughed weakly. "I don't think I want to know."

"Do you like it better than my hand?" If he hadn't known better, he would have thought she was being coy. "Since you don't want to take a chance on babies, I thought this—"

He didn't want to think about what they weren't doing, only what they were. "I love your mouth. You can do that to me every day, if you like."

Her head dipped beneath the water again and he let out a little groan and relaxed to enjoy the way she moved against him.

When he thought she might drown, he twined his fingers in her hair and pulled her bodily up against him and took her mouth, tasting his own salt on her tongue.

"Is it as good?" She couldn't seem to let the subject go.

"Almost."

"Only almost?"

His shoulder blade began to itch. Trouble. She was pure trouble. "There isn't anything a man won't say— hell, anything he won't believe—to be inside a woman. Nothing else feels as good. Men were created that way— I guess to make sure we weren't thinking too hard about babies and marriage and all the tears to come to let it happen."

"Even we women, who are quite sure we don't want the consequences, can forget about those things." She slid herself onto his lap, spread herself over him. "I always thought of myself as a sensible woman, but when I'm with you, I'd rather not think of the consequences. I suppose that makes you a dangerous man."

His laughter was a deep rumble in his chest that he, wisely, did not release. "Save me from sensible women."

She tightened her knees around his hips and rocked against him insistently, still playful. He was too paralyzed with want to move away when she said softly, "I feel it, too—the need for more."

Ros could sense she was winning him over when his voice came low and deep, almost a dare but not quite. "Are you willing to pay the consequences?"

"What if I told you I knew a way to prevent our conceiving a child?"

"Wives' tales."

"No. A tea I have."

He kissed her, hard and demanding, until she gasped for breath. "You've bluffed me once. I won't let you do it again."

But his body told her a different story. "An assured one," she replied, overwhelming him even as the warning sounded in her own head that there was no completely assured gamble.

"How often do you have to drink this tea?"

"Just once, in the morning."

"Should we wait until you've been taking it for a few days?"

"I've been drinking it since the morning after the storm. I don't think we need to wait at all."

"Since the morning . . ." His body stilled. He took her hands in his, halting the play between them. "Why tonight?"

Her fingers twined restlessly in his. "Do you know about my eldest sister—the duchess?"

"Only that she's nothing like you."

"Very true. Miranda believes in happy endings."

"Does she always get them?"

"More than one might expect." She kissed him, full on the lips, soft and spicy and demanding. "Just for tonight I'm going to believe in them, too. For Moses and Ophelia, for Bug and Astrid, and even for you and me."

She pulled away from him, far enough so that she could see the expression on his face in the moonlight when she said, "Make love to me tonight. Pretend we can have a happy-ever-after. Just for tonight."

His hands gripped hers. "I hope you don't regret it."

"I won't know until it's done if I'm disappointed."

"I didn't say disappointment, Rosaline. I said regret. There's a world of difference."

"Then show me." She bent over him and pressed her lips to his in a kiss that said what she wanted so much better than any words she could find. "Because I want to feel you move inside me. I want, for however brief a time, to surround you, to become a part of you."

He sat up, as if he might escape, and then his arms came around her and pressed her to him. His mouth opened against hers, his tongue teased at her lips.

She closed her legs tight around him, refusing to be afraid, shivering with need where he touched, the tender rough touch of desire.

Somehow she found herself by the water's edge. Under him. He lay heavy between her thighs and pressed into her in one fierce movement. It hurt. The pleasure spiraled away, but she welcomed the sting and burn of his entry. Now she knew what it felt like to surround a man, to feel him move inside her.

"Have I hurt you?" She felt him pull away, felt the odd sensation of his body sliding out of hers, but she tightened her knees behind his hips and made a word-less noise of protest, trapping him there.

"Rosaline . . ."

"The first time is the worst, I hear," she said shakily.

*The first time.* Rob gazed down at the face of the woman he'd come to know so well.

He'd been sleeping with her for weeks, knew her body intimately. Knew how to bring a gasp of pleasure to her with a touch of his lips, or his tongue.

And yet he hadn't known this about her. Her mouth, briefly twisted into a grimace, widened into a smile as she looked up at him. "Don't look so shocked. Just get on with it."

The laughter that gusted through him pressed him sweetly deeper and she winced. "We don't have to do this." He began to ease away.

She locked her knees around his hips and stopped him. "I want this."

She moved her hips against his and stopped with a little gasp of pain. "I want this with you. There isn't anyone else I would trust not to hurt me."

They both knew he'd hurt her. A little. But that wasn't the kind of hurt she meant.

He bent his head and pressed his lips to the tip of her breast, overwhelmed at the gift she gave him. He held himself still inside her, letting her adjust to the feeling, as his lips and tongue, hands and fingers worked to overwhelm the pain of his entry with tiny offerings of pleasure.

Soon the tension flowed from her and she arched herself against him, asking for his body to answer hers. He pressed inside her. Deep inside, until he thought he might be lost and die from it.

Her hips lifted to help him, her mouth no longer

twisted with pain but pressed in little panting kisses wherever she could reach.

He began to move, afraid to thrust against her the way his body demanded. Afraid to hurt her. To burst the fragile bubble of pleasure he'd teased from her.

She kissed his chest and he increased his thrusts, closing his eyes as his own need forced their rhythm to quicken.

The shocking feel of her teeth grazing his nipple acted as a catalyst and he plunged into her fiercely, forgetting everything but the desire to bury himself as deeply inside her as possible.

His orgasm broke like a wave, covering him, carrying him toward peace in ever decreasing undulations until he lay shuddering on her breast.

He didn't want to leave her, but the air was cool against their wet skin. He sat up, gathering clothing, wondering what this all meant. "Why didn't you tell me?"

There was a hint of laughter in her voice, though he couldn't see her face. "Did you tell? Your first time?"

He dropped the soft layers of her odd costume in her lap with a laugh. "No." She was trouble. But she was his trouble.


Officers from Fort Laramie were waiting to take Rob into custody for helping a wanted murderer escape when they rode into camp. Jericho had brought the charge.

The emigrants of his company watched him led off in shackles. Some vowed to wait for him to return. Others began to make plans for moving on. Everything he'd feared, and she'd been the one to cause it all.

Ros rode behind the contingent of soldiers taking Rob

away, wondering if she'd finally brought the legendary Captain Hellfire down. And determined to change it if she could.

He didn't want to hear her argument. "You can't take the blame for this."

"Of course I can. It's all my fault. I brought them into the company. You never would have."

Somehow, what had happened between them had shifted things. He seemed to want to protect her even more. No matter that she was guilty and he was not— not really.

"You have to get your emigrants safely to their destination. And you didn't have anything to do with runaways. We both know I'm responsible for that."

He said the one thing that he knew would make her refuse. "The cells are miserable—tiny and dark—you won't be able to bear it."

But that didn't matter. Actions had consequences. And this was hers, not his. "I will."

His gaze focused, warming, as he realized she meant what she said. He leaned forward to kiss her quickly. "Have a little faith in me. I am a legend, after all."

"What?"

"Wait to sacrifice yourself for me until you see if it's necessary."


He looked at the intemperate Lieutenant Grattan. "I tell you, this is outrageous. Do you know who I am? My reputation?"

Ros offered quickly, "He's a legend, Lieutenant. A true legend."

He shook his head in warning, though what he really wanted to do was laugh.

But Grattan was bullheaded. "Jericho here—"

"The man is a bounty hunter. A grasping opportunist. My father, the senator—" He couldn't believe he was bringing his father's name into the discussion. He hadn't done that since he was five years old. He'd promised himself he would never do it. But that promise had been about himself. Not about Rosaline.

She'd sacrifice herself for him, no matter how foolish the action was. And Rosaline wouldn't survive a week in that cell. Not a week. "My father taught me to honor my word, and there is no man here who can say I haven't. You say I let him escape. I say I didn't."

"Your word against his."

"Then let me propose an agreement between gentlemen."

Grattan's commanding officer looked interested.

"Give me a week. I will have this man in custody by then—and I will turn him in myself," said Rob.

"Highly unorthodox."

"My father, the esteemed senator, is fond of unorthodox methods; I learned at his knee. He will be pleased, very pleased, if you allow me to prove my reputation and bring in the man who committed this heinous crime."

Jericho hobbled over on his crutches. "I protest. He could run away."

Ros said, "He's a legend. Legends can't run away."

"Then let her stay—until he returns," Jericho proposed.

Rob returned in two days, hoping to find his wife still sane. "Here's your man."

Grattan looked appalled when he gave him the brown scrap. It had shrunk and dried more in the travel. "How can I know that?"

Rob shrugged. "How many black men with shaven pates are there in this territory?"

Grattan's eyes narrowed. "Who did this?"

Rob had learned to bluff from the best of them. He said, without a tremor of hesitation, "Many Scalps." The Indian was famous for his collection of scalps—won from other Indians, never taken himself. "He says he bought it from a wild band of Cheyenne three days ago. It was fresh then."

Grattan might have objected further, but his commanding officer sighed. "All this trouble for a slave." He held out his hand. "No one would doubt you've done all you could be expected to do, sir. Tell your father we wish him well in his next term."

# Chapter Twenty-five

Ros watched her husband from the curved and elegant parlor windows of Jeanne's home. He was out by the cliff, looking down into the Bay. What was he thinking? Did he worry, as she did, that the bond between them wouldn't be strong enough to stand the test of time?

Helena asked softly, "Whyever did you marry him, Ros?"

"I lost my mind. Bluffing a legend into marriage." She felt so miserable saying the words, but Helena only laughed.

"It isn't funny."

"Of course it is. He's perfect for you."

Perfect. "He and Caroline couldn't make a go of it."

"You are nothing like Caroline. And from what you tell me, your husband is nothing like that lawyer neighbor of hers."

"No. And I am nothing like you and Rob is nothing

like Rand. How can anyone know?" She asked softly, afraid her sister would be offended, "How can you bear to love Rand every minute of the day without fear of disappointing him?"

"My dear sister, if I don't disappoint that rogue at least once a day, I don't consider I've done my duty."

Ros frowned at her twin. "You are making light of this matter."

Helena leaned forward, a serious gleam in her blue eyes. "I have been worried you were dead, or lying seriously wounded somewhere. And now I find that all along it was your heart in jeopardy, not your life. Silly me."

Her heart. Of course. Why had it taken Helena to show her what she needed to know? "I'm going to ask Rand very nicely to throttle you, my dearest sister."

"He won't, you know. I'm to bear another child for him, and he is too pleased at the idea he might have a daughter to spoil at last."

Rob didn't turn toward her when she came out to join him as he looked out at the San Francisco Bay in the pink of dawn. But he knew her by the sound of her step in the grass, by her scent that was only Ros and no other woman. "Gwyneth wants to stay with me. I didn't figure on that."

"No?"

"What can I give her, compared to—"

"A girl just wants her father, even if he isn't perfect."

"I want to do right by her." He sighed. "I suppose it might be time to consider settling down."

"What would you do?"

"They've offered me a job as sheriff in Port Cliff."

He glanced at her. "Would you consider coming with me? I could use your help."

"You're not for one moment imagining that I'll happily settle down to be the town's schoolteacher." Ros shuddered at the idea.

"That wasn't exactly the position I was thinking of." He backed her against a scrub pine. He liked the short skirts of her bloomer costume. He didn't have to wade through as much material to reach her heat.

She pulled her mouth from his after a long while. "Tell me: What *do* you have in mind for me in Port Cliff?"

"How does deputy sound?"

"I guess it's a place to start."

He took her face between his hands and tapped his forehead to hers. "Woman, don't tell me you're after my job already?"

"I'm only trying to keep you on your toes, Captain Hellfire. A man has to live up to his legend, sir, or he embarrasses his children."

He hesitated to ask the question, but it had to be asked. "And his wife?"

"Never his wife. She knows the man behind the legend—and she has a duty to make sure he never forgets that more fallible side of himself."

# COMING IN DECEMBER 2002 FROM
# ZEBRA BALLAD ROMANCES

# <u>BOOK YOUR PLACE ON OUR WEBSITE</u>
# <u>AND MAKE THE</u>
# <u>READING CONNECTION!</u>

We've created a customized website just for our very special readers, where you can get the inside scoop on everything that's going on with Zebra, Pinnacle and Kensington books.

When you come online, you'll have the exciting opportunity to:

- View covers of upcoming books
- Read sample chapters
- Learn about our future publishing schedule (listed by publication month *and author*)
- Find out when your favorite authors will be visiting a city near you
- Search for and order backlist books from our online catalog
- Check out author bios and background information
- Send e-mail to your favorite authors
- Meet the Kensington staff online
- Join us in weekly chats with authors, readers and other guests
- Get writing guidelines
- AND MUCH MORE!

**Visit our website at**
**http://www.kensingtonbooks.com**